The
Bermuda
Affair

A novel with its roots in wartime Bermuda

by
Alan Edmund Smith

D0524306

told
tales"

Not
new!

Copyright © 2000 by Alan Edmund Smith

First Published in 2001

*All rights reserved. No part of this publication
may be reproduced, stored in a retrieval system or
transmitted. in any form or by any means, electronic,
mechanical, photocopying or otherwise,
without permission in writing from the publisher.*

ISBN: 0-9698332-6-1

Design & Layout – Print Link, Bermuda
Cover Design by Print Link, based on a suggestion by the author
Printed in Canada

Author's Note

This is mostly a work of fiction,
although I have tried to make my fictional events
fit into the real background of
Bermuda and the UK in 1943 and 1993.

All characters are fictional,
except Winston Churchill and Franklin Roosevelt.

Alan Edmund Smith
November 2000

Acknowledgements

A dozen or so people have helped me with researching and writing the "The Bermuda Affair" and my thanks go to all of those I list below. However I wish to give extra special thanks to Squadron Leader Colin Pomeroy, RAF (Retd), author of "The Flying Boats of Bermuda", whose help and friendship has been invaluable.

Spanton Ashdown, Jackie Aubrey, Horst Augustinovic, Peggie Bristow, Nick Dicks, Christopher Dobson, Nancy and Peter Hawkins, Margaret Humphreys, Ann Jubb, David Legg, Peter Marsh, Don Mayes, Ted McKie, Sue Wilson and last but not least my wife.

Also the staff at the Public Records Office, Kew, UK; Bermuda Archives and the Riddell's Bay Golf Club.

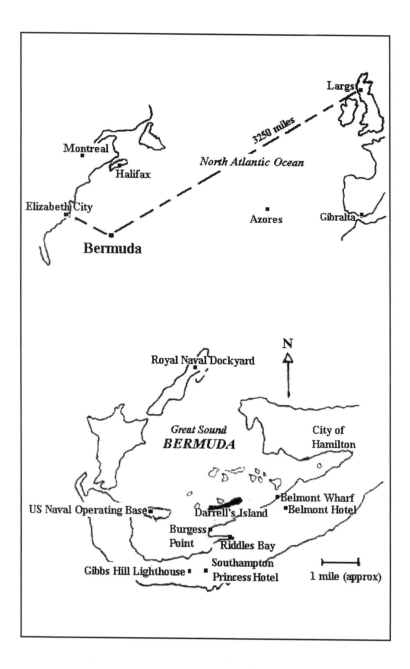

CHAPTER ONE

24 March 1993

It was the Captain who woke Don Newman. Atlantic Airways DC-10 flight 201 was cruising at thirty-one thousand feet over the North Atlantic, on its way to Trinidad.

"Ladies and gentleman, this is Captain Bernstein. I just want to let you folks know what's going on. Right now, we have a medical emergency on board. The nearest hospital from our present position is at Bermuda, so we are now on our way there and should land at Bermuda in approximately thirty-five minutes. I expect us to be on the ground for about half an hour, so all being well we should arrive at Trinidad about an hour late. We have already begun our descent to Bermuda and I will call you again when we start our final approach to the airport."

The Atlantic Airways flight to Trinidad was just an hour and a half out of New York and Don Newman had been dozing. He had left London the previous day and flown via New York so that he could pay a flying visit to his near eighty-year-old friend Hank Humble. But the Captain's surprise announcement quickly brought him to his senses. It wasn't so much the announcement that woke him, but one particular word in it, "Bermuda". When his subconscious heard the word, it reacted! He found his thoughts were suddenly very mixed. Some things that he thought had been put to bed in his ageing mind many years ago, were now suddenly coming to the surface.

The seat next to him was unoccupied and it was easy for him to attract the attention of a passing steward.

"Why are we landing at Bermuda?" he asked, "I missed the first part of what was said." That wasn't strictly true but for some reason he felt he needed to have the message confirmed.

"We have a medical emergency — a passenger in first class. A suspected heart attack. Bermuda is the nearest airport."

"Right — I see — sorry to hear that."

The thick set steward, in his forties and balding fast, wasn't in a hurry to go anywhere. The aircraft was only half full, and he wasn't very busy. He stood in the aisle next to Newman for a while.

"Ever been there Sir?" he asked, after a few minutes. " It's worth a visit."

Newman paused before answering. It was a leading question!

"Yes, during the war, I was in the RAF — the Royal Air Force. I spent a few weeks there, on and off."

"Really Sir. Did you fly?"

"Yes — Catalina flying boats. Cats we called them, I flew Cats to the UK before I joined Bomber Command."

"Oh yes, I know the Catalina Sir. There was one at an air display I went to a year or two ago. They made an amphibious version didn't they — is that what you call it? It could operate from land as well as water."

"Yes, that's right, I only flew the flying boat version. Darrell's Island, Bermuda, was a North Atlantic staging post for flying boats. Kindley Field, the land aerodrome, had only been open a year or so when I was last there. We used the water of the Great Sound as our field — if you know what I mean."

"Right — I guess it was a long flight to England in those days?"

"Yes, we went to Scotland usually — more than twenty-four hours non-stop. As you probably know — it's around three and a half thousand miles."

The steward smiled. "Yes, amazing. What speed did you cruise at then? It can't have been very fast."

"About ninety to one hundred knots, if I remember rightly — say a bit over 100 miles per hour — that was why we needed the wind behind us. If we didn't have that we would never have got there!"

"That's interesting Sir, I've read a bit about the guys who ferried aircraft across the pond during the war, but have never spoken to one before."

Half an hour later the aircraft broke out of a thin layer of patchy cloud over the sea. They were on the aircraft's final approach to the runway and Newman was straining to see Bermuda from his window on the left side of the aircraft. Shortly he caught his first glimpse of the South Shore of Bermuda for nearly fifty years and he felt positively excited. His feelings surprised him. He'd forgotten how blue and clear the water was, how green the Islands were, and that all the houses on the Islands had white roofs for catching the rain. They were now bathed in the lowering sun and it made a truly beautiful and inspiring sight. 'An oasis in the middle of the North Atlantic ocean,' he said to himself, not for the first time.

It was early evening when the DC-10 came to a halt outside the Civil Air Terminal and the engines were shut down. An ambulance was waiting on the tarmac and boarding steps were immediately put in place at the front of the aircraft.

By now Newman's thoughts had settled. His friendly steward had found a visitor's guide to Bermuda which he had passed to him. It included a modern map of the Islands and the airport. He studied it and remembered his first sight of Kindley Field from the air. That was in March 1943, a year or so after the airfield had opened.

Newman studied the layout of the airport now, and noted the direction of its longest runway, which was now its only runway. That didn't surprise him as it was what had happened to dozens, maybe hundreds, of World War 2 airfields, built with three runways for piston engined aircraft, most of which had tail wheel undercarriages.

He concluded that just after take-off — which the Captain now said should be in about twenty minutes time — he might get a good view of the Islands again. He sat waiting patiently, studying the map and picking out some of the places he remembered from years ago. The Great Sound, Darrell's Island, the Belmont Manor Hotel, Riddell's Bay, Burgess Point, and the City of Hamilton.

From time to time he glanced out of the window at the activities on the tarmac. Some passengers were stretching their legs inside the aircraft and pacing up and down the aisles with an air of frustration. Newman sat and thought, mostly about the events of 1943.

"Ladies and Gentlemen, Captain Bernstein. Please take your seats and fasten your seat belts. We are just about to start engines again. I'll call you after we are airborne, give you an update on our estimated time of arrival at Trinidad, and tell you the weather there."

It was dusk as they taxied out for take-off, and although the cabin lights had been dimmed for a night take-off, spots of rain on Newman's window from a Bermuda shower, made it difficult for him to see out clearly. He suspected that his chance of seeing much of Bermuda after take-off was receding fast.

As the aircraft turned on to the runway for a northwesterly take-off, he managed to get a glimpse down the runway. Visibility still appeared good and he hoped that when the aircraft accelerated, the raindrops on his window would be blown away. He couldn't help remembering that years before, when he wanted to see Bermuda better from a Catalina, he used to open the window!

Looking out of his side of the aircraft now, he could see the rain had stopped and it was brighter. There was still enough light to distinguish land from the sea, and beyond a short stretch of grass and a mile or two of water he could see a large building on the far shore line with many lights showing. Newman felt sure it must be the hotel which had been used by the military during the war when the airfield was being constructed. He had known its name once, but just couldn't think of it now.

Nevertheless he was encouraged by what he saw. As he could see the hotel, he felt there was still hope of a nostalgic view after take off. It would indeed be something special if he saw the lights of modern Bermuda. There were no lights in his day since the Islands were subjected to a black out during the war.

To Newman's surprise, the aircraft came to a halt after turning on to the runway for take-off. He presumed it would be a momentary pause. Bermuda was not evidently a busy airport; he had seen only one other aircraft at the terminal, a British Airways DC-10. It seemed unlikely that the hold would be for long. Probably a quick runway inspection, by the US Navy who now ran the airport, or maybe a vehicle crossing the runway, he thought.

Several minutes passed. Newman felt it was unusual to sit on the end of an active runway that long, and he began to wonder if they had another problem. Outside it was getting darker by the minute.

"Ladies and Gentlemen, Captain Bernstein again. This time it's a technical problem, I'm afraid. At the moment we are unable to reach the hydraulic pressure we require for take-off on one of our systems, and we will have to return to the ramp and shut down. Our flight engineer will then be able to investigate more fully. I'm sorry about this, naturally I will keep you informed."

❖

It was nearly an hour after the aircraft had retuned to the terminal, that the Captain came on the air again. This time it was to say that they would have to night-stop in Bermuda. "Bernstein again ... bad news folks ... we need spares which will have to be sent from New York ... hotels being arranged ..." and so forth.

Newman overheard a man some rows in front of him telling a stewardess that he was going to sue the airline for five million dollars. He was hardly surprised. He had come across many litigation obsessionals in his time as an aviation insurance underwriter. Nor was he altogether surprised at the Captain's announcement. It had become obvious, as the delay got longer and longer, that a night in Bermuda was the most likely outcome.

His thoughts turned to the hotel in which he would spend the night. The Belmont Manor naturally crossed his mind. It was marked on the map the steward had given him, as the Belmont Hotel, so it seemed it still existed. But he wouldn't be too disappointed if he had to stay somewhere else, for there must be many more hotels in Bermuda now. The map also confirmed that the building he had seen across the water whilst they were waiting on the end of the runway was a hotel — the Castle Harbour Hotel. Perhaps he would end up there for the night. But his memories of his time at the Belmont Manor were special to him, and that was the hotel uppermost in his mind at the moment. True there were some tough times, but his affair with Lucy had been very special, and he didn't want those memories blemished in any way, even though their affair had not ended as he had hoped.

The passengers were shepherded across the tarmac to the arrival lounge which was deserted except for Flight 201 passengers and airport staff. Their passports were stamped authorising a forty-eight-hour stay and they were told to collect their luggage from the baggage collection area. This surprised Newman. He had expected to spend the night without his luggage but he hadn't reckoned on the need for the cargo hold to be empty so that the hydraulic pipe lines could easily be inspected.

"Ladies and gentlemen," a woman airport official, was speaking. "When you have passed through Customs and Immigration, please make your way to the main entrance where you will find buses waiting to take you to your hotels. There isn't one hotel that can take you all, so those of you who wish to stay together must make sure you get on the same bus. And please also make sure you give your names to the record-clerk when you board the bus. The clerk will be by the door of the bus. This is most important — we must have a record of which hotel you are staying at. And for those of you who may not have been here before, you'll be pleased to hear that we accept US dollars in Bermuda, for anything and everything. Thank you."

Newman felt a strong desire to speak to her, but he wasn't sure why. It was an odd sort of feeling. He had never been any good at guessing the age of a woman, but his best estimate was that she was forty-five to fifty.

Smartly dressed in a dark blue jacket and trousers, which would pass as a uniform or equally as personal attire, he thought she looked a credit to the airport organisation. She didn't notice the distinguished gentleman in a blue blazer and grey flannels, and grey wavy hair, amongst the many passengers.

A porter however had and he approached Newman with a baggage trolley, thinking he looked like a good tipper.

"Good evening Sir. Can I help?"

"Good evening. Yes, I was wondering which hotels the passengers are being sent to?"

"Three Sir, Castle Harbour, the Southampton Princess and the Belmont."

"Oh, right, thank you — just wondering."

"If you especially want to go to a particular one of those three, sir, I'll see what I can do."

Newman decided to try and get on a bus for the Belmont and that if he was successful he would have a few at the bar for old time's sake before retiring. Come to think of it, he would have a few whichever hotel he was sent to. At seventy-one he was past taking life too seriously, but he felt lonely at times. It was something he had gradually got used to in the ten years since his wife had died, and a couple of large whiskies would sort that problem, as well as help him sleep!

"Thanks. Can you get me on the Belmont bus?"

"I'll try Sir."

The porter put Newman's suitcase on the trolley and threaded his way through the other passengers out of the Terminal Building. Newman followed close behind. Warm Bermuda air enveloped him again, and he felt better. He had felt it — and appreciated it — earlier when walking from the aircraft steps to the Terminal. He guessed it was at least 70 degrees, in the Fahrenheit units he was used to — or more accurately, he insisted on using. In the darkness which now shrouded the Islands, he had difficulty fighting off a wave of mild nostalgia! He remembered Bermuda's warm and pleasant climate in 1943, and how very friendly its people were, even though their Islands had been "invaded" by thousands of military personnel and tourism — and its vital revenue — had abruptly come to an end, at least for the time being. Would Bermudian people of the nineties still be as friendly, he wondered? He was already beginning to think they would.

There were five pink and blue coloured buses parked and waiting. He noted that each was showing their destination as "SPECIAL". The porter approached the driver of the nearest coach and Newman heard the driver say "this is for the Southampton Princess. The Belmont bus has already gone, they only had twenty rooms available."

"Looks like you're out of luck for the Belmont. This one's for the Southampton Princess. Is that OK Sir?"

Newman said it was and boarded the bus. There was no reason not to now, and he sat at the front, hoping to get a good view when they moved off. The bus was not designed to take luggage and the driver helped the passengers with their bags. "Put your suitcases on one of the unoccupied seats, Ladies and Gentlemen. We won't have a full load of passengers."

The driver was within earshot and as they drove across the Causeway — which Newman vaguely remembered — he asked him whether the Southampton Princess was near the Belmont Manor. "Well, yes and no Sir," the driver responded, "it's a few miles further on from the Belmont, towards the Dockyard, and it's on the South Road. The Belmont's on Middle Road. The Southampton Princess is much bigger and also much newer. You'll like it there, it's got a marvellous view of the Great Sound. Everyone likes it there when they're not paying!"

Don raised a chuckle. "Right, thanks," he said, " So we won't pass the entrance to the Belmont then?"

"Well we shouldn't, but we could, if you know what I mean. If you've got a special reason to see it, we could go that way."

"Yes — it would be appreciated —I was there during the war — if it's not far out of your way," Newman responded.

"OK Sir, you've got a deal. You leave it to me."

They were now skirting round the southern edge of Harrington Sound. Newman caught sight of the water from the headlights when the bus cornered, but he couldn't remember the Sound's name. The sight of the water came as no surprise. He remembered very clearly that in Bermuda, whichever way you went, you would come to water very soon.

Although it was now eight thirty in the evening there was a continuous stream of traffic going in the opposite direction, but none of the traffic was moving fast. As if reading Newman's thoughts, the driver mentioned that there was a 20 miles per hour speed limit on all roads in Bermuda. A woman passenger sitting behind Newman queried the figure. "Did you say twenty or fifty?" she asked, accidentally puffing cigarette smoke into Newman's airspace.

"Twenty, Mam — two zero."

The woman said something about that being ridiculous. The driver made no comment.

Newman was wondering if this really could be the Bermuda he had visited in the 1940s. The only motor transport in those days belonged to the military. He clearly remembered his first sight of a car on Bermuda; he was staying at the Belmont at the time, waiting for the weather to be right, and his Catalina to be got ready for his ferry flight to Britain, when, on a trip to Hamilton he saw a Ford on Front Street. It caused quite a stir.

"Just coming up to the Belmont Sir, about half a mile to go," said the driver.

"Thanks."

He remembered that the Belmont lay several hundred yards off the main road, so he knew he would not be able to see it properly. The bus slowed and Newman got a glimpse of the entrance road to the Hotel — on their right — which he had passed through many a time, often with Lucy, all those years ago. In truth he didn't recognise it, and was disappointed. He wondered why. For some reason he had the ridiculous idea that it wouldn't have changed in fifty years!

Newman had been wondering if he would try and make a fleeting visit to the Belmont — if he had the opportunity — during his brief overnight stay on the Island. Now, as the bus driver accelerated to his normal cruising speed of twenty miles per hour, he wondered if it might not be wise to let sleeping dogs lie. He had some very pleasant memories of Bermuda and some not so pleasant ones, although that wasn't Bermuda's fault.

Over the years, time had separated them into their own boxes in his mind, and he was able to enjoy the good memories without disturbing the bad ones. However the contents of both boxes overlapped; those of the Belmont for instance, and, yes, if he was to be honest, some of those about Lucy, were in both boxes.

A few miles further along Middle Road, he caught sight of a few flashes of light from Gibbs Hill Lighthouse. He couldn't remember its name but he remembered its existence well enough. On a return flight to Bermuda, when he had been recalled after several hours, whilst on a trans Atlantic journey to Scotland, he had seen it at dusk, from many miles away. It had helped him find the Islands without delay, when he urgently needed to, and it wasn't the sort of thing that was easily forgotten. During his time in Bermuda, it was only turned on when ships or aircraft were arriving. He had always presumed this was to avoid helping the German U-boats that were patrolling the mid Atlantic with their navigation, but he had never actually been told the reason. He had also seen it from the Belmont in the early hours of one particular morning when he was taking Lucy home.

The headlights of the bus briefly shone on a sign outside the Waterlot Inn. The name sounded familiar. He wondered if it could be the Inn that he and Lucy had often visited on their romantic walks together. Almost immediately the bus turned sharp left into a minor road and the driver announced that they were nearing the Southampton Princess. They climbed up a twisting road to a large modern looking hotel, perched on the top of a hill not far from the lighthouse. Newman only had to glance at it to know that it wasn't there fifty years earlier. Apart from its modern appearance, he remembered that there was a gun battery on top of the hill. Lucy had told him that on the day that things had gone terribly wrong, in May 1943. He remembered asking her, "Why aren't they firing then, why aren't they firing?"

It was, he knew, inevitable that memories of that sort would resurface, and he realised that for his own sake he had to keep them in check. But he was finding it difficult.

The bus stopped outside the main entrance, and he was first off. On the way out he slipped the driver a ten dollar bill. He couldn't help thinking that both he and the driver were lucky that US dollars were now acceptable in Bermuda, as he had nothing else.

Whilst walking the few paces to the hotel entrance he heard a sound he hadn't heard for over half a century: the squeaky sound of thousands of calling tree frogs. He had completely forgotten the sound, or he thought he had. Now it delighted him and changed his mood. He was sorry that a fellow passenger had suffered a heart attack, but he was beginning to be glad that the aircraft had a technical problem. Perhaps he should have faced things and come back to Bermuda a long time ago.

The duty receptionist welcomed him. She spoke with an English accent, probably London, he thought. Newman asked her if he could have a room with a view of the Great Sound. She consulted a colleague and after some hesitation, agreed. He was given room 399C and asked if he wanted to make a reservation for dinner. He thanked her but told her he would call room service if he needed anything.

"That's fine, Sir. Just use the phone and talk to Room Service. Your bags will be brought up to you in the next few minutes."

Room 399C, on the third floor, turned out to be good news for Don Newman, although he wasn't to find out just how good until the sun rose the following morning. It was at the north-east corner of the hotel. As a result he had two patio style sliding doors, one on each side of a corner of the room, leading on to balconies which joined each other.

He had shed his blazer on the way to the balcony, laying it on the king sized bed. Now he stood in the warm night air, looking at the panoramic view of the lights of modern Bermuda. The tree frogs provided background music. He couldn't have asked for a better orchestra. He wondered if the frogs and the lighthouse were the only things that hadn't changed in Bermuda.

Gibbs Hill Lighthouse was on his left now, and its beam shone on to his balcony with regularity. It gave him his bearings, as it had done all those years ago, and he had a feeling that if it could speak it would have said, "What took you so long Newman? Bermuda's missed you!"

Newman began to try and make sense of the hundreds of other lights he could see. By far the most lights were to his right and some distance away. They created a bright glow in the sky and he guessed they came from the capital, the City of Hamilton. In the distance, directly in front of him, were numerous lights which he suspected must be at the Dockyard.

He returned to the room, leaving the balcony doors open, and called room service. "Can you send me up a bottle of whisky please?"

"Certainly Sir, and would you like some ice or anything else to go with it?"

"Some ice will do fine."

"And any particular sort of whisky, Sir?"

"No, as long as it's Scotch."

Next he 'phoned his son in Trinidad and told him he wouldn't be arriving until the following day. Then he 'phoned his twin sister Brenda in England. He had promised her he would ring soon after he reached Trinidad. It was already after midnight in London but she thanked him for waking her up. She had left her husband nearly twenty years ago and had moved from Northampton to Staines, so as to be close to Don and his wife. Since his wife's death Don had visited her at least once a week. He enjoyed his visits and she looked upon him as her right arm.

She jokingly told him not to fall in love with a Bermudian girl again as she had got a list of odd jobs for him to do on his return!

When the whisky arrived he invited the waiter on to the balcony and asked him to identify the main lights they could see. His guess about the Dockyard and Hamilton lights were confirmed.

"And what about Darrell's Island, can you see any lights on it from here?"

"No Sir, you can't see any lights on Darrell's from anywhere. There aren't any."

"What! You mean there aren't any buildings on it now?"

"Not to my knowledge Sir. Just one or two unoccupied ones maybe — it always looks deserted when I pass it on the ferry."

"So it hasn't changed much since the end of the war, then?"

The waiter smiled broadly, "Don't know about that sir, I'm only twenty!"

Newman would have liked to continue his cross examination, but he could see the waiter wanted to get on with his job.

"Sorry — yes — interesting. Thank you," he said.

The waiter left and Newman put three or four cubes of ice into a tumbler and poured a generous portion of whisky over them. After a quick swig, he returned to a seat on the balcony, taking his drink with him.

Halfway through his whisky, he made a snap decision. The Belmont couldn't be more than two or three miles away, and if he didn't visit it tonight, he very likely wouldn't get a chance in the morning. Besides, he doubted he would ever return to Bermuda.

There were half a dozen taxis waiting for fares at the hotel entrance and he was soon on his way to the Belmont. The taxi driver, whom Newman estimated to be in his thirties, turned out to be a virtual fountain of local knowledge. In the ten minute journey he learned that the Southampton Princess was opened in 1972, the Waterlot Inn however, which Newman had noticed from the bus, had been there since the seventeenth century. So it was almost certainly the place Newman vaguely remembered from his times with Lucy.

He heard all about the demise of Bermuda's cedar trees, which started soon after he last left Bermuda in 1943, and about the Dockyard and how it had recently been redeveloped.

"And what happened to your trains?" asked Newman.

"Never saw them myself. Before my time, but I know about them. The whole system was taken up and sold to Guiana in the 1950s, I'm told. There's a book about the railway though, done by an Englishman, an ex RAF pilot, they say. Not seen it, but heard good reports about it. You can walk along the track of the old railway, in many places, although the trestles and bridges have gone of course. Watch out for signs for the 'Railway Trail'."

Newman was anxious to ask him about the Belmont Manor, but it was too late. They had just turned left and were going along the drive to the Hotel.

By the time the driver stopped all Newman had learned was that the Manor part had now been dropped, and it was just known as the Belmont. As the taxi went, Newman had other things on his mind. The precise name was not important to him. What mattered was whether it was the same place? The hotel where so much happened! He felt sure it was, but as he stood poised a few feet from the entrance doors he suddenly realised that his memory wasn't as good as he thought it was. The truth be known, he remembered and recognised nothing for certain. It was an eerie feeling, but he knew it was at least the right place. A uniformed doorman had seen Newman through the glass panelled front doors and came out to see if he wanted any help.

"Is the bar open to non residents?" asked Newman.

"Yes Sir," The door was held open for Newman and he set foot in the Belmont with more than a mixture of emotions.

He entered the bar. His initial reaction was that it was so quiet. Where had the raucous laughter gone? What had happened to the continuous banter, line shooting, and corny jokes. He half expected them to come out of the wood work when they realised he was back! But they didn't. The part of his mind that hoped it would be full of flying boat aircrew was out of sync with reality, and he knew it. Nostalgia and whisky. What mixed blessings they brought, he thought.

The room seemed a lot bigger than he had remembered, but at least his memory was right in one respect, the bar was on a corner of the hotel, with windows on two sides.

There were only a few tables occupied. He reached the bar. The barman gave him his full attention.

"Good evening. A large — no — a Dark and Stormy please." He'd remembered it! Lucy had introduced him to Dark and Stormys, so he'd have a few for old time's sake. Rum and ginger beer, that was it. He'd had a lot of those with Lucy, all those years ago.

As he took the drink from the barman he saw that the wall behind the bar was covered in large mirrors, and noticed for the first time that he was still wearing his RAF tie. He hadn't worn it for some years, but some impulse had made him put it on this morning. The barman noticed and recognised the tie too, but didn't comment.

Newman chose a seat at an empty table by the window. Looking out his eyes alighted on the floodlit tennis courts. He had forgotten them, or at least he hadn't remembered them until now. And round to his right was the swimming pool and the lights of Hamilton beyond. The pool was in the same place, but it was an odd feeling to see Hamilton lit up. The blackout in Bermuda during the war had completely hidden Hamilton from the Belmont once the sun had set.

It was inevitable that sooner or later Newman would start chatting to the barman, and it didn't take long!

❖

As soon as the last passenger from the DC-10 diversion had boarded a bus, Margaret Carpenter had quickly made for her car. Visiting hours at the King Edward VII Memorial Hospital were nearly over, but she hoped to snatch a few precious minutes with her mother. The doctors had told Margaret that her mother seemed to be giving up and they were very concerned. Her mother had to be persuaded that there was hope and a reason to keep on living.

Margaret arrived ten minutes before visitor's closing time.

"How are you Mum? You're looking better." She didn't like telling lies, but felt it was justified under the circumstances.

There was no reply.

"Sorry I'm late, but we had an emergency landing."

Her mother gave a just perceptible nod of her head, then closed her eyes and lay motionless in the hospital bed except for the slight rise and fall of her chest.

CHAPTER TWO

Elizabeth City, North Carolina, USA
3 March 1943

This was the day Bermuda started to cast its spell on Newman — for better or for worse. He and his crew were starting their first Catalina delivery flight from the US Navy base at Elizabeth City near the East Coast of the USA, to Britain via an RAF staging post on Darrell's Island, one of the many islands in Bermuda's Great Sound.

❖

"So, how much sleep did you get last night Hank?" Newman asked his co-pilot Hank Humble. His tone showed his annoyance. He already knew the answer having heard from a reliable source that Humble had been drinking in the hotel bar until the early hours of the morning.

"Mind your own bloody business," said Humble curtly as he walked on Newman's right-hand side towards the motor launch which would take them out to their Catalina flying boat. Newman didn't pursue the conversation, but hoped Humble's attitude would improve when they entered the cockpit. On a trans Atlantic flight, tension in the cockpit was the last thing Newman needed.

For Newman, and all but one of the crew, it was their first trans Atlantic delivery flight. Now seven-thirty in the morning, the five crew of the newly built Catalina, JX199, had been up since six. Briefed for the flight, and the necessary paperwork completed, they were walking to the motor launch in their flying suits — which were not ideal walking garments — and carrying their flying helmets and holdalls of personal gear.

Part of Newman's unease about his co-pilot stemmed from the make up of his crew. He was used to flying with an all RAF/RCAF crew, where discipline was tight and orders not queried. However this was no ordinary RAF flight. Only he and the flight engineer were in the RAF; the other three were civilians, and Hank Humble, a US civilian from Texas, was one of them.

Since they had been crewed-up at Montreal five days earlier, Humble had been difficult to get along with. It seemed to Newman that he had been crewed-up with a co-pilot that had a chip on his shoulder, and he wasn't very relaxed about it.

The operations board at EC had announced the delivery flight the day before.

"Movements, 3 March 1943.

Catalina IVA JX199, Crew: -

Captain and Lead Navigator:-

Flight Lieutenant D. Newman, RAF

Co-pilot:-

H. Humble

Flight Engineer (1):-

Sgt P. Ferguson, RAF

Flight Engineer (2):-

None. (To be arranged in Bermuda.)

Radio Operator (1) and Navigator:-

J. Hanson

Radio Operator (2):-

A. Plant

Destination:-

Darrell's Island Bermuda. Briefing 02:00. Take-off 03:00 GMT. Note:-

R/T not yet serviceable on this aircraft. Crystals to be fitted at Bermuda or UK.

All communications by W/T."

❖

They had boarded the aircraft — through the port blister — and started their checks. The auxiliary power unit was started by the flight engineer and the bilge pumps turned on. Soon afterwards they brought both main engines to life and Newman gingerly taxied out into Pasquotank River for take-off. Newman often compared taxying with a juggling act. With no brakes he had to keep the speed down and steer the aircraft by the throttles. More throttle on one side than the other would make the boat turn in the direction he wished, that is if the wind was not too strong and not blowing across the aircraft. He also had to ensure that the engines warmed up and were not allowed to run too slowly, but two years of experience helped and before long he opened up the throttles to check both engines, and then applied full power for the take-off. A minute or so later he lifted the Cat off the water. It was a quarter past eight in the morning, local time, and a bright day with plenty of sunshine, a few scattered clouds, but above all good visibility. That was always helpful to aviators.

The flight engineer retracted the wing tip floats on Newman's orders and they climbed away. Shortly they turned left to an easterly direction and set a direct course for Bermuda, 650 miles away, which they expected to reach in about six hours. As they crossed the coast a few minutes later, Newman reflected that just a few miles away at Kitty Hawk the Wright Brothers had made the first powered flight, forty years earlier.

Fifteen minutes later they reached their cruising altitude of six thousand feet and Newman engaged the autopilot. He glanced over to Hank Humble, sitting on his right. He was keeping a good look out for other aircraft ahead and on his side of the aircraft and from time to time he glanced at his instruments. Newman was doing the same on his side but also keeping an eye on Humble.

Humble was seven years older than Newman. He had much more general flying experience, but the Catalina was relatively new to him. Newman had been flying the Catalina for almost two years as a pilot — and mostly as a captain — with 117 Squadron based in North Sydney, Nova Scotia.

Humble was also paid a lot more than Newman, and since they met for the first time four days before, Humble had taken every opportunity of making the point. At least it seemed like that to Newman, who had come to the conclusion that Humble was a loud mouth who thought he should be the Captain, and who was obviously 'in it for the money'. It was a conclusion that, when he got to know Humble better, he realised was far from correct. But there was a war on, and for the moment Newman knew he had to put up with it and take what was handed out to him. And there was another thing, Humble was definitely an exhibitionist. He always wore an oversized Stetson hat on top of his leather flying helmet. He just wouldn't fly without it.

The noise from the engines made it almost impossible for the two pilots to talk to each other without using the intercom, and Newman lifted his face mask — with its integral microphone — to his face, and tapped

Humble on his left shoulder to indicate he was about to talk to him. He was trying to break the ice which — rightly or wrongly — he felt existed between them.

"If the weather stays like this" said Newman, "it should be cushy."

"Yes, but even if it doesn't, we'd have to be bloody stupid to miss Bermuda!" came the reply.

Newman didn't answer. He hadn't yet got the measure of his co-pilot. To make matters worse Humble took out a packet of cigarettes, tapped one out, and lit it with a gold coloured lighter.

This didn't please Newman one little bit. He smoked himself, but not on an aircraft. But he had heard from several pilots that crews were doing it — against regulations — and apparently civilian crew were mostly involved.

It posed a dilemma for Newman; he might feel like a quick puff himself before the flight was out. If he said anything to Humble now, he could hardly have one later. But anyway, that was an over simplification of the problem. He doubted that Humble would take any notice of him and if that happened it would be an awkward situation.

❖

Three hours later, with the weather still good, the routine — verging on monotony — was broken by an intercom call from the wireless operator.

"Sparks here Skipper — I think we have a problem."

"Yes, Sparks?" said Newman, "what's up?"

"I can't get a bearing to Bermuda. I've been trying for the last half hour."

The broad Scottish accent on the Catalina's intercom, belonged to Jock Hanson, the senior of the Catalina's two radio officers. He had also recently qualified as a navigator.

Although radio officers were invariably called Sparks the world over, Hanson was only happy to be known as Sparks when on duty. When not, he preferred *'Jock'*, except when he was back in Scotland, or in the company of another Scot. Then he preferred *'Sparks'*! But it seemed to him nobody took any notice of what he wanted anyway.

Born in Glasgow thirty-two years earlier, and brought up there, he was a marine wireless telegrapher who had become a civilian Royal Air Force

Ferry Command wireless operator as the result of too much drink one night in Montreal! The drink had resulted in him missing his ship's departure, and him needing to find a way back to Britain. But that was two years ago; he was now a North Atlantic ferry veteran with fifteen deliveries under his belt, although this was his very first flying boat delivery flight.

"Roger, Sparks," said Newman. "Have you tried Gander — maybe Bermuda's down?"

Although the Captain, at twenty-one Newman was the youngest member of the crew. Born in Staines, near London, in May 1921, he wanted to follow in his elder brother's footsteps and at the outbreak of war volunteered to be trained as RAF aircrew. After endless aptitude and medical tests, he entered the "system" and got his wings in Canada in May 1941, at the age of twenty.

"I have Skip — can't raise anyone. The receiver seems completely u/s."

Newman was not overjoyed but not too concerned by the news.

"OK, that shouldn't be too much of a problem. Should be a piece of cake finding Bermuda on a day like this, but keep trying Sparks and let me know if you have any joy."

"Roger, Skipper."

Newman then addressed the flight engineer, who was located high above the rest of the crew in his 'ivory tower'. The Catalina's wing, which carried the two Pratt and Whitney twelve hundred horse power engines, was mounted above the fuselage and attached to it by a tower-like structure and four struts joining the wing to the fuselage, outboard of the engines. To most of the crew, housed in the flying boat hull, it felt as if they were hanging beneath its wing, which in fact they were, but the engineer's station was higher up, inside the tower. From his position he had no view forward, just two windows either side, so that he could look at the two engines, which he had to monitor, and sometimes nurse.

"Fergie," said Newman, "there's just a chance that we may have to go back to EC — what's our duration based on consumption so far?"

"Standby Skipper," there was a momentary pause whilst the engineer consulted his gauges and did some mental arithmetic. "Yes, we're OK for another eleven hours Skipper, based on normal cruising. We can stretch it by maybe an hour if we reduce airspeed straight away."

"OK. No, we don't need to do that now — thanks."

Although Newman and his crew were only a few hours into their trans Atlantic delivery flight they had passed the mid point of their first leg, and Newman decided to continue, at least for the time being, rather than turn around and head back to Elizabeth City.

They expected to spend a few days at the Bermuda staging post before setting off on the long three and a half thousand-mile haul to Scotland, and they were all looking forward to a short break on the Islands which were reported to be a North Atlantic paradise, even in the winter.

On this leg of the journey Sgt Pip Ferguson was the only flight engineer aboard, as they were to pick up a Bermudian in Bermuda who needed to get to Britain to join the RAF. He had already been partially trained in Bermuda as a seaplane pilot and was going to relieve Ferguson from time to time on the second leg of the long trans Atlantic journey from Bermuda to Scotland.

The second radio operator, Alf Plant, a civilian from Adelaide, Australia, was relaxing on one of the two bunks, reading — or looking at the pictures — in a men's magazine. He too would be needed on the second leg, which under some circumstances, could last for up to thirty hours.

"Well, with a bit of luck this'll mean a few extra days in the sun," said Hank.

"Say again," said Newman.

"I said, with a bit of luck it'll take a few days to fix the dam radio in Bermuda, and we'll get more time in the sun!"

Newman, saw an opportunity to score a point. "But that might not be a good thing for you Hank. You might not get so many trips in this month, and then how would you pay the mortgage on your ranch?"

Newman glanced at Humble to see his reaction. Humble didn't return the glance but replied almost before Newman had finished his sentence.

"Well, I guess I'd have to tell my manager to sell a few thousand head of cattle if the bank gets difficult!" he said curtly

Newman didn't respond. He had made a mistake in making his remarks and realised it. The rest of the crew, with the exception of the radio operator were listening to the exchange on the intercom, and he didn't want to encourage them to join in. Too much banter about non essentials was not good. It was important to run a tight ship, he thought. Their lives might well depend upon it, he reasoned, and he censured himself.

They cruised on at six thousand feet in the sunshine. The autopilot was still engaged but Newman had a close eye on the way it was flying the aircraft. He had a bit of a thing about autopilots. He'd once shown too much confidence in 'George' and almost ended up in the drink. He had learned from that experience and was continually checking that the aircraft was maintaining a steady course, airspeed and altitude, whilst scanning his instruments for any sign of abnormalities.

Designed and built by Consolidated, in the United States, the Catalina was known to the United States Navy at first as the PBY-5, but when the RAF ordered the aircraft in 1939 they called it the Catalina. The name was now used by both armed services.

With a wing span slightly greater than a Lancaster bomber, which had gone into service with the RAF a year earlier, but only half it's weight, the Cat was used on anti submarine patrols and reconnaissance, particularly over the North Atlantic, and for air sea rescue operations. Around 250 had already been delivered across the North Atlantic by RAF Ferry Command, initially a civil organisation known as the Atlantic Ferry Organisation, (ATFERO), when formed in late 1941. It was changed to Ferry Command of the RAF in July 1941 when President Roosevelt insisted that Lend-Lease aircraft be delivered to a military organisation. Nevertheless many of the aircrew employed were civilians as was the case with this flight. Apart from Humble and Jock Hanson, there was Alf Plant, an Australian, the relief radio operator.

Newman was trying to adjust to this situation, which he found odd and a bit difficult. In his old squadron he had flown with the same RAF/RCAF crew for almost eighteen months — and consequently knew them very well. They were his mates — and although they were subject to military discipline — he found he didn't have to use his Captain's status to achieve what he wanted. He knew their individual limitations but trusted them, and dare he say it — now he wished they were still with him. His current crew were very much an unknown quantity, but one thing he knew for sure; they were watching him like a hawk. Their lives were at stake, particularly on the long hop from Bermuda to Scotland. This first leg was the leg on which they would make up their minds about him.

He decided to keep them informed. He wasn't used to announcing himself as the Captain. His old crew knew his voice, but things were different now. "Captain to crew — we're having difficulty getting a bearing on Bermuda at the moment, but we have another hour to go to

ETA. When we get near our ETA, I'll let you know. I want as many eyes on the look out for Bermuda as possible."

"Jesus man, we're not looking for a bloody sub," said Humble, through his chewing gum, which he was hardly ever without, "Bermuda's twenty miles long, and believe it or not, I can see something that size!"

"Yes, I know that Hank," said Newman, "I hope you're right!"

❖

When in service, the Catalina normally carried a crew of eight or nine, but on delivery flights, gunners were not carried, even though there was a risk that nearer Europe they could encounter the Luftwaffe. An encounter with an armed, four-engined, Focke-Wulf Condor on long range patrol was always a possibility. However the risk was not considered high and flying armed Catalinas, manned in part by civilians, would have led to all sorts of legal complications. In addition, aircrew were in short supply —particularly for ferrying duties. That was how Newman had entered the scene. The CO at his last squadron had been asked to volunteer two experienced Catalina pilots for Ferry Command. Newman had drawn one of the two short straws. He wasn't quite sure how it had happened. He didn't remember volunteering!

❖

Since leaving Elizabeth City they had been steering a steady compass course, which they had calculated before take-off. This course should theoretically take them straight down the direct track to Bermuda. They had to use the forecast wind speed and direction — given to them by the Met Officer at Elizabeth City — when making their calculations. But Newman expected adjustments to their heading would have to be made during the flight as it was very unlikely that the forecast wind would turn out to be exactly correct. And, on their part, it was unlikely that they would be able to fly the aircraft with perfect accuracy the whole time. So it was essential that the actual wind affecting the aircraft was established at regular intervals if possible.

To do this an 'air plot' was maintained throughout the flight on a large chart on the navigating table, by the navigator if one was carried, or by one of the pilots.

The basis for determining the wind speed and direction was to compare where the aircraft would be if there was no wind at all, to where it actually was. The difference between the two positions was assumed to be due to the wind and, if the aircraft had been flown accurately, would be. Hence the wind direction and speed would be calculated and used to calculate the new course to be flown. This system of navigation — known as *dead reckoning* — was being used by Newman and his crew on their flight. There was in fact no alternative. They couldn't map read their way to Bermuda, the sea had no landmarks! Now there was an immediate need to try and fix their position.

An hour earlier Sparks had obtained bearings from Newfoundland and Bermuda, and he had plotted them. This was their last fix and indicated they were slightly off the required track, but achieving a higher speed over the sea than they expected.

Now, with the radio out of action, they had lost a vital navigational aid at a critical time. Newman had heard at Elizabeth City that the aircraft they were now delivering was one of the last to be delivered without operational radar. In the near future, he was told, all Cats would have this fitted before delivery. In the present circumstances, with some cloud ahead, it would have been ideal, thought Newman, for picking up the coast of Bermuda, but he wasn't worried. Visibility was good, they had been pretty well on track one hour ago, so there was no reason to be concerned, especially when they could stay aloft for another ten hours or so. Nevertheless he felt it would do no harm to take a sun shot with the sextant. It was a time honoured system of marine navigation using the sun, which could also be used as an aid to navigation by aviators, if necessary. But it required a steady hand and eye, with the aircraft flying straight and level.

"What are you like with a sextant," Newman asked Humble, "you taken any sun shots lately?"

Humble, still sitting in the right hand co-pilot's seat, pushed the front brim of his Stetson up, to show more of his leather flying helmet. "I'm bang on with those, do'em regularly," said Hank, smiling for the first time on the flight, as he turned his head, and looked at Newman. "I make one regularly to know when I've reached the boundary of my little ranch — mind you it's not easy taking sun shots on a bloody horse!"

Newman couldn't hear it, but he had no doubt that the rest of the crew were having a good laugh.

"Well, I think you'd better have a go right now then, if you can do it without your horse, that is!" said Newman. "It can't do us any harm."

"No, and it won't do us much bloody good — we can't get a fix from just one position line!"

"I know that Hank, I wasn't born yesterday, but I want one whilst we can. You never know, it could come in handy later."

"OK, but we'll have to keep above this patch of cloud ahead of us. If you take her up and keep her steady, I'll do the rest."

"Take several and average them," said Newman.

"No problem," said Humble, "I wasn't born yesterday, either!" Humble took his Stetson off to make the whole operation possible

Newman called the flight engineer and told him he was increasing power to climb over the cloud ahead, then disconnected the auto pilot, pushed forward the throttle levers — which were mounted in the cockpit roof — and eased the control column back. The Cat responded instantly and started to climb steadily.

At ten thousand feet, above the cumulus clouds, Newman levelled out and re engaged the autopilot. As soon as the aircraft had settled, Humble set to work with the sextant.

A few minutes later RAF Corporal "Tich" Macclesfield, sitting on the grass on Darrell's Island, Bermuda, during his lunch break, heard the Cat pass high overhead, above the clouds. He knew the sound of a Cat's engines. It was unmistakable, and he expected to hear the aircraft circle and let down. He was surprised when the sound continued into the distance.

After ten minutes, when the Cat was several miles beyond Bermuda, heading towards Africa— some three thousand miles away — the clouds broke and Newman could see the sea below and some way ahead of them. Thinking there was no point, he made no attempt to look behind them, and they cruised on expecting Bermuda to come into sight in about half an hour. Humble had taken his shots, and was busy at the navigator's plotting table with Hanson. None of the rest of the crew were looking out of the aircraft.

"Can you see anything yet?" asked Humble, from his new position, at the plotting table, in the hull of the aircraft.

"No, just plenty of sea."

"Well, I've plotted my sun line and it goes right through Bermuda. So if I've done my sums right we've got to go back and then turn left or right and fly down the position line. Trouble is, there's no way of telling which way."

Newman was surprised at Humble's comments. "What ground speed does that give us since the last fix, Hank?" he asked.

"About 135 knots."

"And what was it from EC to our last fix?"

"114."

Newman wasn't happy that all was well with the navigation of the aircraft. It seemed unlikely that their ground speed would change so much, in just one hour.

"Right, can you both run over those calculations again Hank? It seems a big increase, and there's definitely no sign of Bermuda."

"OK, will do. I'll check them and also make certain there's nothing wrong with the fix we got over an hour ago. If that was wrong it could also explain our higher ground speed."

"OK Hank, thanks. Is Jock with you? Let him give you a hand."

"Yes, I'm with Hank, Skipper," said Jock, "we're working together."

"Roger."

"Alf are you there?" asked Newman. He was trying to contact Alf Plant, the second radio operator.

"He's asleep in one of the bunks, Skipper," Jock Hanson replied.

"OK — thanks Jock, wake him up — tell him I want him in the starboard blisters and looking out for Bermuda. And when you're free you take the port blister, there's nothing to be gained by sitting at a dud radio."

"Roger Skip."

"And tell him to let me know when he's in position."

The sun was very bright and reflecting off the sea now, and there wasn't a cloud in sight. Newman put on his dark glasses, and searched the horizon for Bermuda. Searching could be very tiring and he knew it. It was easy to think you had seen land in the distance, only to find it was the shadow of a cloud on the sea, or a trick of the light. He had learnt a great deal during the eighteen months he was in a Catalina Squadron, and some habits he had brought with him. Having his personal ten by fifty binoculars to hand throughout the flight was one of them. Now with *Brenda* the autopilot engaged — he scanned the horizon with them every few minutes. He didn't like the name 'George', he had an aversion to that particular name — so in his aircraft he pronounced that the autopilot was called *Brenda*, feeling, apparently, that he could trust a female autopilot.

The fact that it was also the name of his twin sister, who was friendly and reliable, probably had something to do with it also, but he didn't consciously think of that.

Hank Humble had had rather a lot to say about *Brenda* — the autopilot — when Newman had introduced him to 'her'. He hoped she wasn't a dumb blond, he had said. But it soon became clear that he saw the funny side of things and was happy to play the game.

"Does *Brenda* make tea and coffee as well?" he'd asked.

"No only coffee," Newman had replied.

Newman was scanning his instruments, whilst subconsciously listening to the engines — he knew exactly what they should sound like — then scanning the seascape with his unaided eyes, then with his binoculars, every few minutes.

He was also thinking. He wasn't concerned. They had more than enough fuel to get back to the States, but he hoped it wouldn't come to that. He would consider that a personal failure. "Bermuda where are you?" he muttered to himself.

It was now close to their ETA, and there was no sign of the Islands — although he estimated visibility was up to twenty miles in all directions.

"Any news yet from you navigators?" asked Newman.

"We've just gone over the calculations for my sun line" said Humble, "we can't find anything wrong there — but we haven't checked over the previous fix from the Bermuda and Halifax bearings, I'm just about to look at them with Sparks."

"OK— if they turn out to be OK, then we'll start a square search in thirty minutes time."

"But what if my sun shot was right?"said Humble, with a touch of irritation, "it would mean we've passed Bermuda and we're bloody well heading for Africa!"

Newman sighed quietly. "I take your point Hank — as I say, we'll start a square search if necessary, in half an hour. If it's behind us we'll find it then."

There was no response from Humble.

The outside air temperature was well below freezing, but it had become overly warm in the Catalina's cockpit and Newman leant forward and adjusted the heating controls with his left hand. He then slid open his side window momentarily to get a breath of fresh air.

The rush of cold air brought forth a gaggle of superlatives from

Humble, together with a comment about the Halifax position line. "I can't agree the Halifax line — there's something wrong — just wrongly plotted I think, I'll replot it and be back to you Don."

It was the first time Humble had addressed Newman as Don. Newman wondered if this was significant.

"Who plotted that bearing in the first place?" asked Newman, "You Hank, or Sparks?"

Humble said he did. "Too many beers last night, maybe." he continued.

Newman made a mental note to keep an eye out for Humble's drinking the night before they set out on the Bermuda - Scotland leg.

"Hank can you go over everything, start right back at EC, make sure we used the correct forecast winds and used the right airspeed, and so forth, we must be sure that we've got it right."

"Yes we'll go over it all together, should take us about ten to fifteen minutes."

Whilst Humble and Sparks worked on the charts, Newman was thinking about procedures for the next few hours. He wasn't sure that Elizabeth City would be available for a return night landing. It might depend upon Bermuda advising EC that their Cat hadn't arrived safely. In any event Newman preferred a daylight landing, particularly as he didn't know the Elizabeth City area well. So if they didn't find Bermuda, he intended to set course back to the US east coast, in time to reach it an hour before dusk. He also decided that he would aim for a landfall well south of Elizabeth City so that by following the Outer Banks northwards, they would sooner or later reach Albemarle Sound and then see the Pasquotank River on which Elizabeth City air base was situated.

Having made that decision he conveyed it to the crew. He didn't like indecision, and he wanted the crew to know that he was thinking ahead and making decisions. He'd just finished speaking when he noticed smoke on the horizon, almost dead ahead, and he quickly trained his binoculars on the area. He could see it was definitely coming from a ship, rather than from something on dry land, but the ship was too far away for him to identify whether it was a merchant vessel or a warship. "I've sighted an unidentified ship about fifteen miles ahead of us Sparks," said Newman, "note it in the log will you, I'll let you know what it is when we get closer."

"Right, doing that Skip."

34

Before long Newman could make out enough of the ship to be fairly certain it was a destroyer and he informed the crew that he was going down to get a closer look, "and Sparks, dig out the Aldis signalling lamp, and go down to the port blister, I want you to signal them and ask them for their position. I'll tell you what to say when the time comes."

"Roger Skip."

Newman knew it would take them six or seven minutes to descend to five hundred feet — the height at which he intended to circle the vessel — so he disconnected the autopilot, closed the throttles, pushed the nose down, and started to descend at 125 knots.

As they neared the ship Newman called Humble. "Hank can you come up and take her, I want to try and identify her with my binocs, but I can't do that at five hundred feet in a turn — might end up in the drink!"

"Coming," said Humble.

Humble was soon back in the co-pilot's seat and strapped in. He glanced at the altimeter and saw that they were now at two thousand feet and the ship was a mile or so ahead and slightly to port. After an adjustment to his Stetson to keep the sun out of his eyes, he placed his hands on the control wheel.

"I have control," said Humble.

"You have control," Newman replied.

"OK, Hank, when we get level with her, make a circle to port, so I can get a good look at her — I have a feeling I know her."

"Sounds like the title of a song!" Humble responded.

Newman couldn't resist a smile. It was clear that the thaw had definitely started.

As they drew close, he opened his side window and used the binoculars. At five hundred feet the air was a bit bumpy, but he'd done it many times before and could cope with it. Now he could clearly see the white ensign and the name of the ship.

"I thought so," shouted Newman "its *HMS Brentford.* The Captain was a master at my old school; I had a beer with him a month ago in Halifax."

"You've gotta be joking!" said Humble.

"No I'm not, he's got a nickname, 'Bonzo'. Don't know how he got it but it started at school, and he told me it has somehow followed him on to his ship."

"Sparks, send this message. Are you ready?" Newman asked.

"Yes Skip, go ahead."

"Bonzo from Donald Duck. Please advise your estimated position. "

" 'Donald Duck' Skip?"

"Yes, Donald Duck! It goes back a few years. I was never any good at cricket, never scoring and always making a duck. Eventually I got a nickname, Donald Duck. It sort of just happened."

"Oh — right, Skip," said Sparks, in a tone which suggested he didn't really understand.

A half minute later Newman saw the Aldis on the destroyer flashing a reply, and although Newman was not as fast at Morse code as Sparks, he quickly read the short reply, and it was what he'd expected.

"Standby."

They continued to circle the ship at five hundred feet waiting for the ship's navigator to estimate their position.

"What's all this Bonzo and Donald Duck stuff?" asked Humble.

"It's a way of breaking through the system. I know Bonzo, he wouldn't go giving his position away to anyone until he's satisfied we are bona fide. But this should do it straight away."

"You mean he might think we're the bloody Luftwaffe?"

"Something like that."

They were now starting their third left hand circuit of the ship, and Newman could see that Humble was finding it difficult to keep the ship in sight the whole time, as it was on Newman's side of the aircraft.

"I'll take it" said Newman, "I can see her better. I have control"

"Roger, you have control."

On the fourth circuit the Aldis operator began sending the reply. Newman made no attempt to read it, but he was surprised at it's length. He had expected the latitude and longitude but it was obviously much more than that. He expected to see a lot of numerals in the reply that was being sent — they would be the latitude and longitude figures he was after — but he could only see a few in the answer. He was puzzled.

Sparks came on the intercom as they continued to circle. "Skip, got the reply,"

"Go ahead Sparks."

"SOS. SOS. Our estimated position one two five miles east south east of Bermuda. We proceeding there full speed for urgent medical aid to Captain who unconscious. Can you alight and take Captain to Bermuda? MO says this only way to save his life."

"Jesus Christ," said Humble, "I was right, we've overflown Bermuda!"

Newman didn't say anything instantly, he was thinking. After a few seconds he said, "Sparks, ask them to advise wind and sea state, and name of Captain."

As he said it Newman realised that it didn't really matter if the Captain was his old school master friend or not, for they would help if they could whoever it was, but if it was his friend David Livingstone, which he presumed it was, it would add a very personal angle to the operation.

"They say 'wind westerly, twenty knots, waves three to four feet. Captain's name Livingstone AKA Bonzo," said Sparks.

"Roger Sparks, send, 'Turn into wind and slow. Will land but not stop engines. Bring Captain to starboard blister. Should MO come too. We have radio failure. Instruct RN BDA to advise RAF Bermuda.' "

"Roger Skip."

Newman signalled the flight engineer to lower the wing tip floats. The aircraft was built with a signalling system between the cockpit and the flight engineer's station in the tower, which made this a quick and painless operation. He then told the crew to stand by to alight

Pip Ferguson was not taken by surprise. He had overheard the exchange of intercom messages, and he straight away lowered the floats. A light in the cockpit showed Newman that his command had been executed.

Newman broke off from circling the destroyer and carried out his pre landing check list, then began his approach to 'land'. Meanwhile HMS Brentford had headed into wind, reduced speed and prepared to lower a boat with the sick Captain aboard. Newman was aiming to alight just ahead and to the left of the destroyer. At about thirty feet he checked the aircraft's descent and gradually eased back on the control column until it was fully back. The Cat stalled on to the water and quickly came to a halt. Newman couldn't help thinking that luck was with them. It was rare that the mid Atlantic sea state was good enough for a Cat to alight.

It took fifteen minutes for the patient, Lieutenant Commander Livingstone and the medical officer, Surgeon-Lieutenant Moffett, to come aboard. Newman put Humble in charge of the cockpit and supervised the transfer of the patient through the starboard blister. It wasn't easy in the prevailing sea conditions, but it was achieved after a few attempts.

Newman recognised the unconscious Livingstone instantly, as he was placed on one of the crew bunks with the doctor attending him.

"Standby for take-off" said Newman, as he resumed his place in the cockpit, and strapped himself in.

Their take-off took well over a minute, but it seemed longer to Newman. He didn't want to waste a precious second getting Lieutenant Commander Livingstone to Bermuda.

They were now nowhere near their maximum weight as about a quarter of their fuel had been consumed since they left Elizabeth City, and Newman kept the throttles nearly wide open as they set course. There was no doubt in his mind that this was an SOS situation.

It took them just over an hour to reach Bermuda where, after a quick tight circuit, Newman brought the Cat down in the Great Sound. It was just seven and a half hours since they had departed from Elizabeth City. All the crew had been looking forward to their first glance of the Islands from the air, but they hadn't envisaged the current circumstances, and there was no chattering on the intercom.

They followed the launch to their mooring buoy off Darrell's Island. Newman had mixed emotions as he did so. It was a black mark, missing Bermuda, but on the other hand, if they hadn't, he would not have been able to help his old master, David Livingstone. Perhaps, he thought, the cloud which he guessed had obscured Bermuda when they had passed it was not there by accident! But suddenly a cloud of a different sort descended upon them.

"Bad news, Skipper," said Sparks, on the intercom, "your friend the naval Captain didn't make it. He died just as we were touching down. The MO says there was nothing more he could do. He says he'll talk to you when we get ashore."

Humble removed his Stetson, "Bloody bad luck." he said.

Newman's reaction was one of shock and disbelief. "You can say that again," he responded, with an audible sigh.

❖

Opened as a civil Marine Airport in 1937, Darrell's Island had seen much military aviation activity since the outbreak of World War II. Situated in mid-Atlantic, some six hundred and fifty miles from the US mainland, Bermuda was ideally situated to serve as a base for anti submarine patrols, a staging post for flying boats being supplied to Britain under Lend-Lease, and an advanced base for the defence of the Western Coast of the USA.

"It's a pity it's not about a thousand miles east of where it is," said one flying boat captain he'd met, "but other than that, it's made to measure." The captain, no doubt, had been thinking of the long haul from Bermuda to Europe, which was about four times the distance of the first leg, Elizabeth City to Darrell's Island.

After the necessary debriefing, Newman and the civilian members of his crew were given rooms at the Belmont Manor Hotel. As a non-commissioned officer, the flight engineer, Sgt Ferguson, was accommodated by the RAF on Darrell's Island.

It was late afternoon as they boarded the RAF launch, and with the sun heading towards the horizon behind them, set off on the mile or so ride to the Belmont Wharf. The whole crew were fairly quiet. The death, on their Cat, had shocked them all.

Newman didn't really notice that the air temperature was a comfortable seventy degrees, and that there was hardly a cloud in the sky. Nor that there was a Pan Am Clipper 314 moored nearby. The Royal Navy Medical Officer who had attended Livingstone was also on board, as the launch was going to make a special journey to the Dockyard with him after dropping Newman's crew at the Belmont Wharf.

The MO could see that Newman was quietly distressed. "Had you known him long?" he asked.

"About ten years, I suppose," Newman replied, "I was in his maths class at first and then he was my house master, when I was house Captain, until he left to join the Navy. But he came back to the school regularly when he was on leave. So you might say I knew him well."

"Tough, but I guess these things happen in wartime," said the Medical Officer.

Newman said, "Yes, but wasn't it the sort of thing that might happen, whether there's a war or not?"

"Yes, I take your point — if it was what I think it was."

The coxswain was chatting with Hank Humble. Newman guessed that Humble was asking for a local "briefing".

"That's it up there on the hill," Newman heard the coxswain say, "And the RAF have got offices there too."

As the launch drew alongside the wharf, Newman turned to the MO and offered his right hand. The two men shook and held the clasp for a few seconds.

"I'd like to go to his funeral, if I'm still here. Could you get someone to let me know when and where it'll be?" asked Newman.

"Sure, I'll look after that. I'll ring you at the hotel, or get a message to you somehow. The burial will almost certainly be at the Royal Navy Cemetery near the Dockyard."

"Thanks."

❖

Situated on a green hill on the Bermuda mainland, in Warwick Parish, the Belmont Manor Hotel was a conspicuous building from the Great Sound and from the air. A little over a mile from Darrell's Island, it had an unobstructed, although somewhat distant view of activities there. There was also a more distant and partial view of the Royal Naval Dockyard, some four miles away. Nearer, and to the right, there was a fine view of Bermuda's capital, the City of Hamilton, and its harbour.

That evening Newman had a few drinks in the hotel bar with Hank Humble. The day's events had brought them a bit closer. Neither of them knew what the rules were on Royal Navy vessels, but they guessed that there would be some drinking on *HMS Brentford* too, if the regulations permitted it.

It was eleven pm when Newman returned to his room. He was tired and dispirited, but before turning in he drafted a letter to David Livingstone's parents. He didn't know them, but he felt it was the thing to do. He decided to read it the following day and see if he still wanted to send it, as he had demolished quite a few beers in the bar which might well have affected his style.

CHAPTER THREE

Thursday 4 March 1943

First thing the next morning Newman went over the letter he had drafted to David Livingstone's parents the night before. It took him two hours and five attempts before he was content with his choice of words. He wrote it assuming they would have already been informed officially by telegram by the time his letter reached them, which he was sure would be the case. Then, since he didn't know the parents' address, he addressed the envelope to Mr & Mrs Livingstone, sealed it, and put it inside another envelope addressed to his old headmaster, with a short note asking him to get his secretary to forward it.

Newman's Catalina was being worked on, and he wasn't needed, so he decided to visit Hamilton, find a post office and post the letter. He realised that posting it in Bermuda might not be the fastest way to England, it depended upon how long they would be held up there. And that was anybody's guess. If they got away with their Catalina in the next day or two, he would be able to post the letter in Scotland. But there were a lot of uncertainties: the length of time it would take to get the Cat ready for the journey; waiting for the North Atlantic weather and the weather at their destination to be acceptable; and, of course, for the weather at Bermuda to be OK. So he had decided to post it in Bermuda. At least that way it was out of his control and he wouldn't be tempted to rewrite it yet again.

As if on cue — as he finished sealing the second envelope — there was a knock on his door. One of the hotel staff entered with his "best blue" tunic pressed and buttons polished. Newman tipped him two shillings and asked him the best way to get to Hamilton. The easiest way he was told was by ferry, but he could also get there by train, bicycle, horse and buggie, or even walk. By train or ferry would be quickest, as either way would take him about fifteen to twenty minutes, but he would need to look at the timetables, which were pinned up on the noticeboard. He did that and decided to have lunch, then go to Hamilton by ferry and return by train, so as to experience both.

After a light lunch — he hadn't much of an appetite — he set out for the wharf. It was a fine day with a strong breeze and patchy cloud, with

42

the temperature in the sixties, the sort of day that would normally lift Newman's spirits, but today it wasn't getting through to him.

He found three other people, all in uniform, waiting for the ferry. An RAF Flying Officer with a navigator's brevet, an RAF sergeant wireless operator and a Flight Lieutenant of the RCAF in khaki tropical uniform.

They all looked round in turn as Newman descended the stone steps to the wharf's platform.

"Might be a little while, I think we just missed the one-thirty," said the Canadian.

"Right."

They exchanged notes for a few minutes, then noticed a motor launch approaching from their left. Newman also noticed that the sergeant had moved forward and was gesticulating with his thumb.

"He's trying to hitch hike to Hamilton! Seen him do this before," said the Canadian. "Never had the cheek myself — but it usually works. I suppose there are some advantages — being non commissioned — I mean."

Newman looked a bit puzzled

"Well, you don't have to worry so much about upsetting the King, do you!" continued the Canadian, "if you know what I mean."

Newman wasn't quite sure if the Canadian was making a serious point, or just joking.

"You mean it wouldn't be proper for an officer in uniform to thumb a lift?" said Newman.

"Exactly, unless it was an emergency."

"Yes, I suppose you're right, I've never thought about it, to be honest."

A few seconds later a US Navy launch drew alongside. There were a dozen or so uniformed sailors on board, with an assortment of ranks. Someone — with what Newman thought was a New York accent — shouted "All aboard for New York."

The sergeant led the way and within a few seconds Belmont Wharf was empty. Newman stood beside the Canadian as there were no unoccupied seats.

"You know the US Navy also fly Cats out of here," said the Canadian, as they headed towards Hamilton. "Sub hunting, air sea rescue — you know the sort of thing. They used part of Darrell's Island until their own place was ready at Kings Point."

"Yes I noticed them when I came in yesterday."

As he spoke a Boeing 314 Clipper passed overhead as it circled before landing.

"Bloody great things, aren't they," said the Canadian.

"Yes and I hear they can be tricky to handle on the water sometimes."

"Wouldn't know about that, but they're said to be very comfortable for the passengers and crew."

"So I'm told."

They alighted at Front Street, Hamilton, and Newman asked the Canadian to direct him to the post office, which he did, and Newman set off. A freighter was docked alongside the street, which was bustling with activity. He was amazed at the number of people on bicycles, it was clearly the favoured way of getting around for members of the armed forces, and he decided to enquire if he could borrow one at the Belmont, when he returned there. The horse and the buggy, along with the bicycle, appeared to be the locals' main means of independent transport.

To Newman's surprise a single railway track ran down the centre of the road and disappeared into a tunnel to the west. At least he assumed it was a track for the railway, for he hadn't heard any mention of a tram system in Bermuda. There seemed some confusion as to whether traffic drove on the right or the left side of the road — at least to the cyclists that Newman saw — who appeared to be making their own rules. And the only motor vehicle in sight, a US Army left hand drive jeep, was being driven on top of the train lines, straight down the centre of the road!

On the side of the street opposite the water's edge, there were shops and offices, mostly two or three storey buildings. Some had awnings over the pavement to keep the sun off their windows. He crossed the road, so that he could look into the shop windows as he walked to the post office.

Queen Street was easy to find, and he posted his letter, with a heavy heart. The lady behind the counter told him the way to the cathedral, and he followed her directions to Church Street. He wasn't a very religious person, but there were times when he felt the need for quiet contemplation. This was one of them.

After sitting quietly in the cathedral with his thoughts for ten minutes, he rose and slowly made his way around the cathedral taking in the scene. The RAF ensign caught his eye amongst the colours flying in the Warriors Chapel, which he noted was dedicated "for the use of military personnel of all nations in Bermuda". He paused for a while.

Resuming his stroll in the main part of the cathedral, a particular memorial plaque caught his attention. He stopped and read it, almost out loud.

> "IN MEMORY OF ROBERT JAMES (BOBBY) SPENCE WHO PERISHED IN THE AIR-LINER CAVALIER AFTER HE HAD EXHAUSTED HIS STRENGTH IN SAVING OTHERS 21st JANUARY 1939."

He'd heard about the loss of the Cavalier at the time it had happened, but he hadn't realised there had been casualties. He suddenly had the urge to continue exploring Hamilton and he left the cathedral and made his way back to Front Street. He wasn't sure why, but it seemed to him to be where the action was. He was right.

He was looking at a poster in the window of a liquor store when he noticed her. The poster was advertising a flying display in Bermuda on the first of April to commemorate the 25th anniversary of the foundation of the RAF, but she quickly distracted him. Slim, petite, and extremely attractive, he thought, he couldn't take his eyes off her. In her late teens or early twenties — Newman had never been good at estimating womens' ages — he was instantly attracted to her. In fact the sight of her was enough to remove the depression that had been pervading his thoughts, as a result of events the previous day.

He didn't really need any drink, he could get what he wanted at the Belmont, but he just had to go in and look around! When inside the shop, he couldn't resist buying something from her. He had an instinctive feeling that he wouldn't regret it.

Newman took his peak cap off and put it under his left arm. "Good morning."

She smiled, "Good morning, Sir."

He returned the smile with a little bit extra for luck. "Can you help me, what do I need to make some stormys," he asked, hesitantly.

He was impressed by the way she gave him her full attention. "You mean Dark and Stormy?" she asked.

Newman loved her sparkling blue eyes, and her shoulder length auburn hair. He had difficulty concentrating on the question, let alone thinking of the answer.

"Yes — er — that's it, Dark and Stormy."

"Black rum and ginger beer."

"I see, thank you. And in what parts do I mix them, please?"

She smiled again. It was a smile which would change the mind of a man about to commit suicide, thought Newman, although he hadn't felt quite that bad!

"That's up to you. You'll have to experiment and see what you like. Try fifty-fifty and see how that goes down."

He wanted to ask her to join him with his experiments, but he hadn't the nerve.

"I see, right, I'll take a bottle of black rum, and a bottle of ginger beer. I can always come back for some more ginger beer if I need it, can't I?"

"Of course Sir, come back for anything you need."

Was she choosing her words carefully to include an innuendo, he wondered, or was it his mind playing at wishful thinking. He had to struggle for a sensible answer which he wouldn't regret. A snappy retort might well spoil the cordial atmosphere, he thought.

"Thank you. Much appreciated." he said at last.

He paid her and started to leave when she asked, "This your first time here?"

Newman turned. She had come out from behind the counter now and was in full view.

Wearing a white, knee length, short sleeved dress, belted at the waist, and matching white high heeled shoes, Newman was more than impressed.

"Yes, I came in yesterday," he responded.

"You're a flying boat pilot then?"

She spoke with an air of quiet confidence. He supposed she must chat to a lot of men in uniform, and it came from doing that all day.

"That's right."

She looked impressed. "Oh wizard!" came the reply.

Wizard was RAF slang. Newman had first come across the word whilst he was training to be a pilot in Canada and had heard it practically every day since, but not from a lady shop assistant! When RAF pilots bent their aeroplanes and survived, they were often described as *wizard prangs*. To hear wizard mentioned by a Bermuda girl seemed slightly bizarre. Newman wasn't sure if this was good or bad news. It was then that a thought struck him.

"I wonder," said Newman, "I don't really want to carry drink around with me. Could you hold on to it for an hour or two, for me?"

"Of course — I'll put your name on it — in case I'm not here. I finish work at five."

"Thanks, but I'll be here before five, I want to catch the train back to the Belmont."

"Right. There's a train at five-fifteen, I go on that one myself."

Newman's spirits were lifted even more. "Oh bang on," he said, thinking that the use of another RAF expression would be appreciated, "Would you mind showing me where to get on, and off, so to speak, and where to buy a ticket?"

"Yes — or do I mean no — it runs down the middle of Front Street, and you buy the ticket on the train. Be back here at five and I'll show you."

He thanked her and headed for the door.

"Aren't you going to leave your rum?" she called out.

He turned, full of embarrassment. "Sorry — thanks," he said, as he handed the drink back to her.

"Flight Lieutenant Donald Newman isn't it? I'll write that on it to avoid mistakes."

"Yes, it is, how..."

"Oh, news gets around quickly here, especially when someone does something heroic, like landing in the open sea to save someone's life! There was only one flight in from Elizabeth City yesterday, so it wasn't hard to work out."

He was almost speechless, "Well, it didn't turn out that I saved a life, exactly!"

"I know, sad wasn't it, and I'm told he was your best friend. It must have been terrible for you!"

She sounded so understanding, and so sympathetic — although not factually accurate — that he decided not to correct her. He had a sort of date with her at five, that was the important thing. He smiled politely and put his hat on. "I'll see you at five, then," he said.

"Wizard" she replied. It was a word that Lucy Appledram was later going to use to describe Don Newman for a long long time to her friends. For Don Newman, Lucy was to be "bang on" more or less for ever.

Later that afternoon they caught the train together. Lucy introduced him to Bermuda train travel gently. As they stood at the Cenotaph on Front Street waiting for the train, he noticed the times of trains were painted in yellow on a blackboard on a low building opposite. She laughingly explained that there would be no restaurant car, no corridors and no toilets, and the engine wasn't driven by steam. She said the locals called it 'The Old Rattle and Shake'. He jokingly asked her if there would be any seats in the carriages. She looked at him and smiled, but didn't rise to his bait. He liked her smile.

By the time the train trundled up the street — having left St George nearly an hour earlier —she had told him her name and that she lived with her mother and younger brother at Riddell's Bay, a mile or so further along the line from the Belmont, and that her father was now in North Africa in the British Army. Her mother, he learnt, was very strict and still treated her as if she were a child, which she resented. He wasn't quite sure why she told him this. He hoped she wasn't preparing him for a *no* answer, when he inevitably asked if he might see her again.

It was a four carriage train and Lucy directed Don to the first class carriage, saying officers were expected to travel first class. He didn't query her instructions, but he did wonder who it was that expected it.

There were a few passengers already onboard, some wearing Bermuda shorts, but they had no difficulty finding wicker seats together. They sat on the right side of the train, she took the window seat and he the aisle.

The smartness of the conductor caught Newman's eye, and he wondered how many people had mistaken him for an officer in a military band. In his grey jacket with green piping, and grey trousers with a green stripe, worn with a grey shirt and green tie, topped by a grey peaked cap Newman felt he should be carrying a big bass drum, but he refrained from saying so to Lucy. He also wondered how many enlisted men had mistakenly saluted conductors on Front Street.

Later, with the benefit of a close up inspection — when he had to buy his ticket — he realised that the chromium bell punch and the money pouch hung round his neck, were a bit of a giveaway.

It was an odd sensation as the train moved off, going down the centre of Front Street in between horses, buggies, bicycles and pedestrian traffic and he half expected there to be a collision at any moment. He wondered how quickly the train could stop if the line was suddenly blocked. The thought remained unanswered and they were soon passing through the Crow Lane railway yards and starting to climb an incline. The line was now on its own, the competition left behind. By this time Lucy was asking the questions. Newman told her a little about himself, she asked what

London was like. His present journey reminded him of a journey he'd made by tram along the London Embankment some five years earlier, when going to visit an uncle, and he told her so.

"I've seen pictures," she said, "you can ride on top of the trams, can't you?"

He was impressed by her knowledge.

"Yes, double deckers they call them."

She smiled again and chuckled, then asked about the Battle of Britain and the blitz. He explained that he was in Canada training to be a pilot at that time, so hadn't experienced it himself.

"Must have been terrible." she said, "And those poor people yesterday!"

"Yesterday?"

"Yes in London — Bethnal Green I think they said on the wireless — more than one hundred and fifty people killed. Didn't you know?"

He was shocked at what she said. "No— did you say yesterday?"

"Yes, I heard it this morning."

"Crikey. No I hadn't heard. Was it a direct hit?"

"No, they say a woman carrying a baby tripped and fell down the stairs to an Underground shelter and a man fell over her. Then in the rush many other people fell over him and so on and within seconds over one hundred and fifty people were crushed to death."

"Oh God, how terrible."

There was a slight pause in the conversation. They were both reflecting on the news.

"I've never been off the Islands," said Lucy, starting the conversation again, "and can't imagine what it's like living in a big city, or a country where ordinary people have motor cars." He said that Staines, Middlesex, where he lived was about the same size as Hamilton, so he didn't know what it was like to live in a big city either. But he knew what it was like for a family to have a car; his father had one, although he hadn't been able to use it since the war started as private motoring was banned to save petrol.

She asked whether his father now had a horse. He started to tell her that he hadn't been home for over three years, and was about to say that his father now rode a bicycle, but stopped in mid sentence when he saw the view out of the window. They were crossing the long and high trestle at the Foot of the Lane and could look out over the mangrove trees at the water's edge to Hamilton Harbour and the activity at the Hamilton dockside. The sun was moving towards the horizon, casting long shadows towards them, silhouetting the islands in the Sound and a ferry boat crossing the Harbour. The water was calm and mirror like, and the whole scene tranquil in the extreme. In spite of the news about the accident at Bethnal Green, London, Newman found it difficult to comprehend that there was a world war in progress — the likes of which mankind had never seen before. He thought of his brother in RAF Bomber Command — and guessed that things were far from tranquil for him. And he was right; just two nights earlier Squadron Leader Geoffrey Newman had been the captain of a Lancaster bomber which, together with another three hundred or so aircraft, had dropped nine hundred tons of bombs on Berlin. However Berlin's defences took their toll. Geoffrey Newman's tail gunner was killed over the target and one in twenty of the bomber force did not return.

"What do you think of the view?" she asked.

He paused before answering — he was wondering how the large merchant ship tied up at the dockside had managed to find it's way between the many Islands in the Sound to reach Hamilton Harbour.

"Breath taking, Bermuda's another world isn't it!"

Soon they stopped at the Hospital Station and an elderly gentleman with his right arm in plaster got on. A young man helped him to a seat. The old gentleman thanked him.

As the train continued, now passing between cedar trees, tall oleander bushes and white roofed houses the line started to turn to the west. The wheels rubbed against the rails making a loud squeal.

"It's OK," said Lucy, "it always does this."

The train passed through a tunnel and shortly afterwards they stopped at Elbow Beach Halt. The elderly man with an arm in plaster got off. The driver blew the whistle and the train moved on. Newman was wondering how to ask Lucy if he could see her again, as it couldn't be long before the Belmont stop. But he wasn't too worried, he knew where to find her again.

After more cedar trees, fiddlewood trees and glimpses of back gardens, they passed an Esso tank car on a siding. Lucy told him it contained oil for the Elbow Beach Hotel. There were two more halts before the Belmont Manor Hotel came into sight in the distance.

"The next stop is where you get off," she said, smiling.

He asked if he could see her again soon. It wasn't difficult, she was clearly expecting it. Smiling again, she opened her handbag and gave him a slip of paper on which she had already written her name and the telephone number of the shop.

"You'll have to," she said, "you forgot to collect the rum I was looking after for you, didn't you!"

There was a twinkle in her blue eyes as she said it, which was just as well. Newman would have felt even more foolish without it.

"I usually answer the phone, but if my boss answers, tell him who you are. I'll tell him you may call. OK?"

"Thanks, I'll call tomorrow if I can."

When he got off, she waved to him as the train moved off. He lit a cigarette and headed off along the side of the golf course for the hotel, thinking about her. Just after he had crossed Middle Road and was nearing the hotel, he came across Hank Humble returning from a round of golf.

"I've got a message for you Don," said Hank. "Your navy friend is going to be buried tomorrow. I've spoken with the rest of the crew and we thought we'd come along with you, if that's OK."

Newman was suddenly brought back to the real world, he had been day dreaming rather heavily, "Oh, yes, thanks. Where and when?"

"Eleven hundred hours, at your Royal Navy Cemetery near the Dockyard. I've spoken to someone in admin here — I wasn't sure what time you'd be back from town — and they've organised a motor launch to take us there and back."

"Thanks, Hank. That's one I owe you. I'll buy you a drink after dinner, OK?"

The bar at the Belmont was crowded that evening. Newman found Hank chatting to a Polish Flying Officer, who had flown in on an RAF Dakota, to Kindley Field — the land airfield the US had built at Bermuda — earlier that day. Newman arrived just in time to hear the Pole say, in broken English, "Sorry, can't talk about it, the walls have ears, you know."

It was evident that Hank had made the mistake of asking the Pole why he had come to Bermuda, and instead of making up a story, the Pole had played the 'it's a secret' card. Hank had had a few and said "don't worry I can keep it under my hat!" Newman could see the joke, but the Pole not knowing about Hank's Stetson, made his excuses and left.

"So what sort of day have you had then?" asked Newman.

"OK, a bit bloody depressing though."

"What do you mean?"

"Well I played golf with some guy — forget his name for the moment — who has been through here several times, and he's got all the gen. He says a month or so ago a Cat went missing on a delivery flight, and eventually the Captain was found in a dinghy. The only trouble was, he was frozen bloody solid!"

"Jesus, and what about the rest of the crew?"

"He didn't know, except to say there were no survivors. And there was another lost just before Christmas, he said, and one a week or two earlier near Gibraltar, although he says the crew were saved by one of your destroyers."

"Thanks Hank, you've really made my day."

There was a pause in the conversation. It was an unwritten convention that specific prangs weren't discussed at the bar in RAF messes —and although the bar at the Belmont was not strictly an RAF enterprise — Newman felt it appropriate to try and lead the conversation in a different direction. "It sounds bad Hank, but I've heard that over two hundred and fifty Cats have been delivered to the UK," said Newman, "and think of those poor bods in Bomber Command — I've got an older brother on Lancasters — or your Eighth Air Force, being shot down left right and centre over Germany. We've got much better odds than them, much better!"

"Oh don't get me wrong Don, I'm not bloody scared. But you got to remember I'm a bloody civilian! If I'd wanted danger I'd have joined the Army Air Force."

"Have a drink on me Hank. What will it be?"

Friday 5 March 1943

The following morning Newman checked that he was free to go to Livingstone's funeral and then got to the Belmont Wharf just before ten. He found the whole crew, except Sgt Ferguson, waiting on the wharf. Somehow or other, all the civilians in his crew had managed to borrow black ties, and Newman wondered if there were three RAF officers unable to find their ties that morning.

The launch, coxswained by a young black Bermudian, arrived on time. They made a stop at the Darrell's Island jetty to pick up Ferguson, then Newman and his crew set off for the half hour journey to the

Dockyard. They sat in the small cabin and were mostly quiet. Newman noticed that when they did speak they did so in hushed tones, and he appreciated their thoughtfulness. There were four nationalities among the five of them, and probably as many religions — Newman didn't know — and it didn't seem to be relevant. But he was touched by their decision to lend him moral support. They could so easily have thought it was nothing to do with them, and gone for a swim, or played golf or tennis.

They ran into a rain shower in the middle of the Great Sound, but although it was heavy, it was over in two or three minutes and the sun shone again.

Nearing the Dockyard, Newman saw that *HMS Brentford* was moored inside the harbour, and it looked as though the Coxswain was making for it.

"Where are you going to drop us off Coxswain?" he asked. It was the first time he had spoken for nearly half an hour.

"I'm going alongside *HMS Brentford* Sir, those were my orders."

"Oh, I see. Right."

"I hadn't envisaged that" said Newman, "whose idea was that?"

"The Wing Co's Sir. He said the Navy had specifically requested it. I think it was because you landed on the sea and tried to help, or something like that."

They were now passing the breakwater and nearing the ship.

"But ..."

"Do you want to change the orders, Sir?"

"No — it's just that I've never been on a Royal Navy ship before, I don't know the customs, when to salute, that sort of thing."

"Oh, I shouldn't worry Sir, the rule is — if in doubt salute."

The Coxswain was serious and trying to be helpful, but Hank Humble, who couldn't have looked more obviously a civilian than he did, smiled and nearly laughed. Fortunately Newman didn't notice.

The launch pulled alongside the ship's steps. A sailor at the bottom of the steps saluted and secured the launch. Newman made his way up the steps to be greeted by a young Lieutenant, who introduced himself as the First Lieutenant, and by Surgeon-Lieutenant Moffet, the medical officer who had attended Lieutenant Commander Livingstone on the mercy flight to Bermuda.

Newman followed the Coxswain's advice and saluted. The salute was returned by both officers and he was ushered to the Wardroom.

"Flight Lieutenant Newman," said the Lieutenant, "I'm Raymond Codling, the officer in charge of the funeral party. Tragic business. I'm wondering if you want to say anything at the grave side, or take charge of the guard of honour, that sort of thing. Or would you prefer us to carry on as normal."

"Oh, absolutely, my crew and I are here in a purely private capacity. Please just carry on. We will just be spectators in the background, if that's all right."

"Of course. Do you know where the cemetery is?"

"No, we don't."

"No problem. I'll get Petty Officer Springer to escort you. It's only a few hundred yards down the road."

"Thank you."

And that's how it was. Flt Lt Don Newman and Sgt Pip Ferguson walked with Petty Officer Springer down Malabar Road to the Royal Navy Cemetery, with Newman's civilian crew behind them. They didn't exactly march but they did keep in step.

The Petty Officer led them to the burial site. The only person there was still digging. Petty Officer Springer said the funeral party would be there at eleven hundred hours exactly, then saluted Newman and left.

"Well," said Newman, to his crew, "he's got sunshine for his funeral!"

"A lot of good that'll do him," said Humble.

Newman didn't respond.

Before long, they heard the sound of slow marching feet and a moment later the funeral party entered the cemetery gates. Five officers and a Petty Officer were carrying the coffin on their shoulders. The man digging the grave got out of it quickly and disappeared among the gravestones. If it wasn't deep enough now it seemed it never would be.

The military ceremony was brief, in fact Newman felt it was unduly brief. But he consoled himself that Livingstone had not been buried at sea, due to his, and his crews' efforts. The fact that their Catalina shouldn't have been anywhere near *HMS Brentford*'s position, seemed for the moment, perhaps understandably, to have escaped his attention.

At the end, a guard of honour of naval ratings brought up their Leigh Enfield rifles and fired three volleys into the air. It was the most poignant moment of the funeral for Newman and he saluted, as they fired. As he did so he had a flashback and could see Livingstone standing on the podium as his House Master on a sports day, and after making a brilliant speech, asking Newman to accept the winner's trophy. Newman remembered holding it above his head, to thunderous applause.

They were back at the Belmont by one o'clock, in time for lunch. Newman wasn't very hungry but went through the motions. After lunch he phoned Lucy Appledram. She sounded sweet on the phone and if she had not been at work he would have tried to prolong the conversation. As it was, he just asked her if he could meet her after work again. She said she had been hoping he would call, and would see him outside her shop at what she called 'the usual time'.

He was outside the shop at five minutes to five and caught sight of her through the window. She was wearing a light yellow dress today and looked even more radiant than the day before. She saw him and beckoned him into the shop. The door was open and he entered as though he was entering a church, quietly and thoughtfully, whilst taking off his peak cap.

She surprised him with a suggestion. "Hallo Don, do you feel like a walk?" she asked.

"Yes, that would suit me." He was delighted with the idea, but tried not to show it too much. He wasn't sure why.

"What we could do," said Lucy, sounding excited, "is go over to the Belmont on the ferry, then walk along Harbour Road beside the water to Riddell's Bay. It's a lovely walk on a day like this. I often have to do it, if I work late and can't catch the train. Mummy has got used to me being late when I do that, she won't get upset."

Newman noted her mother was already coming into the conversation again, but he wasn't put off. He realised, on his first real date with Lucy, that she had some special quality which was having a deep effect on him. He'd never experienced it before and he wasn't going to be put off by — what sounded like — an over protective mother.

"OK, fine, I'd like that."

"It would mean you'd have to walk back to the Belmont, though, and it'll probably be dark by then."

"No problem, Lucy, no problem."

At five Lucy collected her handbag and an umbrella, and they started the short walk to the ferry terminus. He asked her if she got home all right the previous evening. As he said it, he realised it wasn't an inspired question.

She was in high spirits and fitted in with Newman's needs like a charm. A breath of fresh air for him, especially after the funeral. She detected his mood and asked about his day. He told her, as they stood waiting for the ferry to come in.

"It must have been terrible for you," she said. "Have you been to a funeral before?"

"Only one," said Newman, "a friend of mine on our course was killed during pilot training in Canada."

The ferry was approaching, she looked up at him as she replied. He caught her blue eyes for just a second.

"I've been lucky," she said, "never had to go to one, yet."

She elected to stand close to him on the quay side and he was tempted to put an arm around her waist, but resisted the temptation, with great difficulty. Telling himself that he hardly knew her and she was different and needed to be treated carefully. There were also thirty or forty other people waiting with them so it was hardly private.

They boarded the ferry *Laconia* for the fifteen minute journey to the Belmont and entered the aft compartment and sat near the stern. Lucy seemed to know most of the people who boarded.

As they moved off, the ferry rocked from side to side and their bodies touched. He wondered if it might get a bit rougher as they moved further out into the harbour, but his luck was out.

Although it was only a short ride, for Newman it was an experience to remember. Not just because it was the first boat ride with Lucy, but also because of the view. The *Laconia's* large rectangular windows were ideal for sightseeing and they looked back at Hamilton, drenched by the setting sun. Lucy pointed out the cathedral towering above everything else. She was clearly enjoying the view as much as he was. He liked that.

"Yes, I was in there yesterday," he said.

The noise of an aircraft drew his attention. Turning and looking into the sun, towards the Great Sound, he could see a large Sikorsky flying boat approaching to land.

"American Export," said Lucy, "they come in regularly."

Harbour Road was almost deserted and they strolled along it as though they had known each other for months or even years. They had to watch their step as the horses of Bermuda — which were numerous and healthy — had left their calling cards very frequently. But it wasn't long before he had his left arm round her waist and they were telling each other all about themselves once more. Opposite Darrell's Island they paused for a few minutes and Newman pointed out his Catalina. He wondered if it was the first time a pilot had pointed out his flying boat to her. He hoped she hadn't heard the patter too often.

They reached a left bend in the road and the road ceased to follow the shoreline. The sun was just disappearing below the Somerset skyline. She told him that she was nearly home and would have to leave him now, and that she would have to use considerable cunning to see him each evening. He liked her presumption that that was what he wanted. She explained that she had to keep him a secret from her mother, as she would watch her like a hawk if she knew about him.

He said he understood, but didn't. At least not completely.

"When you take me home," she said, "we will always have to say our good-byes, before reaching our cottage."

"Is this it then? Do I have to leave you here?" He sounded a little disappointed, as though he was surprised and wanted to extend the walk for a while.

"Yes, but we can meet again, tomorrow. That is if you want to. It's my Saturday off. I only get one off now and again."

"Of course, if I can. I think it will be OK. I'm not on standby."

"We could meet at lunch time if you like, here."

Her enthusiasm was almost overwhelming him. But he knew that sooner or later he would have to fly away. He hoped that there would be delays, so that when he did leave she would feel she was *his* girl friend, and would patiently await his return. He realised he had to make hay whilst the sun was shining, and he didn't hesitate to take her up on her suggestion.

"Wizard. What time exactly?"

Four days later Newman and his crew had to carry out an air test on their Catalina. However there was now a snag with the autopilot which had to be rectified and it turned out that for a variety of reasons, Newman and his crew had to stay in Bermuda for over another fortnight. During this period a statement was made in the British House of Commons that an RAF Transport Command was being formed and would encompass all RAF existing and future ferry operations world-wide. But to Newman and most other RAF personnel at Bermuda, it was a non event, despite rumours — which turned out to be well founded — that three BOAC directors had resigned because of it. Apparently they felt strongly that the whole future of BOAC would be affected by the decision.

One RAF Cat pilot who had had a few in the Belmont bar one night, nearly got himself into deep water by shouting "They're bloody lucky. Can't see anybody allowing my resignation!" when he heard the news. Someone bought him another beer.

During his period of remission, Newman saw Lucy every day; sometimes twice a day. Lucy's mother always went to see her sister on Saturday evenings, so each Saturday night they were able to go to a dance in the local church hall. It was crowded with people from the armed forces and they were able to get lost in each others arms for several hours.

It was at the second dance that Newman realised he had fallen head over heels in love with Lucy Appledram, and he didn't have any doubt that the feeling was mutual. But the evening was marred by a tragedy in the Great Sound. A Catalina which had left Bermuda for Scotland earlier in the day, had returned to Bermuda because of engine trouble and crashed trying to land after dark.

The news reached the dance hall quickly and, although no announcement was made, spread from couple to couple. Newman heard it from his flight engineer, Pip Ferguson, who was there with an English redhead who had come to Bermuda to work on a special wartime project which was being carried out at the Princess Hotel, although according to Ferguson, she wouldn't say exactly what she and the many other English girls who were there were doing.

At first it was thought there were no survivors. Later they heard that there were two, but four of the crew including the Captain were missing, presumed killed. Newman had not known any of the crew well, but had spoken to the Canadian Captain a few times in the Belmont bar.

The accident affected people differently. Some couples left the dance, others — mainly aircrew — headed for the bar. Newman and Lucy decided to stay at least for a while, but it made them realise that their time together was precious. It was a realisation that many couples all over the world were acknowledging. They danced cheek to cheek, and said very little. There wasn't any need to say anything for they were communicating with every move.

CHAPTER FOUR

Monday, 22 March 1943

Newman and his crew were up at four in the morning. After their briefing at Manor Cottage near the Belmont and picking up their rations for the journey, they boarded the Cat at six through the port blister. It was morning twilight, with sunrise due in twenty minutes. The weather forecast was good for most of the route, although they would have to traverse a front five or six hours into the flight, and their estimated flight time to Largs was twenty three and a half hours. They planned to cruise at a height of eight thousand feet for most of the way — although it might be a few hours before they could reach that height — with an expected initial ground speed of 135 mph. There were better tail winds higher up, but as they didn't carry oxygen, they couldn't go above ten thousand feet for long. Their planned great circle route — theoretically the shortest — would take them over 3250 miles of the Atlantic Ocean.

As expected their second flight engineer turned out to be a young Bermudian who was on his way to Scotland to join the RAF. He was as keen as they come, and on Newman's instruction, Pip Ferguson showed the young Slimbridge how to start the auxiliary power unit and then let him observe the engine starting routine. It was virtually certain that Slimbridge would not be called upon to carry out either of these jobs during the next twenty four hours, but Newman wanted to make sure everyone on board, including Slimbridge, considered themselves a vital part of the team.

Newman felt his old self again now that he was in the captain's seat. The familiar and distinctive smell of the Catalina cockpit helped. The smell of fuel, oil, leather and sometimes perspiration wasn't usually noticeable after a short while, and it was the same today.

The crew noticed the change in him as well. He sounded confident and cheerful, and above all, in charge. He was sorry to be leaving Lucy and Bermuda for the time being, but if all went well he hoped to be back in a few weeks. There was always the possibility that he might not be given another Cat to deliver — he was at the mercy of the RAF, and there was a war on — but he thought the chances of being back soon were high.

Lucy was up and about to watch Newman's departure. She could have had a good view from her bedroom window, but she wanted Newman to be able to see her, so she stood at Burgess Point and watched the Cat slip its moorings and taxi out towards Somerset, following the control launch. She was wearing the white dress she had been wearing when they first met, hoping she would show up well against the green background of the shrubs and trees. The local wind was from the north-west, which meant their take-off run would start just beyond Burgess Point, and they would climb away over Watford Island with Somerset Village on their left.

It was a fine bright morning, with just a little high cloud here and there. With the temperature sixty-seven degrees, Newman had his cockpit window open. There was a healthy breeze and the sea state in the Great Sound was just right for a comfortable take-off.

Newman saw Lucy waving as he neared Burgess Point, so did Hank Humble. Neither of them said anything and Newman didn't want to wave back whilst Humble was watching. He was anxious to give the impression that his mind was on the job one hundred per cent, but when it was almost too late he couldn't resist opening his side window and sticking his left hand out. It was more like a salute than a wave, and he quickly returned his attention to the cockpit, where he noted, Humble was just putting his Stetson back on.

Newman was surprised by Humble's gesture — although he very much doubted Lucy would be able to see it. Since he had got to know Humble better at the Belmont bar, and at Livingstone's funeral, he was feeling much more comfortable in his presence.

Pip Ferguson advised that both engines had now warmed up sufficiently for power checks to be made and Newman very briefly opened up both of the Twin-Wasp engines to 2000 rpm and exercised the propeller pitch controls to check their response. He had to be brief as the Catalina still had no brakes!

Satisfied that all was well, he then ran through his take off check with Humble and Ferguson. It wasn't much different from most other aircraft, except that there were no flaps to set. Also it was necessary to check that the wing tip floats were down. Newman knew they were of course, but he was methodical and made the flight engineer confirm it.

He also had the engineer check their fuel status once more — they had already checked it once, before starting the engines. Pip Ferguson confirmed that the main tanks in each wing contained 720 gallons and the cross-feed cocks were off. For this flight, they were also carrying an additional 325 gallons in long range tanks in the fuselage, and both Newman and Ferguson had confirmed they were full prior to starting engines. The fuel in these tanks would be pumped into the main wing tanks later in the flight.

The R/T had been made serviceable at Bermuda and Newman called flying control.

"Darrell's tower, one-nine-nine, take-off clearance. Over."

"One-nine- nine — cleared take-off. Wind, north-west, fifteen knots, gusting twenty. Have a good trip. Out."

Newman addressed the crew. "Gentlemen. Standby for take-off."

He had hardly finished when Hanson the radio operator piped up, "Do you want some rousing music for the take-off Skipper? I've just accidentally — sort of — picked up some wizard stuff."

This was a new one on Newman and he hesitated before replying. It was almost certainly against some RAF regulation or other, but the idea of leaving Bermuda behind to rousing music was appealing.

"OK Jock, but as soon as we set course we must get down to business and listen out."

"Roger Skip."

Then, to the strains of *Beyond the Blue Horizon,* Newman closed his window, pulled the control column back as far as it would go with his left hand and pushed the throttles fully forward with his right. They were on their way!

With a total weight of well over thirty four thousand pounds — the normal maximum weight for a Catalina — their Cat was not about to leap into the air. They gathered speed and spray came over the nose, Humble turned on the windscreen wipers.

"Thanks," said Newman, over the sound of the music.

"No charge," said Humble.

The take-off run seemed to go on forever, but after nearly two minutes their airspeed had reached sixty-five knots and Newman eased the boat off the water. He flew level and let the speed build up to eighty before signalling the engineer to raise the floats, then set the aircraft on a steady climb out at eighty-five knots, and reduced the power. For his part, Hanson gradually reduced the volume of the music and before long they were all left with just the drone of the engines. But the music had been worthwhile and had raised their already high spirits.

Hanson was going to act as radio officer and navigator for the first few hours, and he entered 'airborne 1045Z' as their GMT take-off time in the navigation log, GMT being four hours ahead of Bermuda time. Newman now asked him for the first course to steer.

"Steer zero six seven magnetic, Skipper, zero six seven."

"Roger Jock, zero six seven, magnetic."

They were now passing through five hundred feet and Newman started a gentle right turn on to their first heading. As they came back over Darrell's Island at twelve hundred feet Newman could just make out a white dot on Burgess Point.

"Take it for a bit will you Hank," said Newman.

"Sure. I have control."

"You have control."

Newman took his binoculars — which he always carried in the cockpit — and managed to get a brief glimpse of Lucy before they left Bermuda behind them. With the aid of the ten times magnification, it was as if she was only one hundred yards away, and he could see her waving. But there was someone else standing with her, on her right hand side, it looked like a man in a red shirt or pullover. He wasn't sure, but it puzzled him.

"I'll keep her until we get to eight thousand, if you like" said Humble. "Then I can put her on George — I mean," he raised his Stetson again, "*Brenda*."

Newman smiled, "Yep, OK Hank, you do that. I'm going to make a tour of the ship."

Six and a half hours later they began to see the signs of the front they had been told to expect. The sky became overcast and was gradually lowering. Newman, who was now supervising *Brenda* — whilst Hank was having a break and making coffee in the galley — looked at the outside air temperature gauge. It was just below freezing and when they entered cloud ten minutes later he switched on the deicing boots on the leading edges of the wings and advised Humble and Ferguson.

They had been in the cloud ten minutes when Jock Hanson called Newman. "Skip, we have a recall."

"A recall?"

"Yes, return to Bermuda."

"Jesus," said Hank, "what the hell do they think they're playing at?"

"Do they give a reason?" asked Newman.

"No, Skip."

"Well, ask them to repeat the message."

"Roger."

"So it looks as if you're going to get your leg over tonight after all." said Humble.

Newman didn't respond, he didn't like his relationship with Lucy being thought of in those simplistic terms. Anyway he hadn't yet, and he doubted it was even on the horizon. In some ways he hoped it wasn't. She was a serious girl friend whom he respected, not a passing popsy. But he had to admit that the thought interested him.

Anticipating that Bermuda would confirm the recall, Newman disconnected the autopilot and started a left hand turn on to a reciprocal course. It would need to be adjusted when the new course was calculated by Hanson, but at least they would be going in roughly the right direction in the meantime.

"Got it Skipper. Confirmation. It says 'weather at destination and alternates outside limits. Return BDA.' "

"Bloody hell," said Humble, "somebody really cocked up the forecast — but at least it'll be warmer back in Bermuda."

"OK," said Newman, "I guess you all heard that, we're going back. Give me the new course as soon as you can Jock, and an ETA. I've already done a one-eighty."

"Roger, Skip."

A few minutes later, Jock came up with the new course and the ETA for Bermuda, which he gave as 22:45.

"And what time is sunset?" asked Newman.

"22:28 Zebra or 18:28 Bermuda time."

"Thanks,"

Newman turned to Hank Humble. "I think we had better put some more coal on, otherwise we could be in for a night landing!"

"Yes," said Humble "we should be able to increase our airspeed by ten knots, without too much trouble. We're not going to be low on fuel."

"Just what I was thinking."

Newman informed the flight engineer of his intentions and opened up the throttles until their speed had increased to 110 knots. They were now flying into the wind, so it was slowing them down rather than assisting them, and Newman decided to let the aircraft gradually descend to two thousand feet, where the head wind should be less. It was now a race against the sun, back to Bermuda. A night landing might eventually turn out to be inevitable, but Newman and Humble were keen to get back in daylight if possible.

There were initially a mixture of emotions aboard the Cat as they headed back to Bermuda, but, with the exception of Slimbridge, they all knew that flying was like that. It was evident that it was the weather forecasters for the western side of the British Isles, who had got it wrong. At least the recall had come in time; in another few hours they would have passed the point of no return, and therefore committed to continue.

They were soon out in the sunlight once more, but now the sun was on their left side rather than their right. Slimbridge seemed to come to life on the return journey. He had been very quiet most of the voyage, but nevertheless had made the mistake of making a bet, following an approach from Hank Humble, soon after they were airborne. Humble had bet him a pound that they would see snow within twenty four hours of leaving Bermuda. Slimbridge who had never seen snow or frost, having lived in Bermuda all his life, thought this was a safe bet, since their journey would take them around twenty-four hours, and had raised the stakes to two pounds, which would be more than his first week's pay as an ab initio RAF pilot. Now, with the chances of snow in the next twenty four hours virtually zero, Humble decided to put plan B into operation.

"Looks like we're running into a snow cloud Slimbridge, you'd better take up position in one of the blisters so you don't miss it," he said over the intercom.

There wasn't a cloud in sight and Newman realised Humble was up to something. But at the very least, as long as it didn't get out of hand, it relieved the monotony, and he didn't interfere.

"Really? Right Sir," said Slimbridge.

Humble gave Slimbridge time to get to the blister window, and plug in to the intercom.

"It shouldn't be long now, Slimbridge, we're getting close. Are you in position?" asked Humble.

"Yes, in the starboard blister Sir, but it doesn't look like snow from here."

Humble was relieved Slimbridge had chosen the starboard blister, there would have been complications, if the young Bermudian had sat on the port side of the aircraft.

"Ah well," said Humble, "it takes a lot of experience to recognise a snow cloud. They're not like ordinary clouds, you know."

Humble let a few seconds pass. "Do you see that Slimbridge?" he asked.

"No, not a thing, Sir."

"Well it's definitely snowing now, pouring with snow!"

Newman felt a sudden blast of cold air, and as he looked around to find the reason, he saw that Humble had opened his side cockpit window and taken a brown paper bag out of his flying suit pocket. Humble then proceeded to slowly empty the contents, which turned out to be paper confetti used at weddings, out of the window. It was obvious it would flow back along the side of the aircraft and over and around the blister window and have the appearance of snow. Newman couldn't help smiling to himself.

"I see it, I see it," said Slimbridge. "Amazing, it looks just like small bits of white paper."

"Absolutely," said Humble. "You can pay me when we've landed."

"Shall I report this snow to Bermuda?" asked Hanson.

"No, don't worry, it was a sort of snowstorm in a tea cup!" said Newman, finding it difficult not to laugh at his own wisecrack.

"You happy to take her for the return to BDA?" Newman asked Humble.

"Sure, no problem. I have control."

"You have control - I'm going for a pee."

"Roger."

If truth be known, Newman was happy about the recall and so were all the crew, now that they had got used to the idea. Newman guessed that he wouldn't have been in the UK long enough to see his family anyway, and he now had different personal priorities!

Even Slimbridge — who was keen to get into the RAF and get on with his pilot's training — seemed to have accepted that this sort of thing was part and parcel of flying the North Atlantic.

An hour before their ETA Jock Hanson got a bearing from Bermuda and they altered course six degrees to starboard. Twenty minutes before their ETA — although there was still some daylight — they caught sight of the flashing light of Gibbs Hill Lighthouse about fifteen degrees off the nose on their starboard side and Humble altered course towards it. He estimated they were about ten miles from Bermuda.

"Do you want me to call the Tower?" asked Humble.

"Sure."

"Darrell's Tower, this is one-nine-nine with Stetson approaching from the south-west after a cockup. Over"

Humble's accent was not new to Darrell's Tower and his Stetson had become his trademark in and around Darrell's Island and the Belmont.

"One-nine-nine. Cleared to enter circuit. One aircraft touching down. Wind northerly twelve knots. Call downwind, remove Stetson after landing!"

Newman positively chuckled.

The setting sun was over their left shoulder, behind them, and their distorted shadow hit the water half a mile ahead of them and appeared to bounce from wave to wave. The Southampton shoreline was soon visible and every now and then beyond it, between the cedar trees, they could just make out a train heading towards Somerset. Not for the first time Newman thought of Lucy, and wondered if she had been on it and got off at Riddell's bay a few minutes earlier.

"Looks bloody magnificent, don't you think?" said Humble.

"What the train?" asked Newman.

"No, the whole bloody issue. The green of the trees, the white coloured roofs, the different blues of the sea — it really is a colourful dot in the North Atlantic. Isn't it?"

"You can say that again." said Newman, "and we'd be in trouble if we'd missed it again!"

It was just after sunset when they entered the circuit at Bermuda and ran through the landing drill. Humble signalled to Pip Ferguson, the flight engineer to lower the floats, then waited for the signal that they were down. But the signal on the control yoke indicating that he had successfully lowered the floats, seemed an unusually long time coming. Newman noticed this and looked out of his side of the aircraft. The port wing tip float appeared down and locked but Humble reported it was not down his side. It was at that moment that Pip Ferguson announced, "we have a problem skipper, the starboard float won't lower. I've recycled it three times, and it won't move."

They were downwind at one thousand feet, slightly west of Mangrove Bay, Somerset, heading South.

"OK, Pip, you'll have to try and lower it manually." said Newman,

"Get Slimbridge to help you, we'll continue in the circuit whilst you do it."

"Roger."

Newman pressed the radio telephony button. "Tower, one-nine-nine — we have problems with our starboard float. Attempting a manual lowering. Request permission to stay in the circuit to lower. Over."

"Roger one-nine-nine, permission granted. No other aircraft around now. Out."

Newman was very much aware that it was getting darker by the minute, and was anxious to get the boat on the water whilst there was still at least some daylight. It was only nine days since a Catalina had crashed in the Sound — when he and Lucy were at a dance — whilst attempting a night landing, and they still hadn't found the body of the Captain and some of the crew. But he tried not to let it show, and waited patiently as the flight engineer attempted to pump the wing tip float down by hand.

Newman couldn't see the starboard float from his seat on the left of the cockpit. "Any sign of it moving?" he asked Humble, who was still flying the aircraft.

"Yes it's coming down slowly," said Humble.

"Marvellous! It's getting so bloody dark. Start the approach, we can always go round again if it's not down in time."

"It might bloody help if you took off your sun glasses!" said Humble.

Newman recovered from his embarrassment quickly.

"Yes — I put them on when I was frightened there might be some lightning with your snowstorm!" he retorted.

Humble smiled, but said nothing and started the approach to alight.

They alighted in the Great Sound at 18:47 Bermuda time, and followed the launch to Darrell's. It was always difficult judging height at twilight, but the sea was a little choppy and that helped Humble see the surface and make a smooth landing. Newman was happy with his co-pilot's performance, but didn't say anything. By the time they were tied up at their mooring buoy, it was completely dark, and the near full moon, was rising.

Lucy noticed the Catalina landing as she walked along Harbour Road from the Belmont Wharf. She had missed her usual train, this time by accident, and had taken the ferry to the Belmont and was having to walk to Riddell's Bay by herself. It never occurred to her that the Catalina could be the one she had watched take-off just over twelve hours earlier, and that Don was only a few hundred yards away from her. All RAF Catalinas looked the same to her in their standard grey camouflage.

All through the day she had been thinking of her RAF pilot, Don Newman, and quietly praying that he would return to Bermuda before too long. He was the man she intended to marry, by hook or by crook.

Newman, Humble and most of the crew returned to the Belmont by an RAF launch. It was on the launch that Newman began to wonder again who he had seen with Lucy, through his binoculars, after take-off earlier in the day.

The following morning he phoned Lucy at the shop. She was surprised and delighted to hear his voice, and they arranged to meet at lunchtime.

When they met she was clearly overjoyed at seeing him again, and he didn't mention seeing someone else with her at Burgess Point after he had taken off. He felt it would sound as if he was possessive and didn't trust her. He hoped she might say who it was without him having to ask, but she didn't. At least not then.

They went to Par La Ville park, shared her sandwiches in the sunshine, and made small talk. She wanted to know all about his flight and he did his best to explain. She liked the story about the snow storm, and Newman asked her not to mention it to anyone, he didn't want the whole of Bermuda laughing about it within a few days, especially as Slimbridge hadn't yet realised he had been conned!

She asked him if he might still be in Bermuda at the weekend, so that they could go to the dance. He said he couldn't be sure, but he might be as the weather forecasts for the next few days were not good. They held hands and she looked into his eyes and said she hoped he would be. He could tell that she really meant it, and he decided never to ask her who the man in the red shirt was.

He stayed in Hamilton during the afternoon. They met at five and he escorted her home the long way, by ferry and then walking. They both liked this way as it gave them much longer together, and the road was usually quiet.

As they walked along Harbour Road a Catalina was doing circuits and bumps, in the Great Sound. Newman remarked on this to Lucy.

"You mean circuits and splashes," she said. He tightened his left arm round her waist and they laughed out loud together. Just at this moment, a man in a red shirt and grey trousers appeared on the road about fifty yards ahead of them. Newman wasn't sure where he had come from, and there was something about him that he didn't like, although he would have been hard pressed to say what it was if he had had to.

It was obvious that Lucy knew the newcomer. She waved and when they reached him she exchanged greetings with him.

"Don, this is Helmut Schachmann. Helmut, this is Flight Lieutenant Don Newman."

They stood in the middle of the road, shook hands, and exchanged "how do you dos". As they did so Newman thought of the person in the red shirt he had seen with Lucy at Burgess Point through his binoculars the day before, as he flew over in his Catalina.

Helmut was several years older than him, Newman thought. About the same height, although more solidly built. He was surprised at the name, it sounded German, and Germans hadn't been very popular with Newman for three or four years.

On impulse Newman said. "Didn't I see you at Burgess Point early yesterday morning, Helmut?"

"No, not me!" It was said as a statement of fact, as though there could be no further discussion of the matter. He spoke with an accent, which Newman was convinced was German. The two men were eyeing each other; both seemed uneasy at the other's presence.

But Lucy was not going to let Helmut off the hook. "You were there Helmut. You said you were bird watching, remember?" said Lucy.

"Oh, yesterday morning. Sorry, yes I forgot, that's right, I was there. I bumped into you Lucy dear, didn't I, and went home with you, and had another marvellous breakfast with you. How could I forget that. Yes, of course, Yes."

Newman was not over the moon with the way the conversation was developing. Lucy could see that and stepped in to explain.

"Helmut used to live with us," said Lucy. "He left Austria when the Nazis started persecuting the Jews, and after a spell in England, came to Bermuda."

"Oh, right. I thought I detected an accent. Nice to meet you Helmut," said Newman.

Newman moved as though to walk on, but Lucy, tugged at his tunic to stop him.

"Helmut," she said, "you know you used to say you'd do anything for me?"

"Yes?"

"Well, I want you to do something for me tonight."

"Tonight?" He looked at her with a look of surprise.

"Yes, well you know how strict Mummy is. I want you to cover for me tonight. If I tell her I'm going out with you, she'll be OK, and not stop me."

"To cover — what does that mean?"

"Well, if you see Mummy in the next few days — and she asks if I was out with you tonight — you say 'Yes'."

"Yes, of course I'll go out with you tonight. Where do you want me to take you?"

Newman had strolled a few yards up the road, but could hear what was being said.

Lucy was turning on the charm, and she had plenty of it. "Helmut, stop mucking about. You know what I mean. I want to go out with Don tonight. But I want you to tell Mummy I'm going out with you." She spoke to him as if he was an elder brother, but it was obvious to Newman that he didn't see her as a sister.

Helmut glanced at Newman to make sure he was listening, and said, "OK Lucy, but it's going to cost you!"

"Thank you Helmut, I hope the price won't be too high."

"Probably not. I'll put it on your friend's account. I'll expect a favour from him some time."

Treating the remark as a joke, Newman shouted, "Of course, any time, Helmut."

Shachmann disappeared as quickly as he had first shown up. Don and Lucy walked on arm in arm.

"He lives in a cottage just here, now," said Lucy. "When he's here, that is. He's supposed to be at college in Boston right now, but for some reason he's come back here for a while. I'm not sure why."

"Have you known him long."

"About five years I suppose. He lived with us for three."

Although it was good that he could see Lucy tonight, Newman still wasn't quite sure about Helmut. There was something about him, his confidence perhaps, almost over confident he felt, that put him off the man. He felt instinctively, that when he flew off in a few days time, Helmut might take advantage of the situation, and demand payment in full from Lucy!

"What shall we do tonight, then?" said Don.

"Lets go to the cinema in Hamilton. If you go back to the Belmont now and eat, I can run home, then catch the half past seven train, and you can get on the train at the Belmont stop, and we can meet on the train."

So it was that Lucy and Don had their first evening together at what Lucy called the flicks. They sat in the back row and didn't see much of the film, as they were otherwise occupied. In fact both of them would not have passed the 'what was the film about test,' had anyone asked. Fortunately Lucy's mother didn't.

The following day, Wednesday, was Lucy's day off. Don and his crew were not yet on standby to try and deliver their bird to Scotland again, so Lucy was able to take Don to St George on the train.

Lucy didn't even tell her mother she had the day off. She just got up in the morning and caught the train as usual at Riddell's bay, and Don boarded at the Belmont. She didn't feel guilty. She was madly in love with Don, and all was fair in love and war, she said to herself.

Don only had time for half his breakfast, but that was of no importance. His main priority was to make sure he caught the train that Lucy would be on, and he did. He had to sprint the last hundred yards across the golf course, but that was no problem.

It was a journey of about ten miles from Hamilton, and shortly after passing through a tunnel on the edge of the City, followed the north coast of Bermuda. They had a good view of two merchant ships which Lucy said were in the South Channel and making for the Dockyard, or Hamilton Harbour.

In several places the track ran on trestles on the sea side of the shoreline. Lucy told him that some passengers were terrified going over these trestles. He detected that she wasn't too happy herself, and put his arm round her. He found the views of Bermuda breathtaking.

The longest water crossings were at Flatts and at Ferry Reach, where the train seemed to take an age to reach the other side. At the Ferry Reach crossing, Newman had his first view of Kindley Field aerodrome, which had been opened a year or so earlier, and also of the Causeway, linking the main island with St George's.

As if on cue — soon after the train had finished the water crossing — a Douglas Dakota of the US Army Air Force took-off and passed low overhead.

The train came to the terminus near the quayside at St George and, after a walk around the small town, they found a secluded spot on the high ground above the town and settled down to an afternoon in the grass together. Although they had other things on their mind, they paused from time to time to watch planes land and take off at Kindley Field, or a boat come into St George's Harbour. The weather couldn't have been kinder to them and they got to know each other very well, but not completely.

It was at St George that they found out they had a common interest: birds. They saw a longtail, which prompted Newman to ask what it was. She said there were some wonderful places to bird watch on the Islands and she was determined to show him as many of them as she could, and outlined her plan. Newman was impressed with it's audacity.

The following morning she phoned the shop from a friend's house and told her employer she wanted to take some of her annual holiday straight away, due to a domestic problem. Mr Slater was surprised, but reluctantly agreed. He had the feeling from the way she spoke that she was going to take it whatever he said.

That morning however, the body of the pilot, Alvin 'King' Schmidt, the Captain of the Catalina which had crashed the previous Saturday, was recovered from the Great Sound. The news spread quickly, and soon reached Lucy and Newman, who were playing tennis at the Belmont prior to going bird watching on the South Shore. Newman was told that he was expected to attend the burial at the Royal Navy Cemetery the following day.

Over the course of the next few days, Lucy was to show Don all the local bird watching sites. In some ways the whole of Bermuda was a vast bird watching site, and early on they soon decided they needed to become cyclists to get around. Lucy persuaded her brother to repair a puncture in the back wheel of her bike. She hadn't used it for several months because of it. Newman borrowed an RAF bike from the Belmont.

Newman decided to cycle to 'King' Schmidt's funeral. He felt like the exercise, and he wanted to be able to ride to the Dockyard with Lucy. He had found his last funeral when his old school friend Capt Livingstone had been buried, distressing and, although he didn't know the 'King' well, he felt that a ride to the Royal Navy Cemetery with Lucy would make the whole thing more bearable.

He didn't expect Lucy to attend the funeral. He imagined she would wait outside the cemetery gates, but she insisted on accompanying him to the grave side. She said that she had to go to a funeral sooner or later, and it might as well be now.

Some of the other aircrew there looked at Newman a bit oddly when he arrived with Lucy, but no one said anything. It wasn't the time or place to make ribald remarks.

At the weekend they went to the usual church hall dance. They were a little late arriving and the floor was already crowded. Before long they had lost themselves in the throng.

In the middle of the floor someone had put French chalk on the wooden floor. There wasn't any on the rest of the floor so it took them by surprise. Newman slipped and they bumped into another couple and lost their equilibrium. When they were under way again she thought he seemed in pain. "You OK?"

"Yes, OK, thanks"

"You're not. I can tell you're not."

"I'll be fine in a few secs. I broke my ankle a few years ago. It gives me trouble now and then, that's all."

"You've never told me about that." she said, as they danced cheek to cheek.

"You never asked me about it!"

"Is there anything else you're keeping from me."

"Maybe."

"And what might that be?" she asked.

They collided with another couple. Newman shouted, "Sorry".

"Come on," said Lucy, "out with it!"

"I think you may know, I'm not sure."

"Well, tell me what it is. Then I'll tell you whether you've told me."

"I think you may have guessed — by now — I've fallen in love with you!"

"No, you know you haven't told me. It's the sort of thing I'd remember! But it's the same with me. I know I haven't told you, but you must have guessed. I just can't think of anyone else but you these days, darling."

The following Monday, Newman and his crew were put on standby. This meant they would leave for the UK at the next opportunity, possibly as soon as the next day. Once more, it all depended on getting favourable weather along the route and at their destination and the conditions being all right for take-off in the Great Sound. To some extent it also depended on Newman, as Captain of the aircraft, being happy to undertake the flight after studying the forecast. The ultimate decision lay with him, but he had decided long ago not to be swayed by what he called to himself, the Lucy factor — the desire to prolong his stay with her. If he opted not to go when conditions were suitable it would be obvious to his superiors and other crews.

As it turned out he was still in Bermuda on the Thursday, which was the twenty-fifth anniversary of the formation of the Royal Air Force. To mark the occasion most shops on Front Street had posters in their windows and RAF Staging Post Number 80 at Darrell's Island put on a Flying Display. In London, unknown to the people in Bermuda, the Prime Minister, Winston Churchill, although not a pilot, was presented with "pilot's wings" to mark the occasion, and after that wore them on his RAF uniform.

Newman was instructed to put on a show with his Catalina. He did, and according to several ground witnesses his port wing tip came within ten feet of the top of the Belmont Hotel on two occasions. He was expecting a reprimand from the Commanding Officer after he'd landed, and was relieved when he didn't get one. But later Lucy told him off in no uncertain terms, and told him not to take risks like that again. He accepted it in good spirit and never forgot it.

The following day everything was 'go' for departure and they struggled into the air soon after dawn. Lucy was at Burgess Point. She had realised he was going when she heard the Catalina's engine start in the dawn twilight. She got to the Point just as the Catalina drew level, and waved until he was out of sight.

Their flight to Largs in Scotland was uneventful for the first nine hours. Then things began to get more complicated. They were flying at eight thousand feet in bright sunshine with clear air all around except for directly ahead. *Brenda* was doing the flying and Newman supervising. He and Humble had been alternating supervision every two hours and the system was working well. It gave each of them a chance to go to the galley, have a coffee and demolish some of their rations, do their ablutions, and if they wanted have an hour or so on one of the bunks. They had a long night of perhaps twelve more hours duration ahead of them, during which they would have to keep alert in case *Brenda* malfunctioned and slowly flew them into the sea without them noticing.

Although according to the "agreement" Humble was not required to be in his second pilot's seat at the moment, he was, and Newman decided to discuss with him the heavy cumulus cloud bank — which they could both see twenty or thirty miles ahead of them.

"We can't go round that" said Newman pointing ahead at the line of cumulus clouds, "so it's a question of whether we go under or over."

Newman didn't want to go through them — unless they had to — as he knew there would be a lot of heavy turbulence, which in extreme cases could result in loss of control of the aircraft, and at best would be uncomfortable and tiring for the crew.

"Under, every time." said Humble. "Without oxygen we don't have much choice do we?"

"I think you're right, but it'll probably be a rough ride going underneath, and it looks like it's pouring down underneath them. Let's decide when we get nearer."

"Roger."

Fifteen minutes later they were much closer and able to pick out individual cloud cells that made up the front line.

"We should be able to dodge in between them if we climb a few thousand." said Newman, and without waiting for a response from Humble he opened the throttles and began to climb.

At ten thousand feet, aircrew would normally go on to oxygen, but they didn't have any onboard. He told the crew that they were going on up to twelve thousand feet, but he thought it wouldn't be for long. "So just hang on."

Humble was now very quiet, almost as though he could foresee what was to happen. They levelled off at twelve thousand and Newman chose a gap between two towering cumulo nimbus clouds. They were flying only a few hundred feet above cloud and either side of them heavy, menacing, billowing clouds, towered high above them. Just looking at them close up, it was obvious that they would toss a Catalina around all over the sky given the chance, and more than one person on Newman's Cat had their fingers crossed.

Ahead of the them their path was by no means clear. A thunderstorm cell was directly in their path a few miles ahead, but Newman expected that they would be able to dodge it by going to one side or the other. But it didn't turn out quite like that. When they were closer it was obvious there was no way through to the right, but they might get through to the left if they climbed another thousand feet or so. Newman applied more throttle and started to climb, but the cloud was higher than he thought and at fourteen thousand feet he realised he would have to turn round and go back to the edge of the front, let down to near sea level, and go under it. He commenced a sharp turn to port to retrace their footsteps.

"Sorry gentlemen, we're going to have to go back and go under it," said Newman to the crew. "Everyone OK?"

It was a leading question and he realised it. There was a quick response from Jock Hanson.

"I can't understand it Skip, I've got two radio sets now — only used to have one! Bloody good show, how did you do that Skip?" He sounded happy and a little drunk.

Newman realised instantly that Jock Hanson was suffering from lack of oxygen, and badly so.

"OK Jock, don't use them for now, OK? Have a rest on one of the bunks if you feel like it."

"Roger Skip, won't use either of 'em."

Newman wasn't sure whether Hanson was talking about radios or bunks, but all of a sudden it didn't seem vital to know the answer. They had just completed their one hundred and eighty degree turn and he was looking back the way they had come. It was blocked, the sides of their valley had moved towards each other and in front of them, and on all sides, were towering cumulonimbus clouds. There was no way out, they were trapped in the middle of boiling thunderstorm clouds. Their tops — with the sun shining on them — looked very pretty to Slimbridge who was sitting in one of the fuselage blisters, but Newman and Humble had more on their minds.

"Bloody Hell!" said Humble.

"Sod it!" said Newman.

"The quickest way out must be to go through that muck which has formed where we came in," said Humble, "and the sooner the better, it's building up the whole time."

"You're right," Newman replied. He hadn't anticipated that his escape route might be cut off, and he was annoyed with himself for not realising he was flying into a trap. It was an obvious possibility he should have thought of.

"Captain to crew. We are going to have to go through a bit of rough stuff for a few minutes. Secure yourselves, it shouldn't be for long. We'll descend when we're back out and then go underneath."

Following his announcement Newman wondered why he had chosen to be so formal, but he had said 'Captain to crew' without thinking. He supposed that subconsciously he wanted to make sure they took in what he was saying, and on reflection that was exactly what he wanted.

A few minutes later they entered the cumulonimbus cloud. They had no option. There was no way they could climb above the clouds, as the Catalina was unable to fly higher than eighteen thousand feet or so, and the cloud tops were thousands of feet higher and increasing in height with every passing minute.

Newman had disengaged the autopilot and, although he had flown blind on his instruments hundreds — maybe thousands — of times, this was the first time he had flown into a cunimb. However he knew them by reputation and prayed these cunimbs would not live up to them!

For the first few seconds in the cloud the air was smooth. Newman looked across at Humble, for a split second, who gave him the thumbs up, but it didn't stay like that. A few seconds later they suffered a lightning strike. It was on the nose only a few feet in front of the cockpit and it felt as if their time was up! Completely blinded for several seconds, Newman and Humble were unable to do anything for a while. When they recovered and were able to read their instruments, they were amazed and alarmed to see that they were climbing at four thousand feet a minute, and the altimeter showed them already passing through sixteen thousand feet! Both Newman and Humble instinctively pushed their control columns forward. If they continued to rise at this rate they would soon all be unconscious through lack of oxygen. But it wasn't only that they were climbing when they didn't want to, they were also being tossed around so violently that they could hardly read their instruments. The lightening strike didn't appear to have damaged the aircraft significantly but Newman wasn't about to unbuckle his harness and make a tour of the hull to find out for sure, and he was too busy wrestling with the controls to ask the rest of the crew on the intercom.

The affect of pushing the control column forward appeared to be negligible and the rising current of air continued to push them upwards. They were approaching nineteen thousand feet —if they could believe their instruments — but on the good side, they were still partially in control. Although they weren't in charge of the altitude they were managing to keep going in the right direction, so they must surely soon come out on the other side of the thunderstorm cell.

Newman shouted to Humble over the intercom. "I need both hands on the wheel. Throttle back. We should be out of it soon."

Humble instantly moved the throttles back to idle. "I bloody well hope so!"

It was not connected with Humble's action but just as he took his left hand off the throttles, hail and rain started battering the aircraft. They quickly found that the boat might have a watertight bottom, but it definitely didn't have a watertight top! Water was coming through at several points, but that was the least of their worries — provided it didn't cause any electrical problems.

Suddenly they moved out of the up draft into a down draft and found themselves descending at an alarming rate whilst continuing to be tossed about like a matchstick. To make matters worse their airspeed now was building up dangerously and at 125 knots had already exceeded the maximum speed 'allowed' when flying in turbulence by fifteen knots. They both had to fight the control column and pull it back. Although Newman was technically flying the aeroplane, he was more than happy to have Humble help and between them they managed to arrest their descent at nine-thousand feet only to find they were now climbing again at an alarming rate.

"This is a bloody roller coaster!"said Humble.

"You can say that again" shouted Newman, "but at least we've managed to keep the gyros from toppling. We must have been very close to losing the artificial horizon several times!"

As he said it the Catalina emerged into bright sunshine, clear blue skies and lovely smooth air.

"Hey boy!" shouted Humble.

Newman called each of the crew to check they were all right. They were. Slimbridge asked if they would have to go back to Bermuda again. Alf Plant asked if both wings were still on, to which Pip Ferguson replied "only just!", whilst Jock Hanson commented that "Nobody told me this flying business can be so bloody dangerous!"

Newman brought the Cat down to five hundred feet above the sea, turned it round again, and headed back towards the storms, to try their luck flying underneath them. He soon found that at five hundred feet he was losing contact with the sea due to the low base of the clouds and he was forced to go down two hundred to keep contact with it. With forward visibility down to a few hundred yards in the pouring rain — and sometimes hail — he was flying on instruments with one eye on the sea. But it was a situation he was more used to, having flown low level reconnaissance patrols with 217 Squadron for nearly two years. It was also a more comfortable ride than it had been inside the cloud. The Cat was being tossed around by air turbulence but — although it was bad — it was nothing like as bad as inside the cloud, which none of them would forget in a hurry. After fifteen minutes the skies cleared and they were out in relatively smooth air.

"Nice job Skip" said Pip Ferguson.

"Thanks Pip, how are those engines of ours?"

"Bang on Skip, never been better, never been better!"

"OK to turn-off all de-icing now, and get out the sunglasses?" asked Humble.

"Yes, and let's get Slimbridge to bring us some coffee."

The sun was now setting and the crew were doing their chores before settling down for the long night ahead of them.

After dropping a smoke canister into the sea and checking their drift, they climbed back up to eight thousand feet. Now relatively relaxed, Newman put *Brenda* to work again.

Alf Plant took over from Hanson and got a bearing from Newfoundland which, when plotted, suggested that they were only slightly behind schedule. Newman noted this with satisfaction. He hadn't said anything to the crew, but it had crossed his mind more than once that the lightning strike might have affected the electrical equipment. It seemed that it hadn't.

Before taking a break flight engineer Ferguson had successfully transferred all the fuel in the fuselage ferry tanks to the wing tanks. That was always good news, for if something went wrong with that operation there was no way the fuselage fuel could reach the engines and a forced landing at sea or a diversion to Ireland, and possible subsequent internment, were on the cards. 'So all in all,' thought Newman, 'we have weathered the storm and Scotland here we come!'

Soon the stars were out. Newman dimmed the cockpit lights and searched for the pole star. He just wanted to make a sensibility check— as he called it, when Humble asked what he was up to — to make sure their magnetic compass had not been affected by the storm and they were headed in the wrong direction. He found it and satisfied himself that they were going in roughly the right direction and handed over to Humble.

"If I fall asleep in the cockpit wake me when it's my shift in two hours time." He said it as though it was an order, which it was.

Humble accepted it in the spirit in which it was meant. "Roger Skip. Happy dreams."

Lucy had been thinking of Don all day. Now Don began thinking about her, but he couldn't sleep.

Humble could see that Newman wasn't sleeping. "Do you think you're going to marry her?" he said, to Newman.

Newman pretended to be asleep in his cockpit seat, and didn't answer, but he had to admit to himself that it was a good question, and he began wondering whether they should live in Bermuda, London or somewhere else. He dozed off after realising that Bermuda won hands down!

Their flight to Scotland lasted nearly twenty-seven hours, and within forty-eight hours of reaching the UK Newman and his crew were on their way back to Canada in a BOAC Liberator. They sat or lay in the bomb bay, and slept as much as they could. Newman dreamt that he was delivering another Catalina and Lucy was the co-pilot and that she was wearing a funny hat!

CHAPTER FIVE

April 1943

Newman was given the same crew for his second Catalina delivery, except that Slimbridge had stayed in the UK as intended. An RAF sergeant, Reg Wyborn, had taken his place. Having the same crew came as a pleasant surprise to Newman. He had heard it was unusual. Newman was also pleased that Hank Humble seemed happy about it, even though he had previously told Newman he was hoping to be made the Captain, with his own crew, on his next delivery.

It was a Wednesday in mid April when the crew arrived at Elizabeth City by train from Montreal. They reported to the RAF office in the Virginia Dare hotel, and learned that their Catalina wasn't expected to arrive from the makers, Consolidated at San Diego, until the following Tuesday, as it had been delayed to allow new equipment to be fitted.

Newman couldn't wait to get back to Bermuda and Lucy, and the next few days dragged, but the Cat did arrive as promised and the next day he and his crew made a short air test in the aircraft.

Newman declared the aircraft 'snag free', a rare event — there was usually something which wasn't quite right — and he hoped they would be able to leap off for Bermuda the following day.

It didn't quite turn out like that. The following morning Hank Humble woke up with severe toothache and had to visit a dentist and have his tooth extracted. Newman usually dealt with postponements and delays well. It was par for the course if you were aircrew, but this latest delay got to him. He went back to his hotel and considered writing to Lucy, partly to pass the time, and partly to help cope with his frustration, although he knew it was probably a futile exercise. It was unlikely to get there before he did. He had just written "My darling Lucy" when a thought crossed his mind. Bermuda time was one hour ahead of the USA East Coast, so Lucy's shop should just be opening. He picked up the telephone by his bed. "Can you get me a number in Bermuda, please?"

"Yes Sir, what is the number you want?"

He gave the hotel operator the number of the shop on Front St, Hamilton.

"I'll call you when I've got through."

"Thank you." Newman looked at his watch.

It seemed an age before the phone rang and the operator said, "your call to Bermuda."

"Hallo, can I speak to Miss Appledram, please?"

"Who?"

It was a very bad line, Newman had to put his right hand over his ear and press the earpiece hard against his left ear.

"Miss Appledram."

"Sorry I can't make out what you're saying. Can you call again on another line?"

Newman had one final attempt to make himself heard, but there was no response. The line was dead. He wasn't sure what he was going to say to Lucy if he got through anyway, and he guessed he could be breaking some RAF regulation or other — if he told her where he was — and that he would soon be on his way to Bermuda. So he didn't try to get through again.

There were strong winds and rough water in the Great Sound at Bermuda for the next few days, so it was Easter Monday before conditions were right for them to make the Bermuda flight.

The pre flight briefing was normal, but Newman was surprised to be called into the C/O's office afterwards. Newman saluted.

"Shut the door Newman."

Newman did as he was told.

"Read this, and sign at the bottom when you've done so."

Wing Commander Forbes handed him a typed sheet of paper. It was addressed to F/L Donald Newman, 58986, Royal Air Force. It said:

'SPECIAL INSTRUCTION'

'The Catalina you have been assigned to ferry to the UK via Bermuda has highly secret equipment installed. There is no need for you to know its whereabouts on the aircraft or its function. However, as Captain of the aircraft you should know of its presence.

In the event of the aircraft being in danger of falling into enemy hands, it is imperative, repeat imperative, that you destroy or scuttle your aircraft. Under no circumstances should you allow your aircraft to fall into enemy hands.

'You are the only member of your crew authorised to know the contents of this memorandum. For security reasons, the staging post at

Bermuda will not be told of the special nature of this aircraft. You must bear this in mind at all times and behave accordingly. It is vital that this Catalina reaches the UK safely.

'*Sign below to indicate that you have read and fully understood the above.*

Newman signed and handed the sheet back to the Wing Commander.

"Any questions?" asked the Wing Co.

"Only one Sir."

The Wing Co, looked up at Newman from behind his desk, and put on a wry smile.

"Yes?"

"Suppose one of my crew or some one in Bermuda sees this — whatever it is — and asks questions?"

"Oh, you needn't worry about that. I understand it's not easily seen."

"Right, Sir — and am I to understand that not even the C/O at Darrell's Island will know?"

"That is correct Newman. I don't know why, but I'm told there isn't any need."

"Very good, Sir."

"Have a good trip Newman."

"Thank you, Sir."

Three hours later, on his way to Bermuda again, flying Catalina W4598, at eight thousand feet, the words of the memorandum were still running through Newman's mind.

The weather couldn't have been better for them on this Easter Monday flight. They had clear blue sky with visibility from horizon to horizon, and the crew were in good spirits and looking forward to more time in the sun at Bermuda. They had no trouble with navigation this time. The radio worked like a charm, and after five hours the coral of Bermuda came into view, followed by a distant view of the Dockyard.

Newman started to descend and called Darrell's on the radio for landing instructions. As he entered the landing circuit he signalled the engineer to lower the floats, select rich mixture for the engines, and fine pitch for the propellers.

The wind was from the north-east and his approach to land took him over Southampton Parish and some US Navy Catalinas moored in Port Royal Bay. Newman eased the Catalina on to the water, making the smoothest landing he could remember, at five past two Bermuda time.

"Who are you trying to impress?" said Hank Humble. "She'll be at work!"

By four o'clock he was back at the Belmont and changing into his best blue uniform. He had to clean the buttons himself but managed to catch the four-thirty ferry and be in Hamilton in time to reach Lucy's shop before she left. He hadn't phoned her first; he wanted to give her a surprise.

He arrived at the liquor store at five minutes to five but there was no sign of Lucy through the window. Instead he saw a middle aged, bald headed man standing behind the counter serving an elderly lady wearing a large grey hat. He waited until just gone five hoping that Lucy would emerge, but she didn't.

Waiting until there were no customers, Newman entered and approached the man.

"Good afternoon, I'm sorry to trouble you — I'm looking for Lucy Appledram."

The man took a long look at Newman before replying. "I'm afraid she will not be here for a few days." He spoke in a solemn manner. "She has mentioned that she has an RAF boy friend. Are you a flying boat pilot?"

"Yes, I am. Is she all right?"

There was a long pause again before the reply, which increased Newman's feeling that something had happened to Lucy.

"Well, yes and no."

At that very moment another woman customer entered the shop.

"Excuse me a moment, I'll just deal with Mrs Wicker."

He did that and Newman noticed that he could smile. So appearing solemn evidently wasn't his normal manner.

"Yes, I'm afraid Lucy has had to take some time off, a domestic problem I understand. I don't think she will be back for some time."

The disappointment obviously showed on Newman's face.

"I'm sorry, I can't help more," continued the man.

"She never got round to giving me her address. I suppose you couldn't give it to me?"

"I'm afraid not Sir. She would have given it to you if she had wanted you to have it, surely?"

"Yes, I can see that. Well, thank you for your help, anyway."

Newman took the *Laconia* back to the Belmont. He always found the ferry relaxing, but today its magic didn't seem to be working. He stood on deck where passengers put their bicycles — in front of the engine room — but he could only think of one thing, 'how to find a way of letting Lucy know he was back in town.' A short but heavy rain shower lasting perhaps a minute struck them in mid harbour, but he could see it would be over quickly and didn't move. Even during the shower the Harbour remained tranquil and Newman's thoughts weren't seriously interrupted. His overall feeling was one of determination. He was not going to take this setback lying down.

His first conclusion was that he should have pressed Lucy for her home address before he had left Bermuda. She had told him to write to the shop if he wanted to, but that clearly wouldn't work if she didn't go to work for a few days. It wasn't what Newman would call a satisfactory system and when he did find her he was going to tell her that.

He felt sure he could find her house if he decided to try and do that. He knew where it must be, approximately, and he could ask anyone he saw when he got near. There was a problem however. Lucy had been insistent all the time that he had known her, that her mother wasn't to know about him. If he found her cottage, and just knocked on the front door, he didn't know what sort of reception he might get. Even Lucy might not thank him for doing that, so it was too much of a chance.

As he got off the ferry at the Belmont Wharf, a man in a red shirt was waiting to board. It wasn't Helmut Schachmann, but it reminded Newman of him, and he wondered if Schachmann might be able to help. The ex Austrian apparently had ready access to the Appledram household. If he could find Schachmann, he might be able to persuade him to take a message to Lucy. It was worth a try, and he had a rough idea where Schachmann lived.

He set off along Harbour Road to try and find him. Each time he had walked along the road in this direction before, Lucy had been with him. It made him realise that although Bermuda was a beautiful place, it was Lucy that had made his first trip to Bermuda so very special. Without her on his arm now things weren't right. What could be the problem that was keeping her from her work he wondered? One thing Newman was sure about — her mother must have something to do with it!

Remembering the spot where he had first met Schachmann, Newman looked around. He was almost level with the eastern end of Darrell's

Island, and could see his Cat had gone from the mooring buoy where he had parked it a few hours earlier. It didn't surprise him; it was standard practice to wash the salt water off the Catalinas from time to time, and he guessed that was now being done on the Island. He wondered about the secret equipment that was fitted, and hoped there wouldn't be any complications because of it.

He glanced to his left, another RAF officer of his rank was stepping on to the road from a half-hidden gate.

"Watcha!" said Newman.

"Hi! You just in today?"

"Yep. My second trip. And yours?"

"My fourth."

"Ah, good, you probably know the area then, better than I do. I'm looking for a bod called Helmut — Helmut Schachmann. You don't happen to know him?"

"Yes, I know him, a bit of a clot. He's been living in a room in the same cottage as me." The officer pointed to a cottage on the hillside.

"Great. Is he there now?"

"Yes, he's getting ready to move out. According to him the place is bloody haunted, and he can't stand it any more! Not that I've heard or seen anything."

"Really?"

"Yes, that's what he reckons. You know him then?"

"Not exactly, I've bumped into him once or twice, and I want to find him now to see if he can give me an address of a mutual friend."

At that moment Schachmann appeared from the garden gate, carrying a large holdall and a box like parcel covered in brown paper.

"Helmut, remember me?"

Schachmann put the holdall on the road, taking care to pick a spot which had not been soiled by the road's horse traffic, but hung on to the parcel. Schachmann looked pleased to see him. That puzzled Newman.

"Hello Don."

Newman approached Schachmann. His RAF colleague strolled off towards the Belmont. Schachmann held out his right hand and Newman shook it.

"You're just the man I want to see," said Newman, smiling.

"Likewise," said Schachmann.

Newman wasn't sure if Schachmann hadn't quite mastered the

English language yet, and had chosen the wrong word, or whether he really meant it.

"I've been to the shop to find Lucy — she wasn't there, and......"

Schachmann interrupted, "No she wouldn't be."

"So you know all about it, then?"

The expression on Schachmann's face changed. Newman changed his as well, in anticipation of bad news.

"Yes, her father's been killed, in North Africa. She's looking after her mother."

"Oh God."

There was a lull in the conversation. Newman was about to ask if the funeral had taken place, when he realised the question was inappropriate. Lucy's father would undoubtedly have had a quick military burial in North Africa, if there was time to do so.

"When did they get the news?" he asked Schachmann.

"On Good Friday — last Friday."

"Well, I was hoping to see Lucy again. I'm not sure quite what to do now? Lucy never took me home, and she's not going to the shop, so I can't even tell her I'm back. I was going to ask you if you could take a message to her."

"Going to?"

"Yes, I was looking for you Helmut, to ask for your help, when you suddenly appeared."

"Yes, I can see you have a big problem. Even when her husband was alive Mrs Appledram was a difficult person. But I think I'd better tell you Don that I intend to ask Lucy to marry me. So if you want me to play messenger boy for you, it's going to cost you a lot. Perhaps more than you can afford to pay!"

Newman didn't like the way the conversation was going.

"Anyway," Helmut continued, "I've got new lodgings in Salt Kettle, so I'm going past the Belmont. If you're going back now, we can talk on the way."

They set off back along Harbour Road; Schachmann carrying his bag and his parcel.

"I didn't realise you and Lucy were so close. I wouldn't have had the nerve to ask your help if I had known that," said Newman.

"Well, as I say. It's a question of price. If I were to offer you a million pounds I bet you'd murder your grandmother."

"Helmut," said Newman, "lets keep to reality. What is it that you want from me as payment? A pound of flesh?"

"A ride in your Catalina flying boat!"

"Oh Helmut, you know that's impossible."

"No it isn't. It's well known that some Bermuda people have had rides."

"That's news to me."

"Well, I'm telling you, quite a few people have had rides on test flights."

There was the sound of horses hooves behind them and they had to move quickly out of the centre of the road to let a horse and buggy pass. Newman went to the left hand side of the road, Schachmann to the right, and they came together again as soon as the buggy had passed.

"Anyway, Helmut, why are you so keen on a ride in a Catalina?"

"Not sure, but I see these machines coming and going every day, and I want to know what it's like to fly in one of them."

Newman wasn't really sure what answer to expect, but it sounded reasonable. But he didn't think much of a chap who would help a rival, and possibly lose the woman he wanted to marry, merely to get a short ride in an aeroplane. There was something not adding up properly but he didn't know what it was.

They had to separate again as a couple of American sailors on bicycles were approaching fast. They appeared to be racing each other, whilst having a shouting match.

"I suppose I might be able to arrange something, Helmut, but it could be a few days before I have to make an air test, and I can't promise anything. And I want to get a message to Lucy now, not in three or four days time when I may be about to depart!"

"Well, we could do a deal."

"How do you mean? What sort of a deal?"

"Well, I could let Lucy know you're back later tonight, and if you don't get me a Catalina flight before you go, I'll tell Lucy's mother all about you and Lucy. That will — what do you English say — put the cat among the pigeons!"

"Oh come on Helmut." Newman was shouting, he couldn't help it. "You know there's no way I can do that."

"No I don't. What's so difficult about that?"

A US Navy Catalina passed overhead making a very low circuit.

Newman didn't respond to Schachmann's question, so Schachmann said it again.

"I heard, you Helmut, I heard you. I'm just trying to figure out how it might be done."

Schachmann's face lit up. Newman noticed. 'This clot is really keen to get a ride,' he said to himself. The paper he had to sign about secret equipment on the aircraft entered his mind, but he had also been told that the equipment was hard to find. Nevertheless, one thing was certain, he couldn't tell Schachmann that he couldn't give him a ride because the aircraft had secret equipment fitted to his aircraft!

"I tell you what we could do,' said Helmut.

"What do you mean?"

"Well, it's well known that an English officer can be trusted."

"Is it?" said Newman.

"If you give me your word that you'll try and get me a flight, I'll trust you, and see Lucy tonight to tell her you're back."

Newman was quick to notice that Schachmann had used the word *try*.

"Done," said Newman.

"Mind you, it's just the one message. I'm not going to keep telling Lucy's Mum that she was with me night after night — to cover up for you — until you've told me you've fixed the flight."

Again there were some things that didn't add up to Newman. This clot was prepared to take messages from a competitor to what he considered to be his girl — he had after all said he intended to try and marry her — all for the sake of a ride in a Catalina. It didn't make sense.

"OK, will you tell her I'm back for a few days, I don't know how long, and that I'm staying at the Belmont again. She can find me there, or leave a message for me."

"Yes, if I can borrow a bike I'll nip over tonight with the message."

"Oh, and you'd better say how sorry I am to hear about her father."

"Right, and remember to let me know about the flight? I'll give you my new address at Salt Kettle." He produced a small notebook and pencil from his breast pocket and scribbled the address, tore the page out, and gave it to Newman.

They had reached Belmont Wharf by this time and Newman started the climb up the path to the Belmont. When he got there he went straight to the bar for a pint.

Later that evening, when Newman was paying his second visit to the bar, Helmut Schachmann entered and found Newman drinking with Hank Humble.

"Message delivered, but she doesn't think she will be able to see you, this time. She's written you a note to explain."

Newman's spirits suddenly took a nose dive. He went to open the letter.

"And I forgot to mention this afternoon, that I'm rather partial to beer!"

"OK — let me read this — and I'll buy you one."

Newman opened Lucy's letter. *"Darling Don, I'm so glad you're back. I pray you will be here for a few days, I can't leave Mum at the moment. I'll leave a message at the shop for you — I don't trust Helmut these days, he's changed in the last few weeks — but I trust Mr Slater at the shop, and he won't mind helping. You ring him once or twice a day and ask if I've left any messages for you. All my love, Lucy."*

Newman found it difficult to suppress his pleasure. He wasn't dependent on Schachmann any more. Lucy had found a solution, and contrary to what Schachmann said, it looked as if he would be able to see her this trip. But Newman had been so wrapped up in the letter that he hadn't realised what Hank Humble and Helmut Schachmann were talking about.

"No trouble," he heard Hank say as he put the letter back in it's envelope. "We can get you on board; you don't need a uniform to get on a Cat!"

"In that case the next round is on me," said Helmut.

The three of them spent the next hour talking about the Catalina flying boat. Several times Newman tried to change the subject, but within a few seconds Schachmann successfully brought the conversation back to Cats.

Eventually Schachmann said good night and left.

"I wonder why he's so bloody interested in Catalinas?" said Humble. "He never once mentioned any other aeroplane."

"I don't know," Newman replied, "he's certainly a bit of an odd ball!"

Two days later, on the Wednesday — although it seemed a lot longer — Newman got a message when he phoned the shop.

"Miss Appledram says she will meet you at Belmont Wharf at three o'clock this afternoon Mr Newman."

"Oh, thank you Mr Slater — thanks."

"My pleasure. You've got yourself a lovely girl. You take good care of her!"

"I will Mr Slater, I will."

Newman went down to the Wharf at ten minutes to three, then started to walk along Harbour Road towards Burgess Point. He knew this was the shortest way for Lucy to come, so set out to meet her. As the road followed the shore line it twisted and turned, so he couldn't see the whole length of the road. As he turned each bend he hoped and expected, to see Lucy coming towards him, and as it didn't happen he became apprehensive.

He had walked this road many times before, including the Monday before when he was looking for Helmut Schachmann, but he hadn't realised that it contained so many twists and shallow turns. He hadn't noticed it, but an observer would have noted that at the start of each bend he checked his tie was straight. He wanted to look as good as he could for Lucy!

He came to a straight stretch of road and to his delight could see a figure in a light blue dress in the distance. He waved, it was returned and they started running towards each other. When they met she threw herself into his arms and they kissed passionately in the middle of the road.

When at last they broke off, she said, "Oh Don, it's so good to see you. You haven't been away long, I know. But it's seemed such a long, long time. I've missed you terribly!"

"The same with me. I'm so sorry to hear about your Dad."

She struggled to hold back tears. "Yes, I was so close to him. Much closer than I am to Mummy. It was always that way."

"You remember the garden you took me to once? That must be close to here. Shall we go there again?"

"Yes, good idea. Can I borrow your handkerchief, first?"

The garden hadn't changed very much. Some Easter Lilies were now out, but they didn't notice. They stayed two hours. They both wished it could be longer, but Lucy said she had to get back to her mother, as her mother's younger sister could only be with her for a few hours.

"When can we meet again?" asked Newman.

"I just don't know. It may have to be several days, but when Aunt Sophie goes I'll walk to the road with her and ask her if she can come again as soon as she can. If it comes to it, I can tell her about you. She's completely different from Mummy, I can tell her anything! She's been going out with an American sailor from the Naval Air Station, so she'll understand."

They were able to meet on the Friday afternoon and they spent another two hours at 'their place' in the deserted garden. They had a short interruption due to a rain shower, and had to shelter under a cedar tree for a while, but it would have needed more than a shower to spoil their afternoon together.

Before they parted Lucy told Don that in a few days time her mother was going to stay with her sister in St George's, for a week or two, "so I'll be able to go back to work and we can meet every lunch time and every evening."

He was delighted. "Are you going to be living by yourself then?" he asked.

"No, with brother Jack. He'll be there."

"Ah yes, of course, I'd forgotten about Jack."

"He's not always there though. Last time Mummy went to St George's for a few days, he often went fishing all night!"

Then she said as an afterthought. "But there's no knowing with him. There's no privacy at our place, and he still comes barging into my room at all times of the day and night. He doesn't seem to think I'm a big girl now!"

"I see. I'm lucky! I've got a room to myself at the Belmont at the moment. It's not always like that."

She smiled and looked into his eyes. "Have you now!"

He gave her a final kiss. She said she would talk to her Aunt later, and then leave a message with Mr Slater the following morning for him.

After dinner that evening, Newman found Hank Humble again in the bar. Newman now rather enjoyed his company. Hank had recently acquired the nickname "Stetson". Newman could readily understand why, but he didn't know who started it. He suspected it was Pip Ferguson, his flight engineer.

"I was speaking to some of the guys in the office this afternoon," said Hank, "whilst, I guess, you were snogging your popsy. It looks as if we may be going on standby any day now, and we'll probably be down for a compass swing and an air test tomorrow or Sunday."

Newman didn't like Lucy being called a popsy. She was more than that, but he let the remark pass.

"Right, Hank. Thanks for the gen."

"What are you going to do about this clot Schachmann. He seems to be expecting a ride."

"I don't know. Nothing Hank, I suppose. What can I do?"

"Well you don't want to make an enemy of him, that's for bloody sure. Soon you won't be here to keep him away from your girl, will you?"

"No."

Humble took a large swig from his pint of beer. "Do you want me to handle it?"

"What do you mean?"

"Well if you're caught smuggling him aboard, it could be serious. They might court-martial you, or whatever you call it in the RAF. But they can't do that to me I'm not in the bloody RAF, am I?"

"You mean you'd arrange it and get him onboard?"

"Exactly. If you'll buy me another pint, or maybe two — Skipper."

"That's a brilliant idea, Hank."

"OK, consider it done. Now, how do I contact him?"

Newman passed Hank Humble the scrap of paper with Shachmann's new address on it.

"He told me it's only ten minutes walk from here," said Newman.

"OK, leave it all to me, Skipper."

The following day Newman did have to carry out the air test. Normally the crew all boarded together through one of the blisters, but today it was different. He was told that Humble and the rest of the crew had already boarded the aircraft. He didn't query why because he knew it must be to do with Humble's plan to get Schachmann on board.

He found Schachmann in the cockpit with Humble. "God," said Newman, "You don't need to show him how to fly it, he just wants a ride. That's all Hank."

"Yes, but he's very interested. I was only keeping him entertained."

Schachmann sat in the co-pilot's seat for the whole flight. Newman could easily fly the aircraft for an hour without Humble and — as Humble had arranged everything — Newman didn't want to argue with him.

It was a calm day with little wind and they flew to the south for the first half hour then turned on to a reciprocal course to Bermuda. The air test was routine, although Schachmann had a surprising number of questions.

One of the questions Schachmann asked was how fast a Catalina could be taxied without it becoming airborne. The question surprised Newman and he asked Schachmann why he wanted to know. Schachmann said " He just wondered. That was all."

When they were approaching Bermuda towards the end of the flight, Newman called the tower. He was told to watch out for seven aircraft joining the circuit. Sure enough when they reached Bermuda a few minutes later the sky was full of Catalinas, and he took his place in the queue to alight.

He learnt later that a pack of U-boats had been sighted off Bermuda and the Catalinas had been sent as reinforcements from the mainland.

CHAPTER SIX

Tuesday/Wednesday, 4/5 May 1943

The signal came at midnight the previous night, the Monday night; a single word in Morse code, sent three times at one minute intervals, on the special radio frequency. The dots and dashes which spelt out "Ursula", Schachmann's mother's name, were much louder than the test transmissions he had received a week before. He guessed that a German U-boat had surfaced briefly near Bermuda and sent the signal. He was glad the message had come at last. Waiting for the signal the last few nights had proved nerve racking!

He caught Lucy's brother Jack as he was going to school the following morning and asked him to go fishing with him again that night. They agreed to meet at the Belmont Wharf at midnight. By that time Jack knew that the sleeping tablets which the doctor had given his mother would guarantee she would be sound asleep, and that he could slip out.

Schachmann didn't need to meet Jack at midnight: three in the morning would have been fine, but it would have seemed a bit odd to Jack to suggest that time as they had always met at midnight when they'd been night fishing together before. Schachmann didn't want Jack to think this was anything other than a normal fishing trip in the Sound.

Schachmann got to Belmont Wharf just before midnight. It was a fine, dark, moonless night, with just a few stars, between some scattered clouds. The northwesterly wind was not much more than a breeze. That was his first piece of good luck; he needed a wind blowing away from the south shore of Darrell's Island.

The temperature was in the seventies and the tree frogs were making their usual loud noises. There were other noises too. With thousands of extra military people now on the Islands, it was hardly surprising. Mostly they made a background noise of distant laughter and loud voices, which the Islanders had grown to accept.

Although a warm night, Schachmann had put on a dark blue pullover to minimise the chances of him being noticed too easily. He hadn't mentioned clothing to Jack because Jack might have thought it very odd, but later Schachmann was pleased to see that he too was wearing a darkish pullover. Schachmann had considered putting black boot polish on his face, to make him less noticeable in the dark, but had rejected the idea. If he accidentally came face to face with anyone, he would have a hard time explaining that away! And the first person he would have to explain it to would be Jack, which might well result in the whole operation going down the drain! Anyway, for once, the Bermuda blackout would be on his side. He was well aware that he needed as much help as possible. Over the last few days he had figured his chances of completing his mission at only 10 to 20 per cent!

In the Belmont Don Newman was making love to Lucy. He wasn't to know that this was going to lead to far more problems than he or Lucy could possibly imagine.

Schachmann had left his room at Salt Kettle as he always did, untidy, with a definite lived-in appearance. He had considered whether he should make it look as though he had moved out for good, but had decided against it. It was impossible to tell what might happen in the next few hours. Should he be caught, the state of the cottage had to support his fishing "story", not contradict it. For much the same reason he had not brought any of his personal possessions with him. The only noticeable exception was his fishing rod. Not that he actually intended to do much fishing, but his excuse would collapse without it — for Lucy's brother Jack thought that their sole objective that night was to go fishing! Schachmann didn't intend to tell him the truth until he had to.

The other exception was his one and only letter from Lucy. He treasured it, and just before he left his room he had stuffed it in a trouser pocket.

There was no sign of Jack at the wharf and Schachmann was anxious. The thought that his mother would die if his mission failed, was uppermost in his mind. He had to succeed. It was vital. It didn't occur to him that she might already be dead! His meticulous planning had been an outlet for his nervous energy until now, but waiting around on the Wharf the butterflies in his stomach were getting worse by the minute.

Schachmann's thoughts went back to three months earlier, when there had been a loud knock on the door of his room at his college in Boston. It was a knock he could still hear at unguarded moments.

"Helmut Schachmann?" a man had half asked, half stated, as though he clearly knew the answer already!

"Yes. "

"I have a message from your mother, in Vienna."

He was a tall and well-built man of perhaps sixteen stone. About forty years of age, slightly balding, wearing a dark suit with a grey tie, he spoke with just a trace of a foreign accent. Before waiting for a response he barged into Shachmann's room, sat in the only easy chair and lit a cigarette.

Schachmann took an instant aversion to him. He didn't like his style, he didn't like the look of him, and above all he didn't like the intrusion. Schachmann left the door open wide, even though the intruder claimed to be bearing a message he longed to hear.

"Shut the door and listen!" said the visitor.

Schachmann had the feeling that the man was going to give him real trouble if he didn't execute the order quickly. Reluctantly he shut the door and stood leaning against it. "What is the message from my mother?" he asked.

"She wants to live."

"She wants to live?" Schachmann repeated. As he uttered the words he suddenly felt sick, realising he was about to be blackmailed.

"Yes, so don't stand there. Sit on your bed. We have a lot to talk about."

The intruder's dictatorial manner was annoying Schachmann considerably. He would not have cooperated, if it wasn't for the supposed message from his mother. He moved some clothes from the edge of his bed, and sat facing his visitor. His impulse was to do anything — within reason — to secure his mother's letter, then get the man out of his hair as soon as possible.

The only window in the room was now directly behind his visitor. It was daylight outside and Schachmann moved slightly so he could see better. "Who are you?" he demanded.

"That needn't bother you — call me Fritz."

"How do you know my mother?"

"That needn't bother you either. Just keep quiet and listen."

Schachmann was about to voice his objections to the visitor's tone, but then realised it might lead to complications he could do without. He decided to do as he was told and listen.

"I understand you come from Bermuda," said Fritz.

"Well, yes, I've lived there for a few years."

"That is our information also. You are to return there and do a job for us."

"Us?"

"Yes, we know a lot about you and we believe you can do it."

"How do you know about me?"

"I told you to keep quiet and listen!"

It took Fritz fifteen minutes to outline the "mission".

Before Fritz was halfway through his spiel, Schachmann was in a state of shock with his mouth wide open. This was the stuff they put in movies, he thought!

As Fritz got up to go, Schachmann heard himself asking a question. He felt he knew the answer already, but something made him ask. "And where does my mother come into all this?"

"Wake up Schachmann, she is a Jew. We have her in custody. If you do as you are told, she will live. If you do not, then......."

He gesticulated, and Schachmann was left in no doubt that he meant that she would be killed. And he didn't doubt it. His father had been taken away, never to be heard of again, three years earlier.

"She is not a Jew!" shouted Schachmann. "My father was, but ......not my mother."

Schachmann was lying — trying to take advantage of her appearance — which some said, was not obviously Jewish.

"Whether she is or not, is of no real consequence to me Schachmann. They are treating her as one, and there's nothing you or I can do about it. Except, of course, you can do the Bermuda job!"

Schachmann stood on impulse and confronted Fritz, "But how do I know my mother is still alive?" he shouted.

The two men stood facing each other for a brief moment and Schachmann had a sudden feeling that he had overstepped the mark, and was going to be struck down for his sins. Fritz, self assured and confident, put his right hand into his jacket pocket. Schachmann hadn't yet had time to digest the situation and didn't appreciate that he had to be kept alive for the time being, to do the "job". He sensed that in the next instant he was going to see a gun pointing at him. But he was wrong.

"A letter to you from your mother, Schachmann."

Schachmann took it quickly.

"Read it when I have gone. In a couple of days you will receive more instructions from us. An envelope will be put under your door. Do as instructed, and don't even think of going to the authorities. You would be signing your own death warrant as well as your mother's!"

With a quick Nazi salute Fritz was gone. Schachmann sank back on the bed shaking with a mixture of fear and hatred for the Nazi regime. He had never been trapped like this before! He had left Austria just over five years ago on the advice of his parents and, after a stay in England, had felt secure in Bermuda and more recently at College in Boston. He had even found a girl friend in Bermuda and hoped to marry her one day. But in just fifteen minutes his world had been turned upside down.

He tore open the letter from his mother. He had always been very close to her and struggled with his emotions as he started to read it. He recognized her hand writing. She said she would understand if he didn't do as the Nazis wanted, although she had not been told exactly what they wanted him to do. It was his decision, but she had no doubt of the consequences if he didn't cooperate fully!

There and then, Schachmann decided to try and follow the instructions Fritz had so far outlined. His mother was very special to him, and he would never forgive himself if she was harmed. He just hoped the extra details he would receive within the next couple of days, whatever they might be, would not be too impossible to execute nor involve anything too violent! He knew he could no more murder someone than fly to the moon.

❖

Before long, Schachmann could hear the sound of oars breaking water. Soon he could make out the outline of a rowing boat approaching from the west, keeping close to the shoreline. He started down the stone steps of Belmont Wharf to the water, trying not to think too much about what was in store in the next few hours, days and maybe weeks. If he managed to do his "job" tonight, as instructed, he knew he was heading for the most claustrophobic experience of his life! He kept thoughts of his mother's safety, and the belief that he might soon see her again, uppermost in his mind, and allowed no thoughts of failure to enter.

Jack drew quietly alongside the wharf.

"Watcha," said Jack.

"Watcha."

With the light of a dimmed torch Schachmann climbed aboard the small rowing boat. As he did so he heard the sound of the last Somerset to Hamilton train leaving the Belmont station. Both the train and Jack had been on time.

"Not a bad night — where do you want to fish?" asked Jack.

The question pleased Schachmann. It indicated that Jack was happy to take a subordinate role.

"Yes, not bad at all — head out towards Darrell's Island, I'll show you where when we get nearer."

"Right."

Jack followed the shore line heading westwards towards Burgess point. Neither of them spoke. It was about a mile as the crow flies to the easterly end of Darrell's Island, but he knew the direct route would take them dangerously close to Dagger Rocks. Although only fifteen, he prided himself that he knew the Granaway Deep area better than the back of his hand! He had been boating around there with his late father ever since he could remember.

Schachmann's plan was to fish until four o'clock, then explain everything to Jack, and then hopefully, to start his special task. It would start getting light at five o'clock and sunrise was at twenty-seven minutes past five, so he had chosen five am as his zero hour.

They continued to follow the shoreline, which in spite of the darkness was easily discernable. Whilst Jack rowed Schachmann frequently glanced to Jack's right towards Darrell's Island, looking for any sign of activity, but he saw none. There were no lights to be seen and if he hadn't known that there was an Island there — with maybe forty or fifty RAF men sleeping on it — and with five flying boats on it, and seven more moored close by, he would never have guessed.

He was pleased to see that Gibbs Hill Lighthouse was not shining. It was turned on only when ships or aircraft were expected to arrive at Bermuda in the next hour or two. So clearly no traffic was expected in the near future. That suited him.

The sound of voices occasionally reached them from Harbour Road. Schachmann guessed they emanated from high spirited US sailors who had missed the last train back to their base at Kings Point. He didn't doubt they would be in trouble when they reached it after a further couple of hours.

After ten minutes or so they drew level with Spithead, a small area of land which juts out slightly into the Sound; it was close to the garden where Don and Lucy often spent an hour or two. Schachmann knew that he and Jack were now about half way to their destination. Jack didn't!

"Where off Darrell's do you want exactly ?" he asked.

"Head towards the middle of the Island, I'll explain when we get closer."

"Jack obeyed and they headed in a north westerly direction, towards the Island. Further from the shore now, and heading directly into the wind, the little boat began pitching a little. But Jack was a powerful oarsman and they made steady progress. With his back to the Island, every now and then he would ask Schachmann, if they were "doing OK?". In the darkness Jack couldn't see the Island clearly — and the small boat was not fitted with a compass — but he could make out enough to tell they were going in the right direction.

He guessed it wouldn't be long before Jack repeated the question, and it wasn't.

"This will do fine," said Schachmann, "let's start fishing."

"Why this spot?" said Jack, who found it difficult to believe that Schachmann knew more about fishing than he did. But he had agreed to take Schachmann wherever he wanted to go, so felt he shouldn't be too difficult about Schachmann's decision.

They had been fishing for just over three hours — and had been very successful — when Schachmann decided it was getting near time to tell Jack the real reason for their midnight trip. Although he had rehearsed what he was going to say a dozen times, and tried to make Jack a special friend during the past few weeks, he was concerned that he might not get his help. If he didn't get Jack's full cooperation, he knew his own mother was as good as dead. He had to make Jack understand that.

"I want you to start rowing again in a minute Jack. There's another place I want to go to."

"We're doing all right here," said Jack indignantly.

"Yes, but I have somewhere else in mind. Put your rod down and row towards Darrell's, Jack."

Jack had a great respect for Schachmann. He looked up to him and although he was surprised at Schachmann's order, he reeled in his line and put the rod in the boat.

"Jack, I want to talk to you." There was something about the way Schachmann spoke that surprised Jack. It was more of a command than a request.

"Oh, what about, Helmut?" Jack's surprise showed in his voice, and Schachmann wondered if he was off to a bad start.

"I want you to do something very special for me tonight."

"Special?"

"I want you to help me get on board one of these Catalinas."

There was an instant reaction, and the boat rocked.

"That's a bit risky. What the hell for?" said Jack in a loud voice, "You must be crazy!"

"Keep your voice down Jack," said Schachmann, in a low key voice. "You know how it carries over the water! Just listen, and I'll tell you why."

"I'm listening!" Jack's tone indicated he was not going to be taken in by any cock and bull story. He was the captain of the rowing boat and he wasn't about to have it hijacked!

"Then listen hard, Jack, I'm serious!"

Schachmann gave Jack a somewhat edited version of his story, starting from the knock on the door in Boston, right up to the signal he'd received a few hours earlier. He deliberately left out telling Jack the final stage of the job. He didn't want the whole thing to sound too incredible. He also added a few outright lies that he thought would help persuade Jack.

"And your sister Lucy knows all about this mission, Jack, " he continued, "that's why she's been going out with this RAF officer chap, Newman. It's his plane I've got to get into."

Although only fifteen — nine years younger than Schachmann — Jack grasped the situation. "So Lucy knows all about this and wants me to help you, because if I don't your Mum will be killed?"

"Exactly!"

"Crikey!" said Jack, then fell silent for a few moments.

Schachmann could not see his face in the darkness, and wasn't sure if he had won him over or not. A few stars shone briefly overhead, the boat rocked again with the waves. Schachmann was impatient and wanted to get on with the job. "Well?" he asked.

"What have you got to do after you get inside it, then?" Jack responded.

It was clear to Schachmann that Jack was still considering whether to cooperate or not.

It was the sixty four thousand dollar question, and he knew it. When rehearsing this part he had planned to lie again and say, "Oh, put the radio out of action, a little bit of sabotage, that's all," and then when they were safely aboard, and Jack was already a partner in crime, he was going to tell him the truth.

But he was beginning to get agitated and he blurted out the truth. "Steal it!" he said.

Jack exploded with a mixture of excitement and incredulity. "But you can't fly a plane — and where could you take it?"

"Hey, don't shout, you'll wake up everyone in Bermuda. No, I know I'm not a pilot, I'm going to taxy it. I reckon I can do that."

"You must be bloody crazy Helmut. It's a hell of way to Germany!" Jack didn't usually use expletives, but it seemed to him that if ever there was justification for doing so this was it.

"I know that Jack — I've just got to get it to a U-boat that will be waiting at sunrise."

Schachmann thought this would sound more feasible, which it most definitely was to him, but Jack didn't.

"You don't think they're going to let you taxy it all the way round to St George's and out to sea, do you? They'll blow you out of the water before that. Probably whilst you're still in the Sound. They've got guns on Turtle Hill and lots of other places!"

Schachmann wasn't sure exactly who *they* were, as he was trying not to think about them. He knew there was the RAF on Darrell's Island, of course, but he didn't know whether they kept watch all night. So he had to presume they did and act accordingly. There was the US Navy with their own flying boats at their operating base a mile or two away at King's Point, and the Royal Navy at the Dockyard. In addition there were army gun positions mounted in strategic places — he didn't know, or care whether they were manned by United States troops, British or Bermudian. It didn't make much difference. He presumed they would all be equally proficient.

"No, my orders are to get out to the north. If I get up a bit of speed I can get out of the Sound by the time they realise what's going on, and zoom right over the coral!"

He had worked out that he might have to taxy the Catalina through about five miles of cross fire if things got tough, and he was hoping he would be able to taxy fast enough to give them a much faster moving target than they had been trained to hit. Several months ago he had overheard a conversation in a pub in Hamilton about a triangulation system which was being used to track ships as they came into the Sound. But he was hoping that it would take some time for there to be any response to his actions. He felt sure the RAF would hesitate before giving orders to fire on the Cat, and it would take time for them to be sure that the boat had been stolen — probably twenty minutes to half an hour. If he was right, he would be well on his way by then.

"Maybe, but what's going to happen when you get it to the sub — supposing you do?"

"They'll come aboard the Cat and take out some equipment they want."

"Why do you have to steal the Cat then? Can't you just steal the equipment and get that out to them?"

"No I can't, I don't know what it looks like or where it is on the aircraft."

For a few seconds Jack fell silent.

Then Schachmann said, "Are you with me, or not, Jack — remember it's my mother's life we're talking about."

"You say Lucy knows all about this and wants me to help you save your Mum's life?"

"Yes, it was her that suggested you'd be the best person to help me." Schachmann was lying, but he sounded convincing.

"OK, if I say 'yes', what do you want me to do?"

"Get into the plane with me, and lie low until about four thirty. That's an hour before dawn. Then help me cast off from the buoy so that we drift away from Darrell's. Then as soon as it begins to get light a little, around five, help me start the engines. You can get back in your boat then and row home. I'll taxy her away as fast as I can."

"Right — how are you going to get back then?"

"I'm not. If I get to the sub, I've got to go back to Germany in it."

"Crikey, are they making you do that? Isn't there some way you could stay here?"

"No, it's part of my instructions."

"I don't think Lucy will like that."

"I've told Lucy I'll come back for her if I survive the war!" He was lying again, but past caring.

There was a slight pause in the conversation before Jack continued his cross examination.

"And what do you think will happen to me? It'll be broad daylight by the time I get home, I'm bound to be caught."

"You tell them the truth, you thought we were going fishing."

"So?"

"I pulled a gun on you, and you had to do as I said."

"Yes, I suppose they'd believe that, under the circumstances."

"Good. So you'll help me then, Jack?"

"Yes, OK, just this once. We'd better not make a habit of it!"

It was the first touch of humour in the conversation. And Schachmann found it difficult not to laugh out loud.

"Great Jack, thanks. I know where the Cat we want is moored. It's right next to the big new four-engined flying boat — Coronado I think it's called."

" Yes, I saw the first one land a few weeks ago."

"Right, we've got plenty of time, but we've got to keep very quiet. So go slowly and keep going the way we're heading until I say."

It took them another twenty minutes before they were alongside the fuselage of the Catalina. Five minutes later they had opened the blister — it was the normal and easiest place to enter the aircraft — and both were on board.

At the Belmont, Lucy was preparing to leave. "I must go soon, darling," she said. "Must get home before it's completely light."

"Do you have to?"

"Yes, 'fraid so. Mummy gets up soon after dawn these days!"

"Then I'll come with you," said Newman.

"You don't have to."

"I want to. Can't have anything happening to you on the way home, Lucy."

"Thanks, I'd like that!"

It was four-thirty when they both got dressed. Newman put on his "best blue" uniform, he knew Lucy liked him to wear it. The brass buttons were in need of a polish, but he didn't expect to be seen by anybody else at this time in the morning. Lucy put on the pale blue dress she had arrived in and they made their way quietly and unnoticed out of the Belmont. After making their way down the hill they walked along Harbour Road with their arms round each other, towards Riddell's Bay.

If anyone had seen them, they would have been in no doubt that the couple were deeply in love. Neither of them had been in love before and they were revelling in a world of their own. Although neither of them said anything, they were both wondering what the future held for them. Newman wasn't sure if he would stay with Ferry Command long. It was in the lap of the gods. Although he hoped to be back in Bermuda on another delivery in a few weeks time, he might not be. He decided he would be stupid not to propose to her before he left for Britain in a few day's time, and there might not be a better time, than now. There was no one about at this hour, it was a breath taking morning, and his courage was up.

"Darling," said Newman. "Will....." . He broke off in mid sentence as he heard the sound of a Catalina's engines starting. He had an irresistible urge to check that his Cat was safe at its moorings and in the dim light before dawn he saw that it wasn't. There was only one possible explanation — it had been taken out of the water and was on the hard standing on Darrell's Island for some reason. But then he saw it and his heart missed a beat. It was actually taxying out into the sound, presumably for take off! He knew then that there was something seriously wrong about the situation and he told Lucy so, but it didn't enter his mind that a German 'agent' was trying to steal it. The only thing he could think of was that another crew had taken his boat by mistake, but that didn't add up. There weren't supposed to be any deliveries to Britain for the next two days because of unfavourable winds, and it was far too early in the day for a test flight, and anyway he would normally expect to do that himself if one was necessary.

He had made such a flight only the day before when he had given Helmut Schachmann a joy ride and he wasn't expecting the need for another.

Newman wasn't in the right frame of mind now to propose to Lucy and he abandoned the idea for the time being.

"When I get back to the Belmont, I'm going to find out what this is all about, Lucy" said Newman.

"I can go the rest of the way home by myself if you like," she replied. But Newman was watching his Cat.

"Whoever's taxying it, is out of practice," said Newman. "He isn't keeping it straight, he's all over the blooming place."

Lucy kept quiet. Newman appreciated it. It was typical of her, he thought. She was supportive but not intrusive, and he instinctively tightened his arm around her waist and pulled her closer to him.

The note he'd had to sign in Elizabeth City, about the top secret equipment on board, was uppermost in his mind.

'Nobody in Bermuda will know anything about it. Your aircraft will be

treated just like the rest,' or something like that it had said. *'You will tell nobody.'*

He could still remember his feelings when he had read those words. Now he realised that there could be very serious security complications arising from what was happening. The way the Cat was being taxied there was a distinct possibility that it would sink before too long. What would happen then? Should he say that it was a special aircraft? Perhaps he should try and contact the CO now. If he did so, should he tell him the truth?

But he was getting ahead of himself. It would take him ten minutes to get back to the Belmont if he ran all the way. His Cat would be airborne by then. He decided there was nothing he could do for the time being but watch, and he did so helplessly.

The Cat had turned and was now heading towards the Dockyard and had several miles of clear water in front of it. Newman knew this was when the throttles would be opened up for take-off, if that was the intention of whoever was in the pilot's seat.

There had been at least one previous incident in which an RAF pilot, under the influence of drink, had borrowed a Royal Navy boat and toured around the Sound in a gale. Could this be a drunken sailor from the Navy getting his own back? He doubted it. A sailor wouldn't even know how to start the engines. More likely a drunken RAF pilot, he thought. He knew war had an effect on men, and had noticed that some, when they passed through Bermuda, thought it was the ideal place to let off steam!

"Could someone be stealing it?" asked Lucy.

"I wouldn't think so. Who would want to do that; and where would they fly it to?"

"Couldn't it be a US navy pilot, or somebody trying to defect and get back to the States?"

A story he'd heard some months earlier came to his mind and he realised he'd perhaps underestimated what sailors can do!

"I hadn't thought of that one, Lucy. I suppose it could be. About eighteen months ago I heard that a Russian sailor stole a Catalina from Sevastapol and landed it in the sea near Cyprus! So it's possible."

Lucy couldn't really understand what Don was fussed about.

"Well, there you are then Don!" she said, "Anyway if your plane is stolen you'll just have to stay in Bermuda a bit longer whilst it's all sorted out, won't you. That would be good wouldn't it it?"

Newman didn't respond. His thoughts were interrupted by an exclamation from Lucy. She pointed to a rowing boat heading towards Burgess Point. "There's Jack — looks like he's been fishing." she said excitedly. Lucy and her younger brother had always been very close, and she knew he would help her slip back into their home quietly, if she could get there in time to intercept him. In their household, fifteen year old boys were allowed to go fishing at night occasionally, but since the Islands had been invaded by several thousand troops of various nationalities, nineteen year old girls were not! And her mother was very strict about that. "Let's hurry and we can catch him," she said to Don.

Newman and Lucy still had their arms around each other, and their walking had all but stopped. Now, with Jack in view, it speeded up.

"How do you know it's Jack?" said Newman, thinking it didn't matter who it was.

"Oh, I can recognise Jack and his boat anywhere. Don't know why, just can. "

They hurried on, Lucy forcing their pace until they were almost running. Newman was watching his Cat the whole time.

On board the Catalina, Schachmann was gaining confidence and his butterflies had quietened. Very gradually advancing the throttles, the Cat was gaining speed in the Great Sound. Schachmann estimated his speed was about thirty five miles an hour, far faster he figured, than any motor launch which might be sent out to chase him. He had the control column right back — he had remembered what Newman had said about that the previous day — and, providing no one started firing at him, he felt there was now a good chance of getting the flying boat to the submarine. In case the artillery were preparing to blow him out of the water, he started to weave, changing his direction a few degrees either side of his main heading every few moments. This, he hoped, would make it more difficult for them to triangulate and work out precisely where they should aim their guns.

Newman became convinced that this was a prank by a half drunken sailor when he saw that the Cat was not taking-off, but was steering an apparently haphazard course in the general direction of the Royal Navy Dockyard.

"I bet he's a Fleet Air Arm pilot," said Newman, as though trying to convince himself.

They were now only a short distance from Burnt House Hill, where

Lucy and Don usually said goodbye and she continued on her own.

"Well, Jack may have seen more," said Lucy.

She didn't realise how right she was! "He must have been fishing near Darrell's," she continued. "I know where he's going. He often comes ashore in a little bay near Burgess Point and puts his boat on the edge of the golf course. Let's go!"

They left the road and cut across some rough ground to the golf course, and after that it was easy going to Burgess Point. As they made their way quickly along the northern edge of the golf course a US Navy Kingfisher float plane taxied out from Kings Point and took-off. It seemed the crew were unaware of the Catalina, which was now three or four miles away, and the pilot turned to the left after take-off and climbed into the distance.

"It's the usual dawn patrol," said Lucy. It goes off every morning about this time."

They arrived at the little bay just as Jack was pulling his boat out of the water.

"Crikey, Lucy, didn't expect to see you here," he said, as he spotted the couple approaching.

Lucy wasted no time. "Jack, I want to go home with you. If Mum hears any noise she'll just think it's you. OK?"

"Fine — but I didn't tell her I was going out. Anyway what've you been up to then big sister?"

Before Lucy had a chance to answer Newman asked "Have you been anywhere near Darrell's Island?"

Jack didn't respond at first to Newman's question. He was already starting on his way home and was a few paces away. "What's that to do with you?" he said, eventually turning and shrugging his shoulders.

"Jack wait a minute," said Lucy. "You haven't even spoken properly to Don yet. He asked you a simple question. Don't be so rude."

"Sorry Lucy — Morning Mr Newman."

"Flight Lieutenant Newman," said Lucy.

Don turned and took his eyes off his distant Cat for the first time for several minutes. "Look Jack, you didn't see who got into the Cat that's taxying out there did you?"

Jack walked back to the rowing boat and looked out into the Great Sound watching the Cat disappearing into the distance beyond the Dockyard. He was standing between Don and Lucy, so Newman couldn't see his face as he addressed Lucy. "Oh that Cat. No, I hadn't noticed it up till now."

"Why are you winking at me Jack?" asked Lucy, "there are no secrets between Don and me!" She said it with emphasis, and Jack had no doubt she meant it.

"Oh, I didn't realise you'd told him."

"Jack, what are you talking about. Told Don what?"

Newman moved to stand by Lucy's side, took off his peak cap, ran his fingers through his hair, and replaced his hat. "He knows something, Lucy," said Don, "and I want to know what it is." He sounded 'no nonsense' determined.

"You know Lucy — Helmut told me you were helping him and you knew all about it," Jack responded.

Lucy went to say something but Newman got in first. He got hold of Jack by his left arm and held it tight, so there was no chance he could run away. "Right Jack let's have the truth. Lucy is right, we don't have secrets!"

"All right, you can let go, I'm not going to run."

Newman released him even though he was determined to get to the truth. It wasn't his style to be heavy handed anyway. "Well?"

"You tell him, Lucy," said Jack.

"Tell him what?"

"That you've just slept with him to keep him busy, so that Helmut could steal his Catalina!"

"What are you talking about Jack, that's nonsense. I love Don, now." She emphasised *Don* and regretted the word *now*, as soon as she had said it.

"You knew that he was going to take a Catalina to a U-boat — and that it had secret equipment or something in it. They were going to kill his mother if he didn't. It was you who told Helmut to ask me to go with him."

"No Jack, I didn't. That's not true! That's not true!"

In spite of Lucy's denial, Don Newman had heard enough. With his emotions in turmoil, he left the scene without a word to either of them. It took him fifteen minutes to run back to the Belmont, and he found that all hell had broken loose in the RAF offices. Nobody was sure what was going on. Newman's arrival did something to sort out the situation. He was the last pilot to be accounted for, so they now knew the aircraft was definitely not under the charge of an RAF pilot, and they started appropriate action.

The guns on Turtle Hill were the first to open fire, quickly followed by the Fort at Scaur Hill. Suddenly, because of the noise, most of Bermuda was stirring, including Lucy's mother, Turtle Hill being less than half a mile away. She like many others thought the Islands were about to be invaded by the Germans. She rushed into Lucy's room and told her to finish getting dressed quickly. In fact Lucy was in the middle of getting undressed, but fortunately that thought never entered her mother's head.

Newman didn't realise it, but the guns at Fort Scaur were firing at the U-boat, not at his Catalina! The U-boat's conning tower had been seen through high powered binoculars, by an alert lookout at the Dockyard.

After a few minutes the U-boat dived below the surface and the guns fell silent. Newman presumed they had destroyed his Cat. He prayed that they had, otherwise they would surely still be firing. He felt a strong feeling of relief. The words in the memo, 'You must not allow your aircraft to fall into enemy hands,' had been eating into his soul for the last half hour.

Prime Minister Winston Churchill, on his way to meet President Roosevelt in Washington, was aboard the liner *Queen Mary*. It had left the Clyde a few hours earlier and been chosen because its speed gave it the ability to out-run U-boats. Once out of range of Luftwaffe patrols with their Condor aircraft — which could direct U-boats to their targets — it was thought the *Queen* had little to fear. Thus it was not planned that she should be protected by the Royal Navy, beyond that point.

The news of an attempt to steal a Catalina from Bermuda was received in London with some alarm. With a possible endurance of up to thirty hours, it could be in a position to intercept the *Queen* within the next twenty-four hours. Was it possible that there was a connection between Bermuda events and the Prime Minister's voyage?

In Bletchley Park, England, Brenda Newman, Don Newman's twin sister, was part of a team trying — and often succeeding — in intercepting and deciphering messages between German U-boats and their shore based commanders. But it was not her job to understand messages; she was just a cog in a gigantic wheel and, when she was told to pass the message currently in her hands to the Admiralty instantly, she thought little of it. She had no way of knowing that it concerned her brother's Catalina.

The message — from the U-boat to its home base — merely contained the single word *Hilda*. At Bletchley Park they knew the meaning instantly. The day before they had successfully intercepted and decoded an order to a U-boat which stated that Operation "Onion Meeting" was to be at dawn the following day and that *Hilda* should be transmitted to indicate its failure and *Helmut* its success. However until now naval intelligence in the UK had not been able to determine what Operation 'Onion Meeting' was.

At the Admiralty in London they received the news with some relief. It was received just a few seconds before they heard direct from Bermuda that the Catalina had crashed on the coral reefs.

No one at Bermuda knew about the Prime Minister's journey, but they soon received instructions from higher authority for Newman to be placed under house arrest. Newman wasn't too certain why he was instructed not to leave the hotel until further notice. He was far from happy about that! It suggested that he was in some way involved, and he knew that he wasn't.

Friday, 7 May 1943

Newman knocked on the door of the Belmont Manor Hotel bar, as instructed, at 0900 hours. He had had more than a few drinks in the bar the night before, when he had heard he had to present himself to a — what was it the Wing Commander had called it? — a preliminary investigation, or something like that. By arrangement with the hotel, the bar had been taken over for the morning, since the Commanding Officer's room was too small for the meeting.

A Flying Officer, who Newman had not seen before, opened the door. Newman told him who he was.

"OK, I'll tell them you're here."

The door was shut. Newman waited nervously outside, checking his tie was straight, that all his tunic buttons were done up and his shoes were still sparkling. He had tipped one of the hotel staff to polish the brass buttons on his tunic and press his trousers, and he was pleased with her efforts. She had done an excellent job. The last thing Newman wanted was his appearance to start things off on the wrong foot. A haircut would have completed his attempts to look smart, but he had been told not to leave the hotel. He had complied; there was no point in making things worse for himself than they were already.

They were not ready inside yet, so Newman had time to ponder the events of the last few days. That was nothing new, for he had hardly had any other thoughts since Wednesday morning, and had slept very little. It was bad enough that his Catalina had been stolen, but Lucy's involvement made it ten times worse. Indeed if it wasn't for his association with her, he would be completely in the clear. He hadn't done anything wrong at all as far as he knew. But could he make others believe that? He had considerable doubts.

Up to the 'incident' he would have trusted Lucy with his own life. There was still a part of him that found it impossible to believe that she had used him. Even if he was able to see her again and confront her, could he believe a word she said? The only good thing about the whole occurrence was that Schachmann had failed to reach the U-boat.

Apparently, his taxying had come to a sudden end near the outer reefs. The Cat had partially sunk and although probably irreparable, the Royal Navy had managed to get it back to their Dockyard. He had heard all this from a colleague about eleven o'clock on Wednesday morning. Rumour had it that Schachmann was saved and currently languishing in a police cell in Hamilton.

So the secret equipment had not got to the U-boat. That was the one positive and vital thing which Newman hung on to in his mind. He realised the situation could have been far worse.

The bar door opened. The Flying Officer spoke quietly. "Right, they're ready for you now. I think you'll find the Groupy's OK. His name is Proctor, by the way. Good luck."

"Right, thanks."

Newman entered to find six people in the room. A Group Captain and Wing Commander Wavell were sitting side by side at a table with their backs to the window facing four others, who were seated in a semi circle. Two were uniformed Bermuda police officers, a third was a civilian man, whom Newman was later to learn was in charge of anti sabotage activities at Bermuda. The sixth person was a Flight Lieutenant in the RCAF, whom Newman had previously come across in Montreal. If he remembered rightly, the Canadian was a civil lawyer who now used his legal skills in the Air Force. There was one empty chair at the end of the semi circle. Newman headed for it, stopped behind it, and saluted the Group Captain. "Flight Lieutenant Newman, Sir."

The Wing Commander attempted to explain to the Group Captain that Newman had captained the aircraft on its flight from Elizabeth City.

"Yes, I know. Sit down Newman." Newman took his hat off and sat. From his end seat he could see Darrell's Island in the distance, over the Group Captain's left shoulder. He couldn't help noticing that a Royal Navy ship was at the jetty and off loading a Catalina. He guessed it was his damaged aircraft.

The Group Captain was twice Newman's age, and developing a middle aged spread. Clean shaven with a worn rugged face, Newman gained the impression that he was in for a tough time from the Groupy, in spite of the Flying Officer's remarks at the door. Dressed in RAF battle dress with a pilot's brevet and numerous medals — one of which Newman recognised from the blue and white stripes as the Distinguished Flying Cross — Newman didn't feel at ease. He knew DFCs were not given away as Christmas presents, and he hoped he would be able to keep his head and make his responses in a humble fashion. There and then he decided he would plead that he had been naive, but nothing more.

"You might as well run this show," said the Group Captain, addressing Wing Commander Wavell. "I'll sit in."

"Right Sir — is this to be run like a formal enquiry?"

"No. I hope that won't be necessary. Let's just get to the truth — we can decide then where we go, from there."

"Right Sir."

The Wing Commander leaned forward, put both elbows on the edge of the table, and clasped his hands together. "Newman there are a number of things we want to know from you."

"Yes Sir."

"The first concerns a test flight you made on 4 May. We have been told that you carried an unauthorised civilian passenger, Helmut Schachmann. Is that correct?

"Yes, Sir."

"I see. Was there some special reason you did that?"

"No Sir. Just a friendly gesture, or at least that was what I hoped."

"I see. It has been suggested that you were asked to take Schachmann with you by Lucy Appledram, the sister of Jack Appledram. She was also, I understand, engaged to Schachmann. Is this true?"

Newman felt a sudden pain in his bowels, and momentarily lost his composure. He tried not to let it show. "No, it's not true, I'm sure it's not —Sir!"

"What's not true Newman, all of it?"

"No, I mean she's not engaged to Helmut Schachmann — Sir."

"But she did ask you to give Schachmann a flight in your aircraft?"

Newman was now back to his composed self and resolved to watch himself closely from now on.

"Yes, she was involved Sir, but it was Schachmann who asked me."

The Group Captain scribbled something on the notepad in front of him.

Wing Commander Wavell continued his attack. At least that was what it felt like to Newman.

"Right — now that we've established that she was involved, we need to examine your motives, and before we go any further I should tell you that half an hour ago, we heard from Chief Inspector Clarkson," the Wing

Commander nodded towards the police officer on Newman's left, "that Schachmann is in police custody, and has said that you were one of three others who agreed to help him steal the aircraft, so as to save the life of his Jewish mother. The other two, of course, he maintains, were Lucy Appledram and her brother Jack."

"Sir, I admit to breaking the rules and giving Schachmann a ride. But there's no way I would help anyone steal an RAF aircraft, especially as ...." He was beginning to raise his voice again and he checked himself in mid-stream and broke off the sentence — realising he was about to mention the secret equipment! He regained control and continued. "Schachmann is making this all up in the hope that I'll be put in jail and so won't be able to see Miss Appledram whilst he's locked up too!"

Wing Commander Wavell looked at the Group Captain. Newman took the pause in the attack to play what he thought was his trump card. It showed in his manner as he said, "Sir, can I ask that the police talk to Lucy Appledram. She'll corroborate my story!"

Wavell didn't respond in the way Newman hoped. The Wing Commander unclasped his hands and gestured to the police inspector.

"We have," said the inspector, stroking the back of his hair with his right hand. "We tried to interview her and her brother at length yesterday. She's refusing to answer any of our questions! Her brother's story mostly supports Schachmann's." There was an air of finality in the way the inspector said it that made Newman react. It was as if the inspector was saying 'get out of that one!'

"Oh crikey" Newman muttered. He didn't know that Helmut had saved Lucy's life three years earlier, when they had both been trapped in a house fire together, and that she felt indebted to him. She also knew she would have her mother to face, if she didn't at least appear to support him. The Group Captain and the Wing Commander both gave Newman a stern look.

"I beg your pardon Sir, I wasn't expecting that," said Newman.

A US Navy Catalina was circling, to land in the Great Sound, and the noise of it's engines caused the Wing Commander to glance out of the window, but his attention rapidly returned to the meeting.

"Let's move on now," he said. "Our understanding is that on Tuesday night, the night Catalina 851 was taken from its moorings, you were in bed in your room here at the Belmont with Lucy Appledram. I presume you do not deny that?"

As Newman answered, he addressed, as usual, both the senior offices sitting at the table. The Wing Co was stern but he felt he saw a very slight smile on the Group Captain's face. Their eyes met and Newman felt that he was thinking 'lucky sod,' or something like that.

"No, Sir."

"Well, you won't be surprised to hear Newman, that Schachmann maintains that he asked his fiancée, Lucy Appledram, to seduce you, so as to keep you busy, whilst he and Jack Appledram stole the aircraft."

"No Sir, that's not true. There was no reason to keep me busy. I was a mile away from my aircraft and there was no way I could stop it being stolen. Anyway it was her birthday, and one thing sort of led to another, after we'd had a few drinks."

The Group Captain made yet another note on his pad. Newman wished he could read upside down writing.

The police inspector intervened. "For the record can I just say that Lucy Appeldram was born in February 1924. So if she said it was her birthday she was lying. Isn't that right Sergeant?"

The Sergeant confirmed that it was. Newman was getting concerned at the way the things were stacking up against him!

The Groupy remarked, "She wouldn't be the first woman to lie about her age!"

"Let's just consider that point; I mean the suggestion that you were seduced, Newman." said the Wing Commander.

"Where were you when you first realised an attempt to steal your aircraft was being made?"

"I was on Harbour Road opposite Darrell's, Sir."

"What were you doing there?"

"Taking Lucy Appledram home — Sir."

"So she made sure you were nowhere near the Belmont then?"

"No, it was my idea to see her home."

"But who decided when she had to leave to go home? Schachmann says she timed it so as to get you out of the hotel!"

Newman was beginning to feel desperate. It was true that Lucy had decided what time she had to leave his bed, and he was now starting to wonder if she was on his side or not. He tried to dismiss the thought. It was ridiculous. He leaned forward in his seat, without realising he was doing it, and his general body language made it clear that he was getting agitated.

"Sir, it's true that... Lucy.... Miss Appledram decided when she had to go. Maybe I'm naive in these matters, but I would have thought that was normal under the circumstances. I was in no mood to throw her out of my bed! And I don't see what advantage there would be in me being away from the Belmont."

Before an answer came, the Group Captain intervened.

"Let me take over on this one, George," he said.

"Very good Sir,"

The Wing Commander seemed surprised. He had been wondering why the Groupy had flown in from Montreal, specially to be present at the meeting.

"Newman, before you left Montreal you were given a confidential instruction from the Air Officer Commanding, which you had to read and sign. Is that correct?"

Newman didn't know how to answer, or if he should answer at all. The letter had clearly stated that no one else was to know.

Wing Co Wavell looked at the Groupy, obviously surprised that a Flight Lieutenant would get a letter from the big white chief in Montreal, the AOC. He was even more surprised when Newman didn't respond to the question. Newman was — at least for the time being — one of his pilots and he expected responses.

"Newman you were asked a question!" he said.

Still Newman didn't answer. Eventually, aware that all eyes in the room were upon him Newman said. "I find that question difficult to answer, Sir."

Although he wasn't making it obvious, the Wing Co had come to the meeting, with little doubt that the outcome would be favourable to Newman. He couldn't really believe Newman had cooperated with an enemy agent. Now he didn't like the way things were going, and was beginning to wonder.

"Newman, it's a simple question. Did you, or did you not, read and sign a memorandum from the AOC before you took off from Elizabeth City?"

The Group Captain intervened again. "I can see you are in difficulty here, which is not of your making Newman."

Wing Commander Wavell frowned; the two police officers' faces showed signs of puzzlement.

"Correct, Sir."

"I'm not asking you what the instruction said, you understand, just whether you read it and signed it?" The Groupy's tone was different from the Wing Co's, more understanding, and Newman picked up the change instantly, and began to relax a little.

"Yes Sir, I did."

The Groupy nodded and Newman thought he saw the signs of a very slight smile again.

It was there for only a split second, nevertheless it reassured Newman that the most senior person present was human and understanding. He suspected that the Wing Commander was on his side as well but was hamstrung by the presence of a superior officer.

"Now, Newman, did you tell anyone else anything about that letter?"

"No, Sir, I was instructed not to, and I didn't." Newman sounded confident again.

"Are you absolutely sure about that? You didn't tell Miss Appledram, for instance?"

"Yes Sir, absolutely sure. I certainly didn't tell her or anyone else."

"Good Newman, I'm pleased to hear that! If you're telling the truth, and I'm prepared to accept for the moment that you are, then someone who shouldn't have done so, read it at Elizabeth City." The Groupy produced a handkerchief and blew his nose before continuing.

"Now, it has been suggested in Montreal, that because of what the letter said, you were probably keeping a special eye on your boat — it would be natural. You could see it from here couldn't you? It has also been suggested that Schachmann realised that and was told to make sure you were occupied whilst he did what he had to do."

"But Sir, I'm not usually awake at that time in the morning! I wouldn't know if my aircraft was being stolen!"

The Group Captain gestured to Wing Commander Wavell and he took over the interrogation once more.

"That's what we thought, at first, but on more than one occasion you were up that early, weren't you. Isn't that right inspector?"

The inspector confirmed the allegation. Newman wondered how they knew that.

"Well, yes Sir, there were some mornings that I got up early."

"Yes, he was seen on at least four occasions that we know of," the inspector chipped in.

"Well, Newman?"

"I'm a bird watcher, Sir. Have been for years. I often used to get up early to hear the dawn chorus at home. I thought I'd try it here."

"Nothing wrong in that, but it means that your comment that you would normally be sound asleep at the time Schachmann stole your aircraft wasn't true, was it?"

"No, Sir, I apologise. I'd forgotten the mornings I'd been bird watching."

"Where did you go on these bird watching mornings Newman?"

"Oh just outside the hotel, Sir. Not far away."

"So, if you had decided to go bird watching that particular morning and you had seen and heard your Catalina starting up, what would you have done?"

"I'm not sure, Sir."

"You don't think you would have been tempted to contact the duty officer?"

"I'm not sure. I suppose so, Sir." Newman was beginning to sound dejected and he knew it. Wavell pressed on.

"Now, did you ever mention your dawn sorties to Lucy Appledram?"

"Yes, several times, Sir. She is keen on birds too."

"So you must see that Shachmann's story that he asked Lucy Appledram to, shall we say, keep you busy, is at least a feasible story? They both knew that there was at least a possibility you could get up for the dawn chorus near the hotel, and they decided to make sure you were occupied and out of harm's way. "

Newman was feeling more and more that things weren't going his way. It showed on his face and he was about to say something, when the Groupy spoke.

"Newman, it is a possibility. We are saying, no more than that."

"Yes Sir, but can I say a few words at this point?"

"Carry on, " the Groupy responded.

"If, as has been suggested, Lucy Appledram is Helmut Schachmann's fiancée, it hardly seems likely that he would ask her, as was suggested, to seduce me!"

"Yes, but you must remember that this is war time and that Schachmann really believed that his mother's life was at stake, which is probably true."

There was a slight pause in the conversation as though the senior officers were considering the pros and cons of the matter.

"But there is another complication: the letter," commented the Wing Co.

"I think that's been dealt with. The AOC's memorandum need not concern us any more," said the Groupy, quickly and pointedly.

"No Sir, I'm talking about a letter that was found floating on the water near Darrell's Island yesterday. It's addressed to a *Helmut* and signed by a *Lucy,* and dated 1 February this year, before Flt Lt Newman had arrived at Bermuda. It's very wet, of course, but the Inspector tells me they have been able to read most of it. How it got in the water near Darrell's is not clear, but it has been suggested that Schachmann must have lost it when he was boarding the Catalina. Certainly it wasn't in the water for more than a day or two."

"Yes, it's a love letter which it would be inappropriate to read out here, but it definitely establishes that Schachmann and Lucy Appledram knew each other very well," said the Inspector.

The Groupy spoke. "I understand that it is, as you put it, inappropriate to tell us the complete contents of the letter Inspector, but is there anything at all about Darrell's Island and stealing a Catalina?"

"No, nothing Group Captain, but the general tone of the letter is that she will do anything for him, to keep his love and affection."

That's another nail in the coffin, thought Newman, who now knew for certain that the proceedings were not going in his favour. A sense of injustice was starting to invade his mind, and he didn't like injustice, especially if it involved him. He had been quietly but forcibly told to stay at the Belmont and make no attempt to contact Lucy. But that was unfair. A letter she had written to Schachmann long before he had arrived in Bermuda was being used to suggest she was on Schachmann's side. Hadn't anyone ever heard of a woman changing her mind!

The Groupy turned to the Wing Co and said in a quiet confidential tone, "I think we have enough information, don't you? I'll have a private chat with Newman, but I think you could bring the meeting to a close now."

The Wing Commander thanked the police officers for attending. Addressing them he said "I do understand that what happens to Schachmann is not our direct concern, but equally you'll appreciate that what action, if any, is taken against Flt Lt Newman is up to the Royal Air Force. I know you understand that. Thank you for your help and cooperation."

The meeting broke up. Newman was told not to leave. The room emptied except for the Wing Co and the Groupy who were quietly conversing in the corner of the room, and Newman who had taken the opportunity to stretch his legs and was standing looking through a window at activities at the swimming pool and Hamilton beyond. He was pensive and taut. On the evidence presented today he surely must face a court-martial.

"Newman," the Groupy was talking.

"Sir."

Newman was quickly back facing them over the table, but this time all three were still standing.

"I've been talking with Wing Commander Wavell — I think we have to post you out of here — a new environment — a clean slate. Do you have anything to say?"

Newman was taken by surprise. He'd been expecting to hear he was going to face a court- martial. He found himself saying, "Yes Sir. No, nothing Sir."

"Bomber Command for you, I think then Newman. Come back on my Liberator this afternoon to Montreal. It can be sorted out there."

"Very good Sir."

Later that day Newman boarded the AOC's Liberator at Kindley Field, as a passenger, bound for Montreal. Flying Officer Nick Carter, who had been the "doorman" at the enquiry was also on the flight, and they chatted, shouting to make themselves heard above the noise of the engines.

Carter said "The RAF's way of dealing with problems was to post the people concerned as far away as possible, and bomber command was a long way from Montreal and Bermuda, and needed pilots. Anyway it could have been much worse."

Newman didn't follow Carter's last point. "How do you mean?" he asked.

"Well this bloke Schachmann — he had a good try but he didn't get the Cat to the U-boat did he!"

CHAPTER EIGHT

May 1943

Three days later he was put on a BOAC Liberator bound for Prestwick, Scotland as a passenger. It seemed Montreal wanted to get rid of Newman quickly! Even in the Liberator — which could fly much faster than the Catalina — it was a long flight and he had a lot of time to think. To say the least, he wasn't happy. He didn't know exactly why he was on his way to Bomber Command. It had all happened so quickly. The only thing he acknowledged doing wrong was giving Schachmann a ride in his Catalina, and he had been honest about that at the enquiry meeting.

His mind went over and over the events of the last few days. He realised now, that he had not done himself any favours when he had walked away from Lucy. He couldn't believe that what her brother said could be true. There had to be an explanation, but he couldn't think what it could be. He wished to God he hadn't walked away from her and that he'd given her a chance to talk!

The Liberator landed at Prestwick about seven in the morning on Monday 10 May, after an overnight trans Atlantic flight. It was just six weeks since Newman's previous visit, following his one and only Catalina delivery from Bermuda.

To his surprise he was given a leave pass, ration coupons and a railway travel warrant to Staines, Middlesex, his home town, and told to wait there for a telegram. But Newman had other ideas about getting to London — nearly four hundred miles away. As soon as he was free of the system he made his way to the control tower.

"Just thought I'd ask," said Newman to the Flying Control Officer. "Got any aircraft going South I could get a lift on? I want to get to London."

The Controller was clearly very busy. "Hang on, be with you in a mo."

"*Charlie Freddie,* cleared take-off."

The Controller turned now, and gave Newman his full attention. He was the same rank as Newman but perhaps twenty years older, and spoke with a London accent.

"I've just flown in on the Lib from Montreal," said Newman "and can't wait to get to London!"

"Yes — know the feeling. Haven't been further than Glasgow for six months myself!"

He spoke to a colleague who was looking out on to the airfield with a pair of binoculars. "Burt — the ATA bringing anything in today?"

Unlike the Atlantic Ferry Organisation, which Newman had been a part of, it was not part of the RAF. It was a civilian organisation set up to ferry military aircraft within the United Kingdom and was mostly comprised of pilots who were considered too old for active service in the Air Force, so allowing as many RAF pilots as possible to fight rather than ferry aeroplanes.

Its Headquarters was at White Waltham, near Maidenhead, thirty miles west of London, and fifteen miles from Staines, Newman's destination. If he could get a ride to White Waltham it would save him a long and tedious train journey.

Burt gave a flashing green signal on the Aldis light to the pilot of a Hudson waiting to taxy. "Yes, a Hurricane — it's due in soon,"

"It might be worth hanging around. You could be in luck. The ATA will send an Anson to pick up the Hurricane pilot — that's the way they work. If you play your cards right you should be able to get a seat south on that."

"Wizard. Can you speak to them, or should I?"

"We can speak to the Hurricane pilot when he arrives. With a bit of luck he'll speak to the Anson pilot. He's the one that matters — you should be able to get a lift down to the Midlands, at least."

As Newman drank a cup of coffee he thought it sounded too easy. He feared other would-be hitch hikers might come out of the woodwork as soon as the Anson arrived!

For the next twenty minutes he stood in the Control Tower watching aircraft landing and taking-off. The weather was not the best he'd seen for flying. A succession of rain showers were crossing the field from the sea and reducing visibility to about a mile as they passed. Compared to Bermuda it was decidedly chilly. But Bermuda was another world!

A US Army Air Force Martin Marauder landed safely with one of it's two engines shut down, having flown the last hour of an Iceland - Prestwick flight 'on one'. Flying Control had alerted the Fire Crew and they had their engines running when it landed. Fortunately they weren't needed! But the aircraft couldn't taxy on one engine and the runway had to be closed whilst the aircraft was towed away. As a result a North American Mitchell delivery from Canada destined for the RAF chose to land at the nearby Ayr airfield, because of a shortage of fuel.

Not all aircraft had working radios, so flying control kept a constant watch on the airfield and the sky above and often had to try and guess a pilot's intentions.

"Does this sort of thing happen very often?" Newman asked.

"Yes, I'll say. You name it, it all happens here!"

As if to prove the point Newman noticed a high winged single engined Norseman aircraft circling, just above circuit height. He'd seen many in Canada during pilot training.

"Tower, this is circling Norseman two four five for Edinburgh. Request bearing to Turnhouse, over." The accent made it evident that the Noorduyn Norseman belonged to the US Army Air Force.

The tower knew this one off by heart. They'd had it many times before, along with Renfrew, Turnberry and Scone. "Norseman two four five, Prestwick tower. QDM Turnhouse, zero-five-eight, five-zero nautical miles. Over."

"Roger, dodger. Zero-five-eight."

The Norseman made a sharp right turn and was soon out of sight.

The ATA Hurricane landed a few minutes later without radio contact. The pilot parked the aircraft close to the control tower and mounted the steps to the tower. The FCO was standing watching a USAAF Dakota taking off. He had to watch — as he was the one who had to press the crash button to alert the fire crew — if anything went wrong.

The ATA pilot — whose name Newman was later to learn was Jack Somerville, understood the situation and waited. A tall middle aged man in dark blue uniform wearing a forage cap, and with a pilot's brevet on his chest and two gold bars on his epaulets, he carried a sheepskin flying jacket and flying helmet over his left arm. In his right hand he held his parachute, but Newman didn't notice that in particular. He mostly noticed how calm and relaxed the pilot looked. Just as though he'd just stepped off a train, thought Newman.

The ATA pilot spoke when the Dakota was safely airborne. "Morning Ron."

"Morning Jack, a bit claggy at times today!"

"Yes, very, but I think it'll lift soon! When you let Speke know I got here, will you tell Ron Brown I forgot to give him the ten bob I owe him. I'll settle up with him next time I'm in. That shouldn't be too long."

"Sure we'll do that now."

"Already done it, when the Hurricane landed, sir!" said the Controller's assistant.

"OK, ring them again and give them the message about the ten bob."

"If you want a coffee Jack, we can rustle one up. By the way this is Don Newman — just in from the States, or Canada, whatever — he's been ferrying Catalinas across the Atlantic and is looking for a ride down south, London if possible. Any chance of a lift in your pickup Anson?"

"Ah, a flying boat man, interesting." he held out his right hand to Newman, "Jack Somerville."

They shook hands.

"I should think so. I'll have a word with Betty when she arrives. She's going to drop me at Salmesbury, I've got to pick up a Halifax and take it to North Creake. Probably best you come with me to North Creake, then we'll be picked up there by another Annie and taken to White Waltham — if there's room of course — there should be. That suit you?"

He finished with a broad smile and Newman took to him instantly. He was clearly a jovial character, completely relaxed — done it all— but not boasting about it, sort of pilot.

"Bang on! Thanks, terrific," said Newman, "did you say Betty?"

"Yes, Betty Westhorpe — she's the Anson taxy driver."

"Oh, right," surprise , surprise thought Newman.

"Have you got an ETA for the Anson?" Jack asked.

"No — not yet."

They were distracted by the sight of a Mosquito that had arrived in the landing circuit unexpectedly and was now downwind with it's wheels down and a trace of smoke from it's port engine. The Controller had noticed it a few seconds earlier.

"Give the Mosssie a green — looks like he's got a rough engine and a u/s radio!" he said to his assistant, "and get that Oxford off the runway. Give him a flashing red!"

"It's OK, the Oxford's taking off now, Sir."

"Difficult without our control caravan by the side of the runway — much easier to control the runway from it, but some clot in a Wimpey taxied into it last week. Nearly killed Burt. It'll be a week or two before repairs are finished."

Burt turned and smiled, "He did have brake failure Sir. He didn't do it on purpose!"

Newman asked if the Mossie had flown the Atlantic.

"No, on a training exercise probably. We are expecting Canadian built Mossies may come through here on delivery soon, but we haven't had any yet."

The Controller turned his attention to the ATA pilot again.

"We heard earlier that your Anson's going to Perth first to pick up one of your chaps who's delivering a Miles Master there. Then it's coming here, then on to Carlisle, then Salmesbury."

"That figures, I'm being dropped off there."

Twenty minutes later, at two minutes past ten, the phone rang. Perth advised that the Anson, AW911, had taken off at 9:42 with an ETA for Prestwick of 10:15. Sure enough it entered the circuit without radio contact at 10:13, landed and taxied up to the tower.

Jack Somerville and Newman were waiting on the grass in front of the tower when it came to a halt. The engines were kept running and Somerville gesticulated to Betty, the pilot, pointing at Newman to indicate they had another potential passenger. She smiled and signified her approval with the thumbs up sign. Somerville and Newman quickly made their way round the starboard wing to the door. Newman put his holdall on the floor at the rear of the aircraft and followed Somerville up the short narrow aisle.

There were only two people aboard the eleven seater twin engined Avro Anson — First Officer Betty Westhorpe the pilot, and someone occupying the seat on her right. Presumably the person she had picked up at Perth.

Betty started taxying as soon as the door was closed. That was how it had to be with the ATA. There were six seats on the left, or port side of the aircraft and five on the starboard. Jack Somerville chose a seat amidships, on the left side over the wing. Newman took the seat on his right on the other side of the narrow aisle.

There was one very important other difference, however, between the passengers. Jack Somerville had a parachute, which he had left at the back of the Anson on the floor, when he had boarded. Newman hadn't given a thought about getting a parachute. He was so keen to get a lift south that it never entered his head.

He had never ever before flown without a parachute and he suddenly felt very uneasy. It wasn't that he expected to need a parachute, he just couldn't comprehend flying without one! He guessed that once more he must be breaking some rule, but that was not what worried him. He knew that it might put Betty the pilot in an unenviable position.

He turned and looked at Jack Somerville, only to find he was already sound asleep! It wasn't long before he realised that they weren't flying high enough to be able to use a parachute anyway! The visibility was poor and Betty was following the railway line to the south and keeping low to avoid going into cloud. He hoped that there weren't any tunnels on the railway line to Carlisle, and nodded off himself. He hadn't slept well on the Liberator.

He awoke when there was a slight bump as they touched down at Carlisle, and was surprised to see a Bristol Beaufighter taxying, and many parked on hard standings. Like the Mosquito at Prestwick, it was his first sight of an aeroplane type he had only seen before in pictures and official identification silhouettes.

He was asleep again five minutes later as they climbed away, with an extra passenger, for Salmesbury. There, Jack Somerville and the ATA pilot they'd collected at Carlisle — who was going to act as flight engineer on the Halifax — picked up a brand new, four engined Halifax bomber, and with Newman as a passenger. They had to take it to North Creake, an RAF airfield not far from the north coast of East Anglia.

It was Newman's first ride in an RAF four-engined heavy bomber — and he took a keen interest in what was going on, wondering if he might be flying Halifaxes himself before too long.

They took off to the west and entered a gentle climbing turn to take up a south easterly heading. By now it was a fine day, with mostly blue sky, save for clumps of fair weather cumulus cloud here and there, and good visibility. He sat in the mid upper turret for most of the flight and had an excellent view over the complete aircraft as well as the sky and the ground. Almost like being in the crow's nest of a sailing ship, or so he thought — although he'd never actually been in a crow's nest!

For several minutes the English west coast and Blackpool Tower, some fifteen to twenty miles distant, were clearly visible. They continued climbing to four thousand feet to give them a good clearance over the hills of the Southern Pennines. Newman had no trouble keeping awake on this flight, he just wished he had his binoculars to hand, but they were packed away somewhere in his holdall. The English countryside looked good from his bird's eye view, especially as he had never flown over it before. Having been trained in Canada and spent the following two years mostly flying over the North Atlantic, the green fields of England were a sight for sore eyes. However he couldn't identify with certainty the places they were flying over as he was without a map and had only a rough idea of the location of their destination. But after they had been airborne about half an hour he spotted a cathedral almost straight ahead. Five minutes later his suspicions were confirmed, and they passed just south of Lincoln Cathedral. He knew it well. He had often stayed with an Aunt and Uncle on the outskirts of the City. He tried to find their house but failed miserably.

The Lincolnshire sky was busy and Newman got his second view of a Mosquito that day as one raced close over the top of them going south. It came and went so quickly that he suspected he was the only one on board who had seen it. If it had been fifty feet lower, avoiding action would have been necessary, or there would have been a terrible collision. He wondered if the Mosquito pilot had seen them. He doubted that he had.

It was his first experience of a near collision in the air. He thought of something his bomber pilot brother had told him in a letter a few months ago. "It's not just the ack-ack and the night fighters, it's collisions with other aircraft on the way there and back you have to worry about!" His brother was talking about night time operations where — without navigation lights — the risks must be a hundred times greater. And that was the arena he was heading for! If only Hank Humble hadn't offered to get Helmut Schachmann on to his Catalina for that joy ride, and if only he hadn't agreed.

A little while after that they flew over the Wash and passed over Hunstanton. Less than ten minutes later they were on the ground at North Creake. By then it was two thirty in the afternoon.

There was a wait of several hours for the taxy Anson, and when it arrived there were already nine people aboard. The two ATA pilots climbed aboard, but Newman hesitated. He couldn't see an empty seat. Somerville however gave him the thumbs up sign, and he climbed in. "Sit on the floor at the back," said Somerville. "You'll be OK there." Newman did so, wondering if the pilot approved of what was happening, or even realised he was getting on board.

They had to wait on the perimeter track before taxying on to the runway for take-off as there was an aircraft approaching to land, and the Controller in the caravan by the side of the runway gave them a steady red signal on his Aldis lamp.

The aircraft was about a mile away and most of the pilots in the Anson were casually watching its approach. It was soon recognised as a Mitchell, a twin engined medium bomber with a tricycle undercarriage, built by the North American Corporation and used by both the US Army Air Force and the RAF. But this one was in trouble!

It had only two of its three landing wheels down; its left undercarriage still being completely retracted. To make matters worse the propeller of the left engine was not turning, indicating the engine had failed. It was clear they were all going to witness an accident, and it was probably going to be a bad one. Furthermore one of the three runways at North Creake was bound to be blocked for some time, and there was a strong wind from the east.

Like most twin engined aircraft in 1943 the Mitchell could not climb on one engine, so there was no question of the pilot going round again for a second try if he didn't get his landing approach right.

All eyes stayed on the disabled Mitchell as it continued its approach to land. The pilot was bringing it in steadily and it appeared to be perfectly aligned with the runway, often not an easy task on one engine. It was now a mere two-hundred yards from the beginning of the runway, at a height of around fifty feet. Newman could imagine the tension in the Mitchell. There was a real possibility of a major fire as the aircraft sank on to its port wing after touchdown, and even the chance that the aircraft might cartwheel.

"Wouldn't like to be in his shoes" said the ATA pilot sitting in the seat next to where Newman was sitting on the floor.

"You can say that again," said Newman.

Just as he spoke the airfield controller in the runway control caravan fired a red Very signal into the path of the Mitchell. It went in an arch over the runway, rising to a height of perhaps two hundred feet before falling on to the grass. He was refusing the Mitchell pilot permission to land. It seemed he had only just noticed that the Mitchell's undercarriage was not down properly!

The Anson was instantly filled with expletives.

"Bloody hell - what the hell is that chap doing - he can't make him go round again on one from that height. He'll never get away with it!"

"God, I hope he bloody ignores it" was another comment, referring to the Mitchell pilot.

But amazingly the Mitchell pilot didn't. He opened up his one good engine and flew along the runway at fifty feet, not climbing, not descending. At the far end of the runway, just over a mile away, there was a line of tall trees, with a gap in them a little wider than the width of the runway. The Mitchell passed through the gap with two wheels still down, and continued into the distance. It was soon lost from sight. But it looked as though an accident was inevitable before long.

The airfield controller gave the Anson a green. Someone near the front of the Anson referring to the airfield controller shouted, "He should be bloody well court-martialed."

Another pilot shouted "Yes and then shot!"

Newman arrived at his final destination, White Waltham airfield, in the Anson, at half past seven in the evening and managed to get yet another lift, this time by private car, to Staines. The ferry rides south from Prestwick had probably saved him two or three hours. They had been interesting, almost exciting at times, and the ride in the Halifax from Salmesbury to North Creake had given him the feel of what it might be like flying a four engined aircraft with Bomber Command.

Whilst on the Halifax flight he had made up his mind to write to Lucy. He would have to write to her at the shop because he didn't know her home address. There might however be advantages — her mother was not likely to know about it! He had also decided to take his time writing. If he got it wrong, he knew it would only make a nasty situation worse.

At ten minutes past nine, he reached the front door of his parents house on Wraysbury Road, Staines, for the first time in nearly four years. It was dusk but the house looked just the same, although it looked as if his father had not spent as much time keeping the front garden in trim as he used to.

He rang the bell — it might be a bit of a shock to his parents if he used his key and they heard someone opening the front door.

His mother opened the door. "Hi Mum, still got a bed for me?"

She didn't answer the question, there was no need. And she was practically speechless anyway.

"What are you doing here?" was the first thing she said, "full of smiles and holding back tears of joy, as she took her apron off and quickly checked her hair in the hall mirror. By this time Don was in the living room.

"It's a long story Mum. I've been posted to Bomber Command."

"I can't believe it's you — but you look tired — how long you home for son?"

It was the start of many questions. They came one after another before Don had a chance to reply to any of them.

"Don't know Mum — got to wait for a telegram — probably just a few days."

"A telegram! Oh, I don't like those things."

"Where's Dad, Mum?"

"He won't be home till tomorrow night, he's on Home Guard duty at the factory. Does it twice a week."

Except for the curtains, Newman found his room was just as he'd left it the day he left home to join the RAF. The thin flowery patterned curtains had been replaced by heavy black ones, to satisfy the blackout regulations. He closed them, struck a match and lit the gas mantle in the centre of the room. It was then that he realised his mother was standing in the doorway watching him.

"You will remember the blackout dear won't you."

It was an unnecessary comment since the curtains were already closed, but she continued, "The Warden will be round shortly."

"The warden mother?"

"Yes, Charlie Jackson the Air Raid Warden. Give him half a chance and he'll be banging on the front door shouting 'Put that light out!' And you know your father has never got on with him."

Newman suddenly felt desperately tired.

The next morning his mother remembered to give him a letter that had come for him several weeks earlier. The top left front of the envelope was marked "Please forward" in large letters, but his mother had somehow forgotten to do so. He sat at the breakfast table and opened the envelope to find a letter from Captain David Livingstone's parents. They were thanking him for his attempts to save their son's life and asking him to go and see them when he was next on leave. He decided he would, if he was home long enough.

His mother sat at the table opposite him, "Sorry for not sending it to you. I hope it wasn't important?"

"No, it's OK Mum — don't worry."

"Good. Did you sleep alright?"

"Bang on, thanks Mum."

Newman's mind went back to Bermuda once more. It had a habit of doing that. Was it only nine weeks since Livingstone had died and only a week since Helmut Schachmann had tried to steal his Catalina — he corrected himself — had stolen his Catalina? Back now in his home environment, it seemed at times that he had dreamt it all.

"Good." His mother took a long swig of tea from her cup and carefully placed it back on it's saucer. Don realised she was preparing herself for something. He suspected he was going to be asked why he had been posted to Bomber Command — perhaps a repeat of some questions from the night before — which he knew he hadn't answered very convincingly. But it was quite the opposite.

"There's something I should tell you Don. Didn't tell you last night. Thought I'd let you get a good night's sleep. And I was all excited too — you turning up unexpected."

"Oh!" He couldn't think what it might be. Probably something fairly trivial he guessed, like she'd fallen out with the neighbours, or there hadn't been any apples on the tree in the back garden, the year before.

"Yes, in a way it's turned out well that you've come home now — I was going to write to you — then I thought your letters might be censored. And I wouldn't want anyone else knowing, except your Dad of course."

"Knowing what Mum?"

"You won't tell anyone will you?" She emphasised *You.*

"Not if you don't want me to Mum — what is it. Has Dad got the sack or something?"

"No, if only it was as simple as that." She finished her tea. "It's Brenda — she's four months pregnant!"

Newman practically fell out of his chair. His twin sister pregnant! He could hardly believe it.

Brenda was in the Navy, or more accurately the WRNS — the women's arm of the Navy. She had volunteered two years earlier and was now living in a big house with dozens of other Wrens, near Newport Pagnell and working at Bletchley. She wouldn't tell her family or anyone else what she did; just that it was clerical.

"Who's the father, Mum?"

"A bomber pilot — a Flying Liberator pilot, I think she said. Is that right?"

"Flying Fortress I expect she meant — you mean a Yank, Mum?"

"Yes, an American from Boston."

"Oh Crikey, poor old Bren!" Then seeing how concerned his mother looked, he added "But that's not the end of the world Mum."

There was a pause in the conversation. His mother seemed to be lost for words.

"What's going to happen then. Is he going to marry her?" he asked.

There was another long pause before his mother replied.

"No dear, he can't."

"What do you mean? He's already married?"

"Worse than that. Dead dear, he was wounded over Germany, the day after Brenda was ...... you know what I mean. He died from his wounds just after they landed back here."

"Oh my God, how is she? I must see her — poor old Bren."

"She's very upset! And to make matters worse your Dad is giving her a rough time. She needs our support now — not lecturing — but he just won't listen. I think Dad's worried sick about your brother. Geoffrey's on his second — what do they call it, a tour is it? — He's done over forty raids now. We're both very worried and soon we'll start worrying about you."

She drank some more tea. "We've never worried too much about you up to now. Dad always said you can land a flying boat on the water so the Atlantic's one big aerodrome for Don. So no need to worry about him."

Newman suspected his father didn't really have such a misconception. It was probably his way of stopping his wife from worrying too much.

They talked round and round Brenda's problem until they were repeating themselves. Don was very concerned. He and Brenda were identical twins and had always been unbelievably close. They had no secrets — at least as far as he knew. He couldn't wait to see her.

"You say she'll be home next weekend?" he asked.

"Yes, what day is it?"

"Wednesday."

"Yes, she's due a forty-eight hour pass, so she should be home the day after tomorrow, Friday night."

Mrs Newman started clearing the breakfast things from the table. "She's usually here by ten. Do you think you'll still be here on Friday?"

"I don't know Mum — just don't know. I hope so!"

"Oh, and have you got some ration coupons for me?"

"Yes. Sorry Mum — should have given them to you last night."

His mother went on to tell him that a week ago the government had announced that all women between eighteen and forty-five must do at least part-time work. She said that although she was nearly fifty, she had decided to do her bit — as she called it — and she was hoping to get a part time job at a local factory. Newman heard what his mother said, but his mind was somewhere else.

❖

In Bermuda it was half past five in the morning, and there was still nearly an hour to sunrise. Lucy's mother was awake. She was concerned that even with rationing, there was a serious shortage of food on the Islands, and there were rumours that a senior American naval officer was urging mass evacuation to the United States.

Lucy was just waking. Each morning since Don had walked away from her she had listened for a Catalina taking-off at dawn, which she knew would most likely be a delivery to Britain, but she hadn't heard one. So she felt sure Don was still on the Islands.

She lay in bed thinking of Don and hoping he would ring her at the shop that day, or come to the shop at closing time. She didn't understand how the Air Force worked and comforted herself with the thought that with his Catalina damaged, he was likely to be delayed for weeks, whilst repairs were made to it. She hadn't heard that it had been damaged beyond repair.

She felt sure he would make contact with her, but it was the waiting that was getting to her, and she couldn't understand why Don had believed her brother Jack without even waiting to hear what she had to say! And why Don — to use an expression she had learnt from him — didn't say he 'couldn't care less' about the Catalina being stolen? Surely he wanted to stay in Bermuda longer? She would have understood if he had been jumping up and down with joy when they both saw his aeroplane disappearing past the Dockyard — and she would have joined him in his celebrations. There was something very odd about Don's feelings for his flying boat which she just couldn't fathom. Could he really care more about a flying boat than her?

Relations between Lucy and her mother had now reached fever pitch. Her mother had found out about Don Newman from her son Jack on the day Helmut Schachmann stole Newman's Catalina. Jack and Lucy had had a frantic argument in front of her in the kitchen of their cottage. It was only brought to a halt after an hour or so — and then only for a while — when a police officer came and took Jack away for questioning. Jack had apparently been spotted rowing away from the Catalina just after its engines started. But Lucy's mother immediately blamed Newman for telling the police Jack was involved, although he had told no one about Jack's involvement. She told Lucy that if she ever spoke to Newman again she would throw her out of the house, for good!

❖

In Staines, Don was drafting his letter to Lucy. When his mother noticed him spending so much time at the kitchen table writing, she asked who he was writing to. He was non committal, and just said "Oh, a friend in Bermuda, Mum."

"Did you make a lot of friends there, then?"

He hoped it wouldn't seem rude, but didn't reply, pretending he was concentrating on his writing.

He had lots of breaks from writing and the letter wasn't finally finished until the Friday afternoon. He told Lucy that he had had time to think, and now he just couldn't believe what Jack had said was true. He also said that although he couldn't understand why she refused to help him by telling the truth to the Bermuda police, he had enough faith in her to know that there must be a good reason and he hoped that she would understand that there was a good reason why he was so upset — which he couldn't explain in a letter.

Almost as a PS, he asked her if she would marry him as soon as the war was over. He asked her to write back quickly and addressed the letter to her at the Front Street shop. He posted it at Staines post office, on the Friday afternoon, knowing that it would probably be several weeks before it reached her, but he felt better as soon as it had slipped from his fingers into the post box.

Writing this letter to Lucy turned out to be the main event of his leave until Brenda came home on Friday evening. All his old school friends were now away in the forces, and he found Staines a lonely place. He hummed and hawed about getting in touch with Livingstone's parents and making arrangements to go and see them, and finally ran out of time. In truth he wanted some time to himself. Fortunately the weather was mostly good and he did some walking along the Thames riverbank.

On the Thursday evening he went to the cinema. He had to queue in the rain to get in and the main film was a black & white Western which he discovered he had seen before in Canada, but it didn't matter as it provided just the light relief that he was looking for.

At nine on the Friday evening he went to Staines Central station hoping to meet Brenda as she got off a train from Waterloo. The elderly ticket collector told him there was a London train due at nine-sixteen, and allowed him to wait on the platform without buying a platform ticket. Newman wasn't too surprised, although he knew it wouldn't have been allowed before the war. Earlier he had caught a local bus and the conductor had refused his money when he had offered to pay his fare! He was to discover in future weeks that it was a widespread practice — although unofficial and not universal — to turn a blind eye to service personnel travelling in uniform.

He hadn't seen his twin sister for nearly four years, but they did write to each other regularly. It was a mild night and still light because of 'double summertime' in Britain. It was only seven pm Greenwich mean time, a system that Don's mother said was very popular. She liked it because the long Spring evenings allowed her to tend her vegetable patch in their back garden and, as she put it, follow the government's instructions to *dig for victory*.

The electric train from Waterloo arrived a few minutes late. There weren't many passengers getting off at that time of night — Newman counted seven, and Brenda wasn't amongst them. His heart sank, he so much wanted to see her and hoped her leave hadn't been cancelled at the last moment. They had so much to tell each other.

He asked when the next train would be. Told it would be twenty minutes, he decided to wait, lit a cigarette, and paced up and down the platform like an expectant father with a wife in labour.

The twenty minutes seemed more like forty. She was the only person to get off the next train and didn't notice her brother further up the platform and set off for the footbridge connecting the "up" and "down" platforms. Don hadn't seen her in her uniform before, and now he only had a rear view, but he would know her anywhere. He rapidly narrowed the distance between them and when she was half way up the steps of the bridge he reached the bottom. He called out. "Admiral Newman?"

She knew his voice instantly and swung round in surprise. "Oh the Air Marshall, what a wonderful surprise."

He gave her a quick kiss, picked up her bag and they set off for home.

As they walked down the alleyway to the main road, a passing Air Training Corp cadet gave Newman a smart salute, which took him by surprise, but which he returned eventually with a "Good evening". They walked and they talked. It took them half an hour to reach home on Wraysbury Road — normally a quarter of an hour would have sufficed.

Don found that his twin sister was reluctant to talk about her work. That seemed odd to him, he hadn't expected any barriers, there had never been any before now. It was to be another thirty two years before he found out that his sister was part of a large team of people deciphering highly secret German radio messages and sworn to absolute secrecy.

She didn't seem to know what was going to happen when it got near time to have her baby. He presumed she would be sent home, probably released from the WRNS, but she didn't seem to think it was as simple as that, and didn't want to talk about it. That puzzled him. Nevertheless, by the time they entered their front gate it was almost as though they had never been apart.

Their parents went to bed before eleven and Don and Brenda sat in the living room talking until two in the morning. Don tried to be comforting but when he eventually told her all about Lucy and Helmut Schachmann she burst into tears.

"You may be able to get back together with Lucy, Don, but my Spike has gone forever and my child will never know his father!"

He tried to comfort her, but it was no use, and he gently suggested it was time for bed.

Newman was woken by the air raid siren at six in the morning. It was his first experience of an air raid — or to be more accurate his first experience of hearing an air raid "alert". He wasn't sure what to do. Try and go back to sleep with his fingers crossed or get up and make for the Anderson shelter in the back garden? When the sirens stopped it was deadly quiet, no sound of aircraft or anti aircraft guns. He opened the heavy black-out curtains. It was daylight but overcast, dull and drizzle. Was it possible the warning was a false alarm he wondered. Surely the

Germans couldn't bomb in this sort of weather! He decided to see if his father was awake.

The door to his parents room wasn't shut, he tapped on the door. Just a gentle tap which wouldn't wake anyone who was sound asleep.

"Come in Don," said his mother.

He went in to find his father was just getting out of bed, and his mother already dressed.

"When did this last happen?" asked Don.

His father was slipping into his trousers. "Not too often these days, we usually stay in bed, but we ought to get our Brenda to the shelter — seeing as she's pregnant!"

"Right I'll go and check on her, now."

Don detected a sense of urgency from his parents and hurried. His sister was still sound asleep and he had to wake her. He tried to be gentle by putting his right hand on her left shoulder and rocking her, but it didn't work.

His father appeared behind Don, at the bedroom door.

"Get up, Brenda!" he shouted.

At that precise moment they heard the sound of at least one aircraft. It wasn't overhead but it focussed their minds!

"Get some trousers on Don, I'll look after your sister!"

Don did as he was told. When he got downstairs he found his mother was in the kitchen and had opened the back door. As he entered the room she put the kettle on. "We usually stay in the kitchen until they're close, then we go to the shelter — we may have time for a cup of tea!" she remarked.

His father and his sister arrived a few seconds later. Don thought Brenda looked as though she had been crying all night. "Watcha," he said. She smiled a little.

They could still hear the sound of an aircraft, but it wasn't very near. Although Don could be considered the aircraft expert among them, he wasn't the air raid expert and he turned to his father.

"What do you make of this then Dad?"

"Dunno — a bit odd. Haven't had a raid in this sort of weather before! But it is definitely a Jerry — that throbbing engine noise — definitely a Jerry."

Don stood at the open backdoor and listened. The drizzle had stopped but everywhere was damp, and — at least on Staines Moor — the visibility poor for flyers. Perhaps a mile or so, Newman estimated. It was hard to tell for sure which direction the aircraft sound was coming from. Most likely from the east he thought.

Suddenly it was getting louder. But it wasn't as simple as that, there was a different sound. As well as the sound of the German bomber, which was now very loud, there was a noise which sounded very much like that of the Hurricane fighter which Don had seen and heard land at Prestwick only a few days before.

"Better be on the safe side," said Newman senior, "Get down the shelter now, I'll bring some tea. And Brenda get your old wellingtons out of the cupboard, there'll be puddles on the floor down there!"

Mrs Newman had already got two pairs of boots from the cupboard under the stairs. She gave a pair to Brenda and put on her own. The three of them set off down the garden to the shelter. Newman was wearing his RAF blue battle dress, over his pyjamas and a pair of slippers. Brenda — who was very quiet — was still in her nightdress, with a blanket round her shoulders. Holding the blanket up with one hand, she lifted the nightdress so that the bottom was level to the top of her wellingtons. Mrs Newman was the only one completely dressed. Her husband, who was making the tea, was wearing just his Home Guard trousers and his pyjama jacket. On his feet he wore a pair of sandals.

They were about half way down the garden when they heard the sound of machine gun fire from the sky above! From the sounds of the aircraft engines and the rat tat tat of the guns it was obvious that an ariel dog fight was starting over the top of them, and at least two people were trying to murder each other in the sky above the clouds!

"Get in the shelter, Jerry will jettison his load," Don's father shouted from the kitchen door. He'd abandoned the tea and was now running to the shelter. They all reached the Anderson shelter entrance at the same time.

The Newmans hadn't used their shelter for some months. Also they hadn't thought to look inside recently and to their surprise they found there was much more than a puddle of water covering the floor.

Brenda shouted "it's flooded" and hesitated by the door. At that moment they all heard a loud whistling sound.

"Get in," shouted Newman senior, "it's a bomb coming down!"

"Do they ever go upwards?" asked his wife.

Newman senior tried to laugh, but found he couldn't and was

surprised that his wife had a sense of humour. He concluded it was her way of dealing with the tension they were all feeling.

Now in the shelter, they quickly realised that the water was about a foot deep, and in the scramble to get in both women got their wellington boots full of water.

"Well at least we're all in the shelter," said Mrs Newman, almost laughing over the sound of the continuing battle above them.

Don had read somewhere that if a bomb was going to hit you, then you wouldn't hear it coming. He wondered at the time whether it was true or not, and he was doing so again now.

The shelter was half above ground level and half below. Made of corrugated iron, and covered with six inches of earth, there were wooden bunks inside capable of sleeping at least four people in rather cramped conditions. Don and Brenda huddled together as far into the shelter as they could — they could only stand up in the centre at the far end, because of the curving roof — and waited for the crunch that must come any second. Their father stood nearest the open door.

The whistling stopped abruptly. The air battle overhead continued.

"Must have been a dud," shouted Don.

"Or a time bomb," his father shouted back.

Whether it was a dud bomb or one which would explode several hours later, Don's father knew it would present a problem for the authorities. The hole it would make as it entered the ground would have to be found and the area evacuated. But finding the hole and hence the bomb, could be difficult, time consuming, and above all dangerous. He didn't relay his thoughts to his family. At times like this he considered it his job to be a good father figure, and Brenda had enough problems without him adding to them with his thoughts.

"Be over any minute — they can't keep going at each other much longer!" he said, "can they Don?"

Don was about to agree when they heard another bomb falling. This one sounded different. Don suspected it was more than one. He pulled his sister close to him. No one spoke. It was as though they all knew there was something different this time. Newman senior turned his back on the shelter entrance and moved as far as he could into the shelter, close to his wife. There were no lights in the shelter and Don could see his father's head and shoulders silhouetted against the daylight.

They probably only took five seconds to fall, all three of them, but as

Brenda said later, it seemed like a lifetime. They couldn't tell where the bombs fell but knew that at least one, probably all, were close by. Apart from the deafening explosions and the vibration of the ground, it had suddenly gone pitch black. Their way out of the shelter had been blocked with debris!

In Bermuda Lucy was sleeping soundly and dreaming of Don. But much as he adored Lucy, Don had other things on his mind at the moment. He let go of Brenda, eased past his mother in the darkness and got to the entrance. His father was already there and — unknown to Don — was trying to find his cigarette lighter in a trouser pocket. The air battle overhead had ceased. The German plane it seemed had escaped — probably into cloud — but in the shelter they didn't know that, and anyway another battle was just starting, mostly below ground.

Newman put his right hand out in front of him to try and feel whatever it was that was blocking the entrance. His hand touched corrugated metal, the stuff the shelter was made of. He moved his hand to the left; still the same. Further left, but still corrugated metal.

"Hang on. Found my lighter." said his father. In the confined space of the shelter it sounded as though he was shouting, but he wasn't.

After a few flicks the lighter came alight and lit up the inside of the shelter well. Both Don and his father realised at once that the shelter exit was covered by a piece of corrugated iron that was not the same as that of the shelter. Apart from a different style of corrugation it was painted blue. The shelter was painted green.

"That's come from the roof of the shed," said Newman senior.

"Can you move it?" asked his wife.

"We'll soon know. Don you push this side, I'll push this."

They both pushed together with both hands. It moved an inch or so at the top, sufficient to let in a chink of daylight. It wasn't much, but psychologically it was a mile and they all felt a little relieved when they saw the first sign of daylight. It was clear that they hadn't got tons of earth on top of them.

It took another twenty minutes to clear the entrance and when they all emerged it was with a mixture of relief and apprehension about what they would find. Don expected that his parent's house had taken a direct hit and would be a pile of rubble. He and his father were first out but Don's worst fears were not realised. The house was still standing, although all the windows — at least those he could see at the back of the house were gone — and the roof was in ruins. He glanced to the right to their neighbours — their house had been completely flattened! A burst water main was spurting fifteen feet into the air. The wooden boundary fence between the two properties was nowhere to be seen. Don rushed towards the pile of rubble, which at it's nearest point was only twenty paces away.

His father shouted, "It's alright, the Jackson's are away in Wales, Don. There's no one living there!"

Don stopped in his tracks and sighed. "Thank God for that," he said.

It was a week later when the Jacksons' bodies were found that his father heard he was wrong! It was believed that they had come back the day before the raid to collect some belongings. But he had told the police the house was unoccupied. It was an honest mistake — his neighbours should have told him they had returned for the night — but he was devastated by the news.

The Newmans spent the whole weekend clearing up their own house. It was Spring time, almost Summer, so they could manage without glass in the windows for a few days, and they did. They were happy to be alive and both Don and Brenda had a new perspective on their problems.

CHAPTER NINE

Monday 17 May 1943

Early Monday morning two elderly workmen arrived at the Newman's residence and began to measure up to replace the broken glass. The previous evening Don had travelled up to London with his sister and seen her safely on to the train for Newport Pagnell.

One of the workman saw Newman in his RAF uniform and asked him if he'd heard the morning news.

"No, we haven't had the wireless on this morning." Newman replied.

"Well some of your RAF guys have given the Jerries something to think about!"

"Sorry?"

"They've knocked the bloody sh.. out of 'em. They've flooded the Rhur!"

Newman didn't understand. "Flooded the Rhur?"

"Yes they've bombed some dams and let all the water out!"

"Wizard."

Newman decided he must listen to the next news bulletin in an hour's time. A few minutes later he saw Mrs Townsend hurrying up their front path. She had been at school with his mother and now lived a few hundred yards away. She greeted Don, "Heard you were back home — saw your Mum yesterday. Good to see you."

"Morning Aunt Rose." She wasn't really an aunt but he'd been brought up to call her that.

Aunt Rose and her husband had a telephone in their house and thus were highly regarded by the local community. The Newmans — like most people — couldn't afford their own telephone.

"Good news. Tell your Mum I've had a message from a friend of your brother this morning. He says 'he's eaten his breakfast!' "

Newman didn't understand and didn't reply. He wondered why on earth his brother would phone to say that. He stood on the path turning the message over in his mind.

"Can't stop," said Aunt Rose, "You make sure you tell your Mum right away, won't you!"

With that she was off down the road, stepping between the rubble of the ruins next door.

The workmen had overheard the conversation. Both of them looked at Newman as he walked to the front door. Neither of them said anything, but both seemed to be saying, "She's lost her marbles?"

As he expected his mother was in the kitchen, washing up the breakfast plates.

"Mum, Aunt Rose has just given me a message for you. I don't understand it. She says that Geoff has eaten his breakfast!"

"Oh marvellous, that's a relief, he's been training for it for quite a few weeks!"

Don looked miffed. "I don't follow Mum — why does he need to train to eat breakfast?"

His mother didn't see the joke, even though it was the sort she had been known to make.

"Well," said his mother, sitting down at the table as she spoke, "Your Dad and I have been very worried about Geoffrey doing all the bombing raids, and he sort of understood that. He didn't say much — in fact I don't think he knew much himself — but he told us that he hasn't been on a proper raid for some time now. Apparently he's been training for some very special raid. We got the idea that as it was special, it was bound to be more dangerous. So, as we were more worried than usual, he decided to send us a message when the raid had been carried out and he'd got back alright."

"So this message means he's OK?"

"Yes, exactly. He expected to go to bed as soon as he got back — not that he even knew for certain that it would be a night raid — so he said he'd get someone to phone Aunt Rose at breakfast time."

"Was that the only message he arranged with you?"

"Yes, there was to be no message if he didn't get back to his station. He said they might have to land at another airfield, and he didn't want his friend telling Aunt Rose that he hadn't eaten his breakfast! It could be misleading and upset us."

It was as well that Aunt Rose had delivered her message swiftly, as a quarter of an hour later there was a loud knock at the front door. Mrs Newman answered it; Don stood behind her. The telegram boy looked solemn. It was his usual way, for he'd been the bearer of bad news so often. But Mrs Newman didn't feel weak at the knees on seeing him.

"Telegram for Flight Lieutenant Newman," said the boy.

Newman's instructions were to report to RAF Station Littleby, Lincolnshire, by midnight the following day. It said that a travel warrant was in the post. He referred to a pre war automobile road map and found Littleby was not far from Lincoln — the city he'd recognised from the Halifax six days earlier. It was also within twenty miles of RAF Scampton where his brother was stationed, and that held out the prospect of seeing his brother again before long.

Satisfied that it would be fairly straightforward to get to, he visited Aunt Rose and telephoned Kings Cross Railway station to find out the times of trains. He chose one at 16:05 the following day. It would get him there with plenty of time to spare.

The daily papers the next morning reproduced a reconnaissance photograph showing the breach in the Möhne Dam, with the caption "The Smash-Up: RAF Picture Testifies to Perfect Bombing." Newman looked at it with one of the workman who was back again, replacing glass at the front of their house.

"Bloody good show and all that — Sir — but I hope the Jerries don't try and do that to that one!" He pointed to the King George VI reservoir, the high walls of which could be seen a mere four hundred yards away.

"Well I guess we'll have to keep our fingers crossed," said Newman, hoping that his mother hadn't heard any of the conversation. She would be bound to lose sleep over that possibility, if she'd heard about it.

"It's bad enough we're going to be living by the biggest bomber station in the country soon," the workman continued, pushing his cap back to expose more forehead.

Newman didn't know what the man was talking about, and it showed on his face. The workman didn't like being disbelieved.

"Yes, got a letter about it from the Air Ministry, last week, they're talking about buying my house — and I've lived there all me life! And they use the word compulsory — you know what that means! They'll give me almost nothing for it! "

"Where do you live then?" asked Newman, curiosity getting the better of him.

"Heathrow — you know it, a mile or two beyond the reservoir. There's a little grass aerodrome there."

It was over two years before Newman returned home and found the airfield was being built. A score of years later it was the busiest international airport in the world.

He arrived at RAF Littleby, early the following evening. The station had been built a few years before the start of the war as part of the RAF's expansion programme, and had comfortable and permanent brick built accommodation. However its runways were not as long as those on airfields built more recently, which sometimes caused a problem.

It didn't take him long to find out that it was a Bomber Command OTU — an operational training unit — and that he would be flying twin-engined Wellington bombers. He had arrived a week after the five week course had started and found he was to take over a crew whose skipper had fallen from the ladder of his Wellington when leaving it in too much of a hurry during the first week of the course, and had broken his right arm.

When he entered the dining room the following morning Newman found the breakfast conversation was almost entirely about the RAF raid on the German dams the previous weekend. There was a lot of speculation as to exactly how it was done. Newman didn't say much, he knew he would get the truth from his brother one day. Hopefully not before too long, as he intended to try and contact him as soon as he had settled in at Littleby.

Newman had no difficulty with the Wellington or his new crew, and he soon caught up with the rest of the course. After thirty-five hours of flying, and a similar amount of ground instruction, the whole course, except for one crew, was posted to the Heavy Conversion Unit at Scanton in Yorkshire. The exception was the crew that had crashed on the approach to land one night. There were no survivors.

He was given a flight engineer at Scanton — they weren't carried on the Wellington — and there followed a six week spell converting to the four-engined Lancaster. The course included several long cross country practice flights, mainly at night, lasting five or six hours. By Newman's standards, flights of this length were short ones, and he had no trouble with them. There was another accident half way through the course when an aircraft overshot the runway and ran into a ditch after landing. Fortunately no one was seriously injured but the aircraft was a write-off. At the end of the course, on 17 July, Newman and his crew were posted to 695 Squadron at RAF Sandstone, Yorkshire.

They left Scanton mid morning on the Saturday, in an RAF bus for the twenty-five mile journey to Sandstone. Newman sat at the front near the WAAF driver. The vehicle was an American left hand drive bus capable of seating twenty or so. From the WAAF he learnt that Sandstone was a new wartime airfield which had been open only a few months and that accommodation was very basic. It wasn't long before he found out just how true that was!

They crossed the River Humber just north of Goole and soon afterwards the airfield's black painted water tank could be seen. Mounted high above the ground, on strong metal girders, it was a common sight at wartime airfields. Shortly after Newman could make out, over the tops of the hedges, the tails of several Lancasters at their dispersals. There was one different one, the tail of an American B-17 Flying Fortress. He thought of Brenda and the bad luck of her American pilot. Later he found out that the Fortress had been forced to make an emergency landing at Sandstone, after losing two engines on a daylight raid to Bremen and becoming considerably off course on the way home.

Finally they were at the main gate and guard house. The driver brought the bus to a halt and a corporal from the guard house checked the crew's papers. Newman was directed to hut 127 for the night and the crew told to report to C Flight at 0800 the following morning. The WAAF bus driver volunteered to drop him at the hut and did so five minutes later.

Newman found hut 127 deserted. There were a dozen or so beds in rows on each side of the hut, with plenty of evidence that they had been used recently, but not one obvious vacancy. Newman put his bags on the floor near the entrance and walked the full length of the hut looking for a bed which looked as though it might not have an owner. He was checking out a bed at the far end of the hut, when he heard someone open the door behind him.

"That's it Sir, you've got it. That one."

Newman turned to see a corporal approaching. He stopped ten feet or so from Newman and saluted. "I'm the hut orderly Sir, Corporal Skinner. That one's free."

"It doesn't look it Corporal— looks like someone's just got out of it!"

"Ah yes. Sorry about that Sir — been a bit busy — that was Flying Officer Jackson's bed, but he won't be needing it. He got the chop last night. Crashed on take-off with a full load of bombs on board. No survivors."

"Oh, I see. Is there another bed I could have corp?"

"Only that one Sir," the corporal pointed to a bed on the other side of the hut.

It looked used like all the others. "And what's the story with that one?"

"Spun in Sir, over the Ruhr. Nice bloke too!"

❖

It was whilst Newman was trying to find a bed, that Hank Humble and Lucy had bumped into each other on Front Street. He told her that Don had left Bermuda — he was surprised she didn't know — and been posted to RAF Bomber Command weeks ago. Humble had delivered two Catalinas to Britain since then.

"I got to like Don" he told her, "and I'm sure sorry the way things worked out."

She was very upset and distressed and asked him if he knew Newman's home address. He said he didn't but that if she knew his RAF number she ought to write to him at the Belmont, and that maybe the letter would eventually catch up with him, wherever he'd got to. But she didn't know his service number.

When Lucy got off the train that evening it was raining. She had walked the short distance home in the rain many a time, but tonight it seemed to be the last straw. Reaching home she found her mother in their small kitchen preparing the evening meal. That was how it was usually.

Jack was at a prefect's meeting at school. He had not been punished for his part in the Catalina incident, mostly because he was only fifteen, but also because his story — that he was forced into being Schachmann's waterborne chauffeur by a confidence trick. This was accepted by the police.

Mrs Appledram could see that her daughter was more upset than usual, and asked her why. "And what's wrong with you?" she said to Lucy, drying her hands on a towel as she spoke, with such force that Lucy thought she was going to tear it to pieces.

Without thinking, Lucy sat down at the end of the kitchen table. It was the seat that her father had always occupied at meal times — before he left to fight the Germans. Since he left, it hadn't been sat in. Lucy's mother had never wanted her husband to volunteer for the army, and the sight of Lucy sitting in his old chair put her back up.

Before she could say anything, Lucy told her mother what had happened to Don Newman, and said Jack had ruined her life by telling lies about her. Her mother, who had a German grandfather, had always had a soft spot for Helmut Schachmann — ever since he became a lodger with them, when he first came to Bermuda before the war started — and would have none of it. She stopped laying the table and stood beside Lucy, as though she would hit her if she continued in this vein.

"Helmut was only doing what any good boy would do to save his mother's life," she shouted, "I would expect you to do the same for me. What he did was magnificent, did you hear that, magnificent, and he nearly succeeded too! It was only bad luck that he didn't get to the submarine. I would be proud to have him as my son." Then as an afterthought, she added "Or my son in law."

Having said her piece, she stormed back to the sink, turned on the tap and washed her hands again, attacking the towel with renewed vigour. Lucy got up.

"Mummy, I liked Helmut at one time, but that was before I met Don. I'd never marry Helmut now. There was no need for Jack to blurt out all those lies when Don and I met him after he had helped Helmut. He must have known that Don would be very upset by it."

"Jack's a good boy Lucy, and you must remember Jack also wants you to marry Helmut — when the time comes, of course. He's only a boy, and he's very attached to Helmut — and he misses his father as much as I do — and he wouldn't deliberately do anything to hurt you!"

"Well maybe, but I wouldn't marry Helmut Schachmann now if he was the only man on earth!"

"You will— you will! Mark my words, you'll soon forget this RAF man — he was just playing with you, whilst he was waiting for his aeroplane, or something or other, to be ready!"

"But Mummy."

"Lucy listen to me." Her mother was shaking the index finger of her right hand at her, "I will not have Don Newman mentioned in this house ever again. Never, for as long as I live. Do you understand?"

Lucy knew her mother meant it and she didn't answer. There was no point in arguing any more, and she went to her room and sobbed.

After a while she composed herself and wrote her first letter to Don. She poured her heart out to him with the truth. She addressed it to Flight Lieutenant Donald Newman, RAF Bomber Command, Great Britain.

A day later the letter was opened by the Terminal Censorship unit at the Princess Hotel. Lucy had made the mistake of referring to Helmut Schachmann and his stealing of the Catalina incident in too much detail, and the decision was made to censor the letter in case it fell into the wrong hands. But when they blacked out the offending words the only words left were *My darling Don* and *I love you, Lucy.* Thereupon someone decided it wasn't worth sending, and took the decision to 'lose it'. Two more letters were 'lost' during the course of the next year; one due to U-boat action in the North Atlantic and one when a German bomb fell on a RAF sorting office in London.

Newman had a short flight on the Tuesday with the squadron commander, Squadron Leader Jack Aubrey, who was carrying out an air test on a Lancaster after it had been repaired following flak damage. Newman assumed that it was a way of checking him out — although this wasn't mentioned — especially as he was told to make the landing. The flight went well, even though he had never flown a Lanc from the right hand seat before.

"We should have a couple of new Lancs delivered by the weekend," said the flight commander as they left the aircraft. "I've promised one of them to a skipper who's done twenty-three ops on an old clapped out Lanc that's seen better days. You'll probably get the other."

"Wizard," said Newman, "what'll happen to the clapped-out one?"

"Can't say at the moment. It depends on whether we lose any more in the next few days."

"So when is our first op likely to be?"

"For you it may be tonight," said Aubrey. "You'll come with me for experience on our next op. That way the flak and the searchlights won't seem quite so bad the second time, when you go on your own. You get used to it — a bit. We'll know in the next hour or two. For your second op and your crew, it'll depend upon when the new aircraft arrives."

The weather was bad over most of Europe that night and it was the following night that Newman had his indoctrination trip over enemy territory, a trip to the Ruhr. He had heard from some of the other pilots that most of them had been thrown in at the deep end without a trip with another crew first. Newman wondered why he should be so lucky — or unlucky — it depended upon how you looked at it! He was told it was because there was a shortage of Lancs, at the moment, and there just wasn't one available for him and his crew.

Like Newman's brother, Aubrey had already completed one tour of thirty operations and was now half way through his second, so Newman was looking forward to being taught some new tricks by the old dog. Take-off time for the first aircraft was scheduled for 2300 hours. Engines were started at 2245 and the airfield came alive, first with the sound of eleven Rolls Royce Merlin engines starting up, followed by another eleven, then another eleven until finally all eleven Lancasters had their forty-four engines running.

It was 2305 as Aubrey opened up the throttles and B for Baker started to roll down the two thousand yard runway. All ten aircraft in front of them had climbed away safely over the crater just off the end of the runway, caused by the Lanc which had blown up on take off, a few nights earlier. It was perhaps as well that it was dark and the crews couldn't see it.

To Newman the take-off run was particularly long although, as it was the first time he had flown in a fully loaded Lancaster, he half expected it. Aubrey climbed the Lanc away from the airfield on his instruments and when they reached one thousand feet set course for Lowestoft, where they were due to cross the English coastline. It was a fine night with little cloud and the forecast for the target area was good.

"ETA Dutch coast five minutes, Skipper," said the navigator over the intercom.

"Roger, Nav. I'll let you know when we cross it."

Newman had done nothing so far, except watch and inwardly digest. He was very impressed with the operation so far. Every single member of the crew sounded alert and competent, and they clearly had tremendous confidence in their captain.

"We're at the stage now where we can do with your eyes, Newman," said Aubrey. "Keep a good look out to front and starboard. There are several hundred other aircraft out there somewhere, not counting the Jerries! We can do without any collisions, they can be bloody dangerous!"

"Roger, Skipper."

❖

In Bermuda, Lucy was arguing with her mother again. They had just finished their evening meal and Lucy announced she was going out and would be back in half an hour.

"Where are you going Lucy."

"Just a walk Mummy, I want to be alone and think."

"A walk to where?" asked her mother.

"Oh, here and there."

As Helmut Schachmann had been interned at a house in Paget where, according to local gossip some German prisoners of war were also being kept, Lucy's mother knew her daughter could not be going to meet him.

In truth, Lucy was going to the Belmont to see if she could find any of Don Newman's old friends who might be able to give her more news of him, and she opened the front door and walked out before her mother could reply. She never got there because her mother called after her and made her come back before she was through the front gate.

Lucy's relationship with her mother had got worse rather than better in the few months since her father had been killed. It was now almost open warfare.

❖

Newman had his first experience of open warfare when the German anti-aircraft batteries on the Dutch coast opened up on Lancaster B for Baker. It seemed to Newman that all hell had broken out. Aubrey said it was always like that, but he wasn't strictly accurate. Their port inner engine had just been hit — that hadn't happened to Aubrey before — and was starting to run rough, then beginning to vibrate. The engine was stopped and the propeller feathered, but there was still vibration running through the aircraft.

"It's the port outer Skipper, it's losing oil pressure rapidly," shouted the flight engineer, on the intercom, "we'll have to feather that too!"

If they did that they would have just the two working engines on the starboard side, and Aubrey wanted to be sure it was absolutely necessary. "Is it still falling?" he asked the flight engineer.

The words were hardly out of his mouth when another salvo rocked the aircraft. Almost instantaneously shrapnel struck and shattered the instrument panel in front of the two pilots. The whole of the blind flying panel — the basic instruments needed to fly the aircraft — were pulverised.

The flight engineer never answered the Skipper's question, because he had been killed instantly when another piece of shrapnel had penetrated his heart. Newman, terrified and expecting the order to bail out, looked across at the Skipper, silhouetted now, against a fire which had just erupted in the port outer engine. He was motionless and Newman feared the worst. As far as he could see in the darkness, the Skipper's hands were not on the controls. Newman grabbed the control column on his side of the cockpit, in an effort to take charge and fly the aircraft. "I have control," he shouted into the intercom, hoping to hear a "you have control" response from the Skipper. He didn't get one.

Newman didn't need the instruments to know that the nose of the aircraft had dropped and that they were diving fast and turning to the left. He thought he could see flashes on the ground from more anti-aircraft guns ahead of them. In fact they were the guns that had hit them The aircraft had already turned through 180 degrees and was heading back towards the coast. He throttled back all four engines, pressed the fire extinguisher button for the port outer engine and pulled back on the stick, gently at first, for he didn't want to pull the wings off the aircraft. They were at 18,000 feet when they were hit, so they were in no danger of hitting the ground for the moment. But the aircraft didn't respond, and the engine fire was getting worse. The lack of response on the controls was a nasty feeling: a bit like a car with failed brakes and steering, but worse!

Momentarily he thought of shedding the bomb load to make the aircraft lighter. But he knew they were over Holland and rejected the idea quickly. He didn't want the bombs dropping on innocent civilians. He pulled harder on the control column and called the crew on the intercom. "Crew this is Newman; co pilot. The Skipper's been hit. Nav come up and have a look at him. Crew standby to bail out. Repeat, standby to bail out."

The navigator came up behind Newman like a gun out of a bullet, even though he had to scramble over the body of the flight engineer.

"Have a look at the Skipper" Newman shouted to Nav.

Whilst all this was going on, Newman was using the trimmers to try to bring the aircraft out of the dive and level the wings. He was winning, but it was taking time. He stopped it turning and gradually increased power on the two good engines whilst increasing the rudder trim to continue keeping the aircraft going straight.

"He's had it." Nav shouted. "Half his bloody head's been blown off!"

"OK, I've got her fairly level, but that bloody fire's still going. It's going to burn the wing off!"

"Better get the hell out of it, before it's too late!" shouted the Nav.

"Bail out, bail out, bail out. Go!" shouted Newman, over the intercom.

Newman was the last to go, and as his chute opened, there was a gigantic explosion in the sky almost above him. Lancaster B for baker, with the bodies of the captain and the flight engineer aboard, had exploded into thousands of pieces.

Newman feared that he would be hit by the falling debris, but realised there was nothing he could do about it. He glanced around, looking for the 'chutes of the rest of the crew below him. He counted four, there should have been another. He hoped it was there somewhere.

It suddenly became quiet, so quiet, it seemed unreal. The anti-aircraft fire had ceased and the sound of aircraft engines had gone. Although it was dark his eyes picked out a white parachute not far below him, perhaps only two or three hundred feet. He was sure it must be the navigator who had bailed out immediately before him. He thought of trying to shout to him, but decided there wasn't really much point.

Newman didn't know the height at which they had bailed out, since the altimeter had been shattered, but he guessed it was about fifteen thousand feet. He could see the coast not far away and suddenly wondered if he was going to end up in the sea. His mind was not as clear as he would have liked and he couldn't remember the wind direction the navigator had been using. He wished he could, but that suddenly became academic. The sudden noise of a large aircraft grabbed Newman's attention and before he realised what was happening another aircraft passed directly below him and between him and the navigator's chute. Like a super-fast express train passing through a suburban station it was gone in a flash. Newman clearly saw four red hot engine exhausts and realised it was probably a Halifax. They flew lower than the Lancs, but there was no time to identify it for sure. It was so near to him that he was tossed around by its slipstream and he feared his parachute might collapse.

It was then that he felt cold. He hadn't noticed it before now, but all of a sudden he was shivering. He couldn't see the ground clearly in the darkness and was taken by surprise when he hit it just one hundred yards from the shore and fifty yards from a German anti-aircraft battery. There was no point in trying to escape, a bright torch was being shone in his face even before he could get up off the ground. Even in his state of shock, he realised he was going to spend time in a prisoner of war camp. He would have to leave trying to escape until then.

Late the following morning the telegram boy stopped outside Newman's parents' house in Staines, leant his red bicycle up against the front fence and walked slowly up to the front door. He was supposed to move quickly and purposely when doing his job — but he had never had to deliver two telegrams to the same house at the same time before. He didn't like being the bearer of bad news, and it seemed he was doing it far too often. He found he could tell when it was bad news by the supervisor's manner when he gave him a telegram to deliver!

Perhaps it was fortunate that Aunt Rose was with Newman's mother when she learned that her son Squadron Leader Geoffrey Newman had been killed when his aircraft collided with another RAF aircraft over East Anglia the previous night, and that her son Flight Lieutenant Donald Newman was missing in action over enemy territory.

A few days later, the letter which Don had written to Lucy whilst on leave in Staines arrived at its destination. But Lucy's mother had already spoken to Lucy's boss at the Front Street shop and sought his cooperation. He passed the letter to her and she tore it into a thousand pieces. Lucy never saw it nor knew of its existence.

Newman wrote three more letters from his POW camp. Two suffered the same fate, one was lost in the Atlantic.

CHAPTER TEN

24 March 1993, Again
The Belmont Hotel, Bermuda

It wasn't long before Fred, the forty-five year old Belmont barman and the seventy-one year old Don Newman were chatting as if they had known each other for years.

"So when was it, did you say, you were here before with the Air Force?" asked Fred.

Newman took a long swig of his drink, and then paused before answering. He was pondering whether to try and develop the conversation in an attempt to find out what had happened to Lucy. It was unlikely he would ever come back to Bermuda again, so if he was going to satisfy his curiosity — and he was telling himself that was all it was — it was probably now or never. Not that he actually expected the barman to have any instant answers, but there was just a chance. Bermuda was a fairly small place.

"Nineteen forty three. The Spring."

"Fifty years — that's a long time!"

"It certainly is, although sometimes I find I can remember things that happened fifty years ago better than a week ago!"

"Sounds like you enjoyed your Bermuda stay, Sir?"

"Yes — well — never forgotten it, Fred."

"So why did you take so long to come back?

"Ah well, that's a long story!"

Fred detected Newman's hesitation. "Sorry, didn't mean to pry, Sir."

A young couple whom Newman had seen on the DC-10 flight with him, entered the bar and drew the barman's attention. It gave Newman time to sort out his thoughts. He decided he was making a mountain out of a molehill, so when Fred returned Newman said.

"You lived on the Islands all your life, Fred?"

"Yes, and in the same house!"

"Nearby?"

"Yes, up near Riddell's Bay. Don't suppose you'd know it. It's a mile or two up the road, near Burgess Point."

Newman spluttered and nearly choked on his drink at the mention of Burgess Point. He put his drink down on the counter.

"Yes, I know where you mean, I used to have a friend who lived somewhere up there."

"Really! Yes you get really good views of the Sound from some of the greens."

"That's a coincidence. My friend — my girlfriend at the time, you understand — used to wave to me from Burgess Point when I taxied out in my Catalina, for take-off."

"You're empty Sir, same again?"

"No thanks Fred I've had more than I should already. I'll have to get back to the Southampton Express — I mean Princess — soon."

"Sure Sir?"

"Well maybe. Yes — one for the road, as they say."

Fred gave Newman his drink then leant forward over the bar. Newman responded by doing the same, sensing that Fred wanted to introduce a touch of confidentiality.

"If you don't mind me asking Sir, I was wondering about your friend. Have you kept in touch?"

"No, I lost touch with her. I was posted to Bomber Command." He glanced round the room to see if he was being overheard. He wasn't. "Bit of a problem with my Catalina here. Ended up in a Prisoner of War camp in Germany, so I don't know what became of her."

"How did you end up as a German prisoner because of a problem here?"

"As I say, I was posted to Bomber Command and got shot down."

"Ah, yes, I follow. Sorry. This friend, maybe I know her. What was her name?"

Newman hesitated. He didn't want to send out the wrong signals. If Fred thought he was still carrying a torch for Lucy at his age — which of course he wasn't — it would be most embarrassing. He tried to sound very casual.

"Appledram — Lucy Appledram — I think it was," he said, knowing full well he wasn't fooling Fred one little bit.

"Appledram. Yes, I know the name. Several Appledrams on Bermuda. I'm not sure, there may have been an Appledram on the Plough, the first ship that came from England with settlers, in sixteen-twelve, you know. Don't think I can remember a Lucy, though." He laughed. "I don't mean on the Plough, I mean at Riddell's Bay. You sure that's where she lived?"

Newman joined in the joke. "No she wasn't that old. Yes — quite sure — or near there."

The barman stroked the right-hand side of his face and chin with his right hand. "And nineteen-forty-three, you say this was?"

"Yes, the Spring of forty-three."

It was nearly eleven pm, and through the mirror behind Fred, Newman saw the other couple from the DC-10 get up and leave. Fred the barman, and Newman were alone in the bar.

"I know who would help us though." Fred was now talking as though he was really enjoying himself. "My parents. My dad was in the war, but my mother was here all the time. She's sure to remember, I'll give her a ring."

Newman was just swallowing some more of his Dark and Stormy. Suddenly it went the wrong way and he made his second splutter of the evening. He sensed that things were going to get beyond his control. That was the last thing he wanted.

"No, no, no," he said "I didn't come here to...."

"Hang on a minute Sir, I'll ring her before she goes to bed."

Fred left the bar before Newman had a chance to respond. He felt uneasy, although he was genuinely interested to know whether Lucy still lived in Bermuda, if of course she was still alive. But it seemed a little odd, almost ridiculous, to be enquiring after all these years. Some unseen force seemed to be sending him down a road which was not properly mapped. It suddenly came to him, it was the drink. He wasn't thinking clearly. He should get back to the Southampton Princess straight away and go to bed.

Fred had disappeared into a room behind the bar. Newman heard him dialling a number. His bill for his drinks was on the bar top in front of him, and he picked it up. It was just over thirty dollars. He took two twenty dollar bills out of his wallet and placed them under his empty glass.

"Goodnight Fred, must go — good to chat," he called out, and left.

He felt a bit of a heel, but barmen must get used to people drinking too much in their bar, he thought to himself! And Fred seemed the sort who would understand.

At the front entrance he asked the hotel porter to call a taxi for him, and sat under the porch in a wicker chair and waited. He was annoyed with himself. He had been behaving like a teenager, but he had to admit he hadn't felt so much alive for a long time!

The taxi arrived after ten minutes. The hall porter opened the taxi door for Newman and told the driver his fare was for the Southampton Princess. Newman boarded. At that moment Fred the barman appeared shouting, "Hold it Sir, hold it!"

It was a warm night and the windows of the taxi were open. Fred handed a note to Newman through the nearest window.

"She's still alive and living in Flatts. This is her phone number. My mother says she's heard that she's been very ill lately. Her daughter will tell you, she lives with her."

Newman took the note, "Thanks,"

"By the way Sir, I didn't catch your name. My mother was most insistent I ask you. I'd better take it, if you've no objection."

Newman felt he had already been rude in walking out, he didn't want to make things worse. "Newman — Don Newman. Thanks for your help."

The taxi ride back to his hotel was uneventful, except for what Newman considered a near collision with a moving bright light on the wrong side of the road, which turned out to be a motor scooter. The taxi driver said he was used to it. "Good job it isn't wet," he said. "He'd have come off driving like that!"

Newman was very tired, as the four hour time difference between London and Bermuda, meant his body clock thought it was three in the morning. The one night stop in New York seemed to have done little to help, and he was soon sound asleep in room 399.

He awoke early the next morning and got up immediately. Sliding back the curtains and opening the balcony door, he found he had a breathtaking panoramic view, starting with Gibbs Hill Lighthouse on his left, the Great Sound and the distant Dockyard in the middle, and the outskirts of the City of Hamilton on his right beyond the Warwick foreground.

To his delight — the hotel being on the top of a hill and his room being on the third floor — he had practically the same view of the Great Sound as he'd often had from the cockpit of his Catalina when coming into land all those years ago. Then a thought came to him; the hotel must have been built more or less on the spot where the Turtle Hill guns used to be. They were the guns that were responsible for the U-boat having to crash dive!

He found out later that the site of one of the guns mounts still survived in the hotel grounds.

He was looking at Burgess Point and Riddell's Bay when he heard his room telephone ring. He supposed it would be the airline telling him about the arrangements they'd made for the DC-10 passengers to continue their journey. He sat on the bed and picked up the phone, hoping he wouldn't have to rush straight to the airport.

"Donald Newman speaking."

"Good morning, Mr Newman." It was a pleasant sounding woman on the other end of the line. Newman picked up a pen and prepared to make a note of the instructions he was expecting — time to be picked up from the hotel — take-off time, and so forth.

"Good morning."

"Mr Newman, you won't know me. My name's Margaret Carpenter. I understand you were making enquiries last night at the Belmont about my mother. You knew her by her maiden name, Lucy Appledram".

Newman was completely taken off guard. "Well, yes — hello — it was just a casual inquiry. I was on a plane that was diverted here yesterday, and it's the first time I've been back to Bermuda since the war. I'm sorry, I shouldn't have enquired. It's none of my business; it was all a very long time ago. I do apologise."

"Oh it's all right Mr Newman, perfectly all right. You see my mother has often spoken of you — at least I think it must be you — that's why I'm phoning. But she is ill now. So, as you were enquiring about her, I was just wondering if we could meet and maybe, as it were, exchange notes. That is, if that would be of any interest to you?"

All of a sudden things were getting complicated for Newman. He was more than sober now. He hadn't anticipated that the chat the night before with the Belmont barman might lead to this, but he just couldn't resist the opportunity to meet Lucy's daughter, and anyway it would be rude to say "no".

"Well that's very kind of you," said Newman, "I'd like that very much. The thing is — I'm waiting to hear from Atlantic Airways. I was on a DC-10 of their's that was diverted here yesterday, so I'm expecting to have to get back to the airport soon."

"Yes I understand. I work at the airport, so I can help you there. The airline is bringing in a replacement aircraft this afternoon — so you don't need to rush to the airport at the moment."

"Oh, right, I hadn't been told that yet."

"Can I suggest something, Mr Newman?"

"Please do."

"I don't have to be at the airport until mid day. Nothing comes in before then. If I came round to the Southampton Princess, could we have a coffee or two, and sort of take it from there?"

"Yes, of course."

"Great. How about nine-thirty. Is that too early?"

"No fine. Where shall I meet you?"

"How about Windows On the Sound?"

"Sorry?"

"It's one of the dining rooms, the main room. You can have breakfast there. It overlooks the Sound."

"Right — and how will I know you?"

"No problem, I'll find you."

"OK, understood. I look forward to seeing you then at half past nine."

He put the phone down, 'Wow, the chap who'd had the heart attack on the DC-10 had really started something!' he muttered to himself.

He showered and shaved and went down to Windows on the Sound at nine, telling the clerk at the desk by the entrance, that he was expecting to be joined by a Ms Carpenter later. He was given a window table with a perfect view of the Sound on his left, but he hardly noticed it for the moment, and found himself drinking large quantities of orange juice and wondering if he was about to make a fool of himself. Or could it be that he'd already done that?

Over the years he had learnt the advantages of thinking through a strategy before a meeting and out of habit he started to do so now, but it didn't last long. It dawned on him that he wasn't about to face a business opponent, but the daughter of a very special girl that he'd once proposed to — although admittedly he wasn't sure that she'd actually received his proposal, and they had had a very big tiff when his Cat was stolen — so he would play it by ear. Anyway, what happened in 1943 was hardly Lucy's daughter's responsibility, and she certainly wouldn't know — or want to know — anything about someone trying to steal a flying boat.

She was ten minutes early. Almost too early for Newman's comfort. He had just dropped a large dollop of marmalade on to his grey trousers and was trying to carry out some emergency cleaning. Fortunately his blazer and tie were untouched.

His attire made him stand out like a sore thumb from the coloured shirts and shorts of the holiday guests at other tables, and it was his different dress style, coupled with his age, that enabled Margaret Carpenter to approach him from behind with confidence. Also a quiet word with the lady at the desk at the entrance to Windows on the Sound helped.

"Mr Newman?"

He almost jumped. Looking up he saw that the woman airport official who had spoken to the passengers at the airport the day before, was standing by his table.

"Yes, Don Newman. Come to tell me about the flight arrangements?"

She smiled. "No, I'm Margaret. I spoke to you an hour or so ago."

Newman shot to his feet, smiling broadly. "Oh so sorry! I saw you at the airport yesterday — and put two and two together." He offered his hand, and they shook. "Do sit, Margaret"

A waiter appeared from nowhere.

"Have you had breakfast?" asked Newman.

"Yes thanks, but I can use some coffee, I didn't leave the hospital until late last night."

Although Newman had only seen her for a few moments the day before, he felt he knew her. It was an odd feeling, which he'd never experienced before, ever.

Dressed in the same outfit as the day before, a smart two piece dark blue suit that would suit all occasions, she was an attractive and intelligent looking woman.

She was smiling again, "Mr Newman , I'm not quite sure where we start. Perhaps I should start by telling you the current situation, and the reason why I'm here. Is that OK?"

Newman suddenly felt she was approaching the meeting in a rather businesslike manner and wondered if he had been wrong to approach it so differently. He didn't realise she just had to control herself.

"Of course. Why don't you call me Don, by the way," he said hoping this would introduce the casual air he was after.

"Thanks."

"Well Mummy has been in hospital nearly two months now." She spoke quietly, with a touch of sadness in her voice, but was deliberate and very composed. "She went in last January after suffering a stroke. She was expected to make an almost complete recovery, but I'm afraid she's not progressing as hoped."

"Oh, very sorry to hear that. How has it affected her?"

She's lost the use of her right leg and right arm and she can't speak properly. But she has been subject to bouts of depression for the last twenty years or so, and it seems to have returned."

He looked concerned but understanding, she thought.

"Hardly surprising — must be terrible to be partially paralysed and not able to speak properly, " he said.

She sighed. "Yes, that's how it is. I'm very worried. She seems to be slipping away fast."

"What about her husband?"

"She's been divorced over thirty years now. He was a rotter by all accounts."

"Are you the only child."

"Yes, but she's got a brother He's not a bad sort."

He felt she was talking to him rather frankly considering they had only just met.

"Is that Jack, can I ask?" he asked.

She smiled in surprise. "Yes, you remember!"

"Yes, I remember him well."

"Jack seems to think something has happened to her attitude. It's not clear whether it is a result of the stroke or not."

Newman had difficulty associating the young vivacious Lucy he was in love with fifty years ago with the person Margaret was talking about, and was about to say how sorry he was again, but thought better of it. It would be better to let her finish first.

"The specialists don't understand it. They say she seems to be dying of a broken heart, although I believe technically that's supposed to be impossible. She seems to be progressively living in the past, and she keeps talking about *'Don,'* and doesn't seem to understand why *'Don' didn't write to her.'* I don't know of course if you are the Don that she is talking about, but when I found a message from a friend on my answer phone last night, saying that someone called Don Newman — who hadn't been to Bermuda for fifty years — was asking about Mummy, you'll understand, I just had to try and speak to you. And you say you remember Jack, so..."

She stopped and looked at him, as if to say, 'I've finished for the moment. The ball is in your court.' Something in her expression touched his heart. She was clearly very attached to her mother.

Newman didn't rush it. "I suppose you don't know if your mother knew any other *Dons*?" He asked slowly.

"No, not to my knowledge. Certainly none that were RAF pilots."

"So this Don was definitely an RAF pilot, was he?"

"Yes, definitely, and he got into some sort of trouble here — RAF trouble, I mean. Mummy would never tell me the full story, although she told me some of it. She tried to tell me everything once but she got too upset and had to stop! But she did say that it was this trouble that caused the break up of her romance — and probably was the root cause of the failure of her marriage."

By this time Newman was in no doubt that he was the 'Don' in question and he felt obliged to tread softly.

"And when exactly would your Mother have known this Don?"

There was a slight pause before she answered. "I've worked that out exactly, it must have been in May 1943."

Don Newman knew then that he was now going to have to own up. But he had a heavy heart. According to Margaret's story, it sounded as though her mother had been blaming him for their break up, fifty years ago. True he had walked away from her at Riddell's Bay, but the RAF enquiry — or whatever they called it — seemed to show that she had aided and abetted Helmut Schachmann. Some would say the real villain.

"Margaret, from all that you say, I do feel I am the 'Don' your mother talks about."

She smiled but didn't speak, sensing that he was going to say more.

"But I can't understand why she asks for me — as you say she does."

"I think perhaps there is a good reason. I'm not sure."

"I'm not sure I follow you Margaret. We had a very special romance and something happened that finished our relationship abruptly. But these things happen. Life is like that, especially in war time. She surely must have got over it!"

Margaret was looking sad. A waiter refreshed their coffee.

"You say something happened. Would that be about the stealing of a flying boat?" she asked.

"Yes, that was it."

He was surprised that she knew about it. "The RAF forbade me to speak to your mother again, and posted me to Bomber Command. She was thought to have been helping the person who stole the Catalina flying boat: Helmut Schachmann."

"Mr Newman — she corrected herself — Don. Mummy's told me about it, more than once, and it wasn't true. Her brother Jack thought it was because he believed Helmut Schachmann. But Helmut was a liar through and through."

He noticed that she was now saying that her mother had told her about it, whereas a minute ago she said her mother hadn't told her everything. But Margaret had the sweet smell of honesty and integrity about her, and he liked what he saw. He believed her. There must be something else she was trying to get to.

She had raised her voice and Newman felt for her. "Margaret, maybe we should leave things as they are. I came here to Bermuda by accident. I have deliberately kept away for fifty years because I felt I would only end up being upset if I came back and perhaps upset others. Now it appears I was right, and that my accidental return is causing you distress. I'm so sorry. I should never have gone to the Belmont last night."

Her table napkin was taking a lot of punishment; she had almost made mincemeat of it. She put it on the table. It looked like a deliberate move to Newman, rather as if she was clearing the decks to play a trump card. He couldn't help thinking she was a most attractive woman.

"Don, I'm sorry, I didn't mean to get uptight. I don't usually, but there's a reason."

Newman was a little confused. Margaret had lightly touched on Lucy's role in the stealing of the Catalina. He would like to have heard the whole of Lucy's story, even though he feared it was a simple case of Lucy not telling the truth to her daughter.

"Believe me, I understand, " he said in a soft voice, wondering about the reason she mentioned.

As he looked at her, hoping that he wasn't distressing her, he suddenly realised that he could see Lucy in her. Even some of her mannerisms reminded him of Lucy. It was an odd sensation, both pleasurable and painful at the same time.

She sensed that she had prepared the ground sufficiently. "Have you guessed yet?" she asked looking straight into Newman's eyes. Newman thought he detected a special look in her eyes, as though she was going to cry if he didn't come up with the right answer!"

Desperately trying to show that he was following the conversation, he said, "What is it — is it that Helmut Schachmann is your father?"

"Good God no! No, no, no, no!"

The tears started rolling down her cheeks, uncontrollably, and she struggled to continue. "You — the Don that Mummy has kept talking about — are my father! The father I've yearned for ever since I can remember!"

Newman was knocked for six. It had never occurred to him in all these years and his wildest dreams, that his one and only night of passionate love making with Lucy had left her pregnant. What a fool he was. Why hadn't he thought of at least that possibility before now? His overall feeling was one of great joy, but it wasn't as simple as that. It now seemed even more wrong that he had walked away from her at Riddell's Bay all those years ago. He should have waited to hear what she had to say, especially as he had been a vital part in her pregnancy.

He felt guilty, terribly guilty. Lucy was evidently now near death's door, and he had not been at hand to help her or his daughter for fifty years. He had obviously shot himself in the foot fifty years ago. He had been too ready to believe Lucy's brother Jack and what was said at the RAF Enquiry. He should have had faith in Lucy and listened to his heart, which, at the time, was telling him that Lucy slept with him because she was truly madly in love with him, and she would marry him. Not for any other reason. He had been taken in by the evidence, a mistake which was understandable maybe, but a mistake with terrible consequences, and it was his fault. Entirely his fault, and only his.

Margaret was sobbing. It was perhaps fortunate that Windows on the Sound was now deserted, except for a waiter discreetly clearing tables and the two of them. "I'm sorry," she said, "It's tears of happiness. I feel so relieved to know that I've met my Dad! I've been wondering about you for so very long. Not having a Dad has been the problem of my life."

Newman stood on impulse. He didn't consider why, he just did it. She followed his lead and they met half way, beside the table. Newman was emotionally exhausted, and as she stood in his arms, with her head over his left shoulder, he struggled to get to grips with his emotions. One of them was to accept that it was his daughter he was hugging, not Lucy. They were so alike.

After what seemed a life time, but was only a few seconds, they broke off, and returned to their seats. Newman wasn't thinking particularly clearly — it wasn't the sort of situation he'd been in before — but felt it was his job to take the lead from now on.

"I hardly know what to say," he said. "When can we go and see your Mother?"

She wiped her tears and composed herself. "Three o'clock is the official opening time for visiting hours, but we might be able to get in before. I can speak to the sister on the ward. Your flight will probably go before then."

"Forget the flight Margaret. I didn't expect to come here, but now I'm here I want to stay until a lot of things are sorted out," he said it in a decisive manner. Newman had always wanted a daughter, and now that he had a delightful and ready made one he wasn't going to let her down, as he felt he had Lucy. "Let's go at three then. I'll explain to the airline."

"Fine, you can leave the airline to me if you like, and the immigration. They may want you to purchase a ticket to New York or somewhere or other before they will let you stay on, but I can explain that it's a matter of life and death. There'll be no problem. I've got to go into work at midday. I can sort it all out then and explain to my boss that I just have to go to the hospital with you this afternoon. He will probably collapse when I say I'm going there with my father!"

She seemed more relaxed now, and Newman picked up the mood. "Shall we sit here for the moment, or shall we find somewhere else to chat?" he asked.

She smiled. "If you want, we could go outside and sit in the fresh air on that bench seat, and talk." She pointed to a wooden garden seat on the lawn outside. "I don't even know whether you're married, or whether I've got any half brothers or sisters. I'm dying to know."

"Lets do that. I can answer your questions, and there are a lot of things I want to ask you."

They left Windows on the Sound and Margaret asked to be excused for a few moments. Newman strolled around the lobby awaiting her return in a daze. When she did, they left the hotel by a back door, and crossed the road on to a flat piece of grass — almost a lawn — then to a wooden seat. It meant that they sat side by side, rather than opposite each other as they did in the Hotel, so they both sat at an angle to make it easier to continue their frank revelations.

Newman took the lead. "You were asking if I had any other sons and daughters?"

She looked at him, smiling. It was the same smile Lucy had; at least that's how it seemed to him.

"Yes, Margaret, you have a half brother, that's all. I was on my way to visit him when we were diverted to Bermuda, and he has two children."

"And your wife?"

"She died nearly twenty years ago — of cancer. I was very upset, but life goes on!"

"Yes, sorry to hear that. Had you been married long?"

"Eighteen years. When did your mother marry?"

"Nineteen fifty two, but it didn't last. She says it was a big mistake."

"A local man?"

"Sort of, you'd have heard of him."

"What was his name?"

She was about to answer — or he thought she was — when a hotel waiter appeared with a small portable table which he put down in front of them. Newman was wondering why, when a second waiter appeared with an ice bucket and two champagne glasses.

"I hope you don't mind Daddy, I thought we should have a celebratory drink together!"

Apart from a big smile, Newman didn't respond. His brain was going numb.

"Shall I pour Mrs Carpenter?" asked the waiter.

"No it's OK, I'd like to do that. Thank you anyway."

Although he was feeling overwhelmed, he picked up the 'Mrs Carpenter' quickly.

"I'm pleased to hear you're married, Margaret."

"Was," she said. "It was all over ten years ago, now."

"Sorry to hear that. About your Mum — who did she marry?"

Lucy handed him his glass of champagne and picked up her own. They clinked glasses.

"What shall we drink to?" she asked.

"To Lucy's recovery?" he suggested.

"Yes, to Mummy."

They sat and drank champagne together. Margaret was aware that she hadn't answered Don's question about who her mother had married. She wasn't sure how he might react, so was pretending to have forgotten the question. It hadn't escaped Newman that she hadn't answered. He wondered why she avoided the question. Anyway it was none of his business.

Newman stood, and walked a few paces to a low hedge at the edge of the lawn. He wanted to get a better view over the Sound and let his mind settle. She followed, topped up his drink, and stood beside him.

"There's one thing at least Don, I should warn you about," said Margaret, "Mummy has her ups and downs. If she's better today, she may ask you why you didn't write to her — I just thought I should warn you."

Newman was quiet for a few seconds. He was getting too many surprises! How many more surprises were there going to be?

He turned towards her and looked straight into her eyes. "Margaret," he said at last, "I wrote to your mother, several times. She never answered."

"Oh dear, oh dear, oh dear! She's told me that she wrote to you several times to tell you that she was pregnant. She felt sure you must have got some of them, but you never answered. Mummy said she knew you would want to know that, and would do what she called 'the right' thing. She had complete and absolute faith in you, she said. But even before that she apparently wrote to you and explained her side of the story, about the Catalina, which she says was completely different from what you thought."

Newman didn't answer instantly. He hadn't received any letters from Lucy — it was hardly a thing he would forget. He sat on the seat again and looked out over the Sound, his expression impassive. She sat, this time closer to him, almost as though she felt he needed consoling.

"I'm sorry I had to mention it, Don."

"It's OK. You were right to warn me."

"And I don't want you to think that I don't believe you. I do, now that I've met you."

Newman shrugged his shoulders. "Yes, but it means that for all these years your Mother must have felt I let her down!"

"Yes, but I don't think she blamed you. She blamed her brother Jack and Helmut Schachmann. I suppose Helmut had to lie, it was the war! You mustn't blame yourself. You didn't know the truth."

"No, but I didn't give your Mum the chance to tell me the truth, did I? And from what you say that has affected her whole life." He might have added that it would have changed his life completely as well, but he chose not to. He wasn't the one who was lying in a hospital bed, seriously ill.

Margaret could see all this had been a bit much for her father. "Maybe, but so many things we do nearly every day can have a big impact on our futures," she said. Then as an afterthought, feeling she was being rather too serious, she added "Even the time we get out of bed one morning can change the rest of our lives."

He said nothing and gave her the benefit of the doubt. He felt sure Margaret had not realised the significance of what she had said, but he couldn't help thinking that if he and Lucy had stayed in his bed an extra ten minutes at the Belmont in 1943, they would never have met her brother Jack, nor seen the flying boat being stolen by Helmut Schachmann!

CHAPTER ELEVEN

Thursday, 25 March 1993

Margaret suggested that he might like to take the early afternoon hotel ferry to Hamilton. It would, she said, give him a chance to see Darrell's Island again as he sailed past, and she needed to leave him for the time being to sort out airline and immigration matters. She would pick him up at the Hamilton Princess soon after the ferry arrived. Before they parted she asked him for his passport. He gave it to her without hesitation.

Back in his room, Newman was restless. Now that Margaret had gone, he realised even more how complicated the situation was becoming. His daughter seemed to think he had some magic power to bring Lucy back to reality, but surely it could have the opposite effect? It was all a big shock to him, but he wasn't ill. Who knew what effect it might have on Lucy? It might give her a heart attack or another stroke.

He had half a mind to tell his new found daughter, when he next saw her, that he doubted the wisdom of what she was proposing. He would think about it on the ferry. That wouldn't be difficult. He wouldn't be able to think of much else.

Just after one he went to the lift and down to the foyer, where he spoke to the duty receptionist about staying another night. Smiling profusely, she said she already knew. "Your daughter has told us," were the exact words.

He was beginning to realise that his initial impressions of his daughter were correct; she was indeed efficient and organised.

At the front door he asked about the hotel ferry and was directed to one of the two green buses waiting to the left of the entrance. After checking with the driver he boarded and sat on a wooden, two seat bench near the door. It was an unusual vehicle, at least Newman thought so, with large decorative windows and left hand drive. From the outside it was the most un-streamlined vehicle he had ever seen, like an oblong box, with a wheel at each corner. But there was something oddly attractive about it.

A woman asked the driver if this was the jitney to the Waterlot. Newman hadn't heard the expression before, and wondered if he was hearing right. "Step right up madam," said the driver, "we're about to go," and they did.

It was only a few minutes journey to Middle Road where the jitney journey ended close to the Waterlot Inn. The driver directed passengers to the jetty behind the Inn. Newman could now see the building in the daylight and tried to remember what it was like in 1943, but he couldn't. The demise of the railway made a big difference, and he couldn't quite get his bearings without it. But the name definitely rang some bells with him. He felt he should remember more, but he'd forgotten that when he'd been with Lucy his attention had been on her, not very much on their surroundings.

He followed several other people along the left side of the Inn and on to the jetty. There was no sign of the ferry and he sat and waited at one of the white outdoor tables. The March sun was warm and he relaxed in it; the champagne earlier also helped.

It wasn't long before he saw the ferry nosing along the inlet towards the jetty. The name *Elizabeth* soon clear on the bow. A few minutes later the incoming passengers had disembarked and the Hamilton bound passengers — having displayed proof of their hotel room numbers — had boarded. He sat in the open air on one of the many portable chairs on the upper deck, determined to make the most of the trip.

Soon the boat was under way and the *Elizabeth* eased out into the Little Sound. As it headed north-east towards Burgess Point, Newman looked back and up at Gibbs Hill Lighthouse. The view was vaguely familiar, but there seemed to be many more white roofs dotted around the landscape now. The same with Burgess Point. There were a few more houses on the edge of Riddell's Bay Golf Course now, but he could pick out where Lucy had stood and waved to him as he had taxied out for take-off.

They continued along the shoreline and passed Darrell's Island on their left. Newman wasn't surprised that the old marine airport looked derelict. The waiter had hinted as much in the conversation they'd had on the balcony of his room the previous night. Apart from a piece of the terminal building which was still standing, and the concrete ramps which were used to get the flying boats in and out of the water, it was as though the airport had never existed. Indeed if he hadn't been there before he would have passed by Darrell's Island and not realised it had a big place in Bermuda's history. He had expected at least, to see a large sign saying it was the site of the old Marine Aviation airport, 1936 - 1948. Perhaps there was one on the north side of the Island. He wandered forward and asked the helmsman, who was using the wheel on the top deck. "No, don't suppose anyone ever thought about it. The older locals will know about it, the younger ones and the visitors probably wouldn't be interested!"

Newman was not over impressed with the answer, but it had the ring of truth and he had to accept it. It reminded him of the reaction he had from local villagers some years earlier when he had been passing through Yorkshire and had made a detour to Sandstone, the RAF base he'd taken off from before being shot down. Admittedly that was only an airfield for three years — Darrell's Island must have been in use for three or four times that — but there had been a lot of action there. A lot of lives had been lost in crashes, but most of the locals he spoke to in the local pub seemed completely disinterested, and no attempt had been made to put a notice at the old main entrance showing its historical significance. The only notice said "Main Entrance: Yorkshire Fertilizer Company."

"What about the Dockyard?" said Newman. "Anything going on there?"

"Yes and no. The Royal Navy gave it up in the fifties. Some of it has been turned into a Museum, there are a few shops and some cruise ships now dock there. It's beginning to come back to life. The Government ferries are maintained there, that sort of thing. "

They were passing through Timlin's Narrows now and Newman got his first modern view of the City of Hamilton. Mainly in sunshine but with the shadows of small clouds dancing on the roof tops, the multicoloured buildings with the cathedral topping them all made Hamilton a splendid sight. He remembered his first ferry ride with Lucy on the *Laconia*, and how they had looked back on Hamilton as the ferry made its way to the Belmont Wharf.

"What do you think of that view?" asked the helmsman.

"Marvellous, absolutely marvellous. It's good to see the city's skyline is still dominated by the cathedral. It must be one of the few cities in the world these days not dominated by skyscrapers."

The ferry docked at the Hamilton Princess Hotel, and Newman mounted a flight of stone steps which brought him up to a terrace near the swimming pool. Margaret had said that if she didn't meet him as he got off the boat, he should sit by the pool and wait for her.

There was no sign of her and he chose one of the many chairs and tables and sat looking at the boats coming and going in the harbour. He regularly scanned for any sight of his daughter approaching from behind him, but after half an hour there was no sign of her and he began to be a little concerned. He stood to get a better look, but it didn't help. There was still no sign of her.

A couple of young girls were making a lot of noise in the pool, and for a fleeting second he wished they would make less noise — not that he would dream of saying anything to them. He realised it was because he was tired and emotional. They were just having good friendly fun.

There was a small bar at one corner of the pool. He wandered over and asked for a coke.

"The ferry from the Southampton Princess — does it always dock here," he asked, "or is there another place in Hamilton it goes to, as well?"

"No Sir, just here."

"Thanks."

Newman returned to his seat, feeling uneasy. His instincts told him something was wrong. The image of his daughter, which admittedly he had built up in just an hour or so, was one of reliability and consideration for him. He felt she wouldn't be late. Perhaps there had been some misunderstanding, but he couldn't think what that could be. He had already checked that he couldn't be waiting at the wrong place.

After an hour, and three cokes, there was still no sign of Margaret. Newman was considering his options. It was then that he suddenly realised there was a lot he didn't know about her. He didn't even know where she lived. Then he remembered he had been given her phone number by the Belmont barman. It was a bit like not knowing exactly where Lucy lived in 1943. He reluctantly decided that he would just have to wait, but eventually, if it came to it, he would have to go to the police and ask for their help, or maybe get in touch with the airport. Most likely he felt, she had been involved in an accident after she'd left him. He couldn't think of anything else!

For a while he gave up sitting and strolled back and forth beside the pool, trying to deal with the tension which was building up. The pool was now empty and looked inviting. Under different circumstances he might well have been tempted to take the plunge, but at the moment nothing was further from his mind.

The barman, who had nothing to do now, had been observing Newman and realised he must be waiting for someone. As Newman passed him for the umpteenth time he asked him if all was well. Newman explained he had been waiting for a friend, as he put it, for an hour and a half.

"Do you want me to see if there is a message for you at the front desk?"

"I hadn't thought of that. Yes, please. "

He gave his name and the barman rang the front desk.

"Yes, there is a message for a Mr Don Newman."

"That's me."

"Your daughter has been delayed unexpectedly, Sir. She sends her apologies and asks you to wait for her. She will be as quick as she can."

That was the second time someone had mentioned "his daughter" to him. It was going to take a lot of getting used to.

"Oh fine, thanks very much," said Newman, then as an afterthought, "I'll have a Dark and Stormy."

The barman had it ready for him quickly. "You going to sign for it Sir, or is it cash?"

"It'll have to be cash, I'm staying at the Southampton Princess."

"No problem Sir, if you've got your hotel card I can put it on your account."

"Right, thank you. I hadn't realised that."

Newman signed for it and gave the barman a large tip — which wasn't strictly necessary — and went and sat at his table again. He was feeling in better spirits now. But somehow or other he had missed lunch and he felt he ought to eat something. The barman ordered a sandwich from the kitchen for him. It came promptly, and he ate it sitting in the sunshine.

He heard her footsteps first. Ladylike, but with a sense of purpose. He looked up and saw she was heading for his table. But she looked distraught, the smiles of the morning had gone, and her body language was different. It looked as though every step was hard and painful. He could tell that there was something wrong.

He stood and offered her a chair when she finally reached him. She stood beside it, opposite him and he looked at her face briefly. If he was not mistaken, she'd been crying.

"Sorry I'm so late — I'm afraid I've got bad news."

"Don't worry about being late Margaret."

He sat on his pool-side chair. Then, remembering his manners, got up quickly and stood until his daughter had taken her seat. They sat facing each other.

"After I left you it occurred to me that it might be a tremendous shock to Mummy if I took you to see her, without at least trying to talk to her first and telling her you were here."

"Yes, I wondered about that, too."

"So I went to the hospital and explained the situation to her doctor. I didn't go into all the background, but I said you were my father and that Mummy often talked about you. They seemed to think it could do no harm to tell her and might do some good. So they let me in to see her. They told me to gradually work round to telling her you were here, and that's what I did.

She wasn't too bad to begin with, but she began to get emotional when I told her you were here. She clearly understood, but being unable to speak properly she got very frustrated — at least I think that was the problem — she was animated and excited. I called the doctor and he decided to give her an injection, presumably to calm her down. But shortly afterwards she lost consciousness! Apparently she's had another stroke. They are doing everything they can but I have a feeling they don't think her chances of pulling through this time are very good." She paused, "And I was hoping so much that she'd get better now that you are here."

"Oh God," said Newman, "Oh my God! If only I hadn't gone to the Belmont last night."

Margaret was sobbing quietly. "You mustn't think like that Don. How were you to know she was unwell and in hospital? You might as well blame the man on your plane who had the heart attack. And anyway, I would never have met you if you hadn't, would I? "

They sat quietly for a few minutes, exchanging a few words now and then, but mostly just thinking and contemplating. It had been a roller-coaster of a day for both of them.

The hotel ferry docked again and inbound and outbound passengers mingled and juggled for space on the quayside. One, in a rush to get to the stone steps that led to the gang plank accidentally brushed against the edge of their table. It wobbled momentarily and some Dark and Stormy splashed over the lip of Newman's glass on to the table. He was looking down at the table when it happened, but ignored it. He raised his head and looked at her. She had not lost her composure completely, but was clearly struggling to keep it.

"I think I'd better get a flight out tomorrow," he said in a quiet voice, "I've done enough damage in Bermuda."

She didn't reply instantly. She was considering all the implications. "Please don't make a decision right now," she said eventually. "In another day or two we should have a better idea of her chances. And if she should start to recover and find you've run away again...... sorry I didn't put that very well.......I'm upset...... you know what I mean."

He was glad she had corrected herself. He felt like smoking a cigarette. He hadn't had one in twenty years, but now he could do with one. He hadn't had that feeling since his wife had died. "You want me to stay?" he asked, leaning towards her, and gently touching her right hand with his left.

Suddenly there were tears in her eyes again. "I wish you could stay for ever!" She stood, moved to the parapet so he couldn't see her face and looked out over the harbour. He rose and stood beside her. A glass bottomed sight-seeing boat slid by making its way to Albouy's Point. There was not a cloud in the deep blue sky. It was warm, and calm, unusually calm in fact.

"I think this may be the calm before a storm" said Margaret.

He thought she might be right in more ways than one.

"Yes."

For fifty years, Lucy hadn't been in his life, only his thoughts from time to time. Now he was more concerned about his new daughter. There didn't seem to be a man in her life, at least she hadn't mentioned one.

He could see the Belmont on the skyline of the far shore. He wondered if Fred the barman realised what he had started when he phoned his parents the night before. Then he realised that was unfair. He was only trying to help.

"Margaret, I've only known for a few hours that I've got a daughter, but if you are sure you want me to stay, I will." He wasn't expressing himself very well and he knew it. He was struggling to get his mind working clearly. He soon wished he hadn't opened his mouth.

"It's different for me, I've known for nearly fifty years, I had a father called Don, but I didn't know how to find him! Please don't go away again until things settle down."

He understood. His sister Brenda's daughter, Elizabeth, was almost the same age as Margaret, and she often said how much she missed never having known her father. All she knew was that he was an American bomber pilot who had lost his life in the war. Newman sensed his daughter was worried that he might go back to England and never return or contact her again. It was as though she was echoing her mother's anxiety of fifty years ago. He wanted to allay those thoughts forever.

"Of course, I'll stay — for a few days at least. And you must come to London."

"Thanks Don — I'm not sure about that, I expect I'll be looking after Mum — I can't think very well at the moment. But look at it this way. If Mummy comes round — and is compos mentis — and finds you've left the Island again, she'll be disappointed and upset all over again. That won't do her any good. After all she knows you are here now. That's why she got so excited."

"What about your Uncle Jack. Shouldn't you ask him what he thinks?"

She had regained her composure now and sat at the table again. It seemed his words had reassured her.

He followed suit. The poolside waiter approached and mopped up the spilt drink.

"Do you want a drink or coffee?" Newman asked her.

"A coffee please."

"Make that two."

"He's in New York at the moment. Be home tomorrow. I'll phone him later and tell him about Mummy, and I'll tell him about you tomorrow when I meet him."

In truth she wasn't sure how her Uncle would react to the news of her father's reappearance. She had a feeling that Jack had felt guilty for many years for having ruined his sister's life. He had seen his sister change following the Catalina "stealing" incident and felt he was to blame. But his mother — now ninety-two — confined to a wheelchair, but still very much in command, had steadfastly maintained that it wasn't his fault. He had tried to convince himself that she was right but he was by no means certain.

"I'll have to tell Grandma as well, soon, " Margaret continued, "I don't want to get in her bad books!"

Newman was quite prepared to stay longer, but he was still doubting the wisdom of it. It looked as if he was bound to become the focus of bitter arguments which would serve no purpose and achieve absolutely nothing. He folded his arms and leant forward, putting his crossed arms on the edge of the table.

"Margaret, I have an idea."

She looked up and put on a brave face, almost a smile.

"Go on."

"Suppose we keep me a secret. Don't tell anyone else? Sounds like your Mum won't be able to tell Jack — unfortunately," he added quickly.

"Daddy, I want everyone to know you're here. It's the best thing that's ever happened to me!"

"Well, why don't you keep it to yourself for the moment. We can talk about it tomorrow."

"Yes I suppose I could do that."

She drove him back to the Southampton Princess in her Honda and they discussed practical matters on the way. She returned his passport, explained where to get money on his credit cards at the hotel bank, and gave him her telephone number at work. As he opened the car door outside the Southampton Princess she said she would ring him after she had been to the hospital that evening.

He stood by the car looking down at her through the open window of the car door. She was looking at him as he said.

"Fine. By the way — if I ring the hospital to find out how she is — who do I ask about? I don't know your mother's married name."

She stopped looking up at him and it seemed deliberate. After a long pause, she turned and looked up at her father again. There was a sad and — Newman thought — guilty look in her eyes.

"Mrs Schachmann," she replied.

A look of disbelief appeared on Newman's face.

"You mean she married Helmut Schachmann?"

"I'm afraid so Daddy. It was Grandma. Mummy says her mother made her do it."

A hotel bus was behind them, patiently waiting to move forward. Margaret realised and started to move off. "I'll tell you more when I ring you later Daddy."

When he got to his room Newman poured himself a whisky and took it on to the balcony. He wished he still smoked too, he could do with a cigarette. But just at the moment he wished all sorts of things.

CHAPTER TWELVE

The Southampton Princess

Newman woke in the middle of the night. The wind was howling and it sounded as if it was raining hard.

Margaret had phoned the night before, as she had promised, and told him there was no change in her mother's condition. She apologised for having to drive off just after she had told him her mother had married Helmut Schachmann. She hadn't told him earlier because she was afraid it might affect his decision to stay a few more days. He said she was a naughty girl but he forgave her, and they laughed together.

"I'll have to make up time at the airport tomorrow," she had said "I've had so much time off lately. So would it be all right if I phone you at the same time tomorrow?"

He said it would.

The arrangement suited him. It meant he could have a restful day and let the events of the last couple of days sink in.

He got out of bed, pulled back the curtains. His eyes confirmed his suspicions. The covered balcony was wet from heavy rain being driven under the roof by a strong westerly wind. It was still dark and the rain had reduced the visibility. The lights of the Dockyard and Hamilton had disappeared. Every ten seconds the balcony was illuminated by the light from Gibbs Hill Lighthouse, but even that was struggling and lacked the apparent brightness it had a few hours earlier. He went back to bed and tried to sleep, but he didn't succeed.

He rose at seven thirty. It was light now but the wind and rain had not abated. He opened one of the sliding doors on the north facing balcony just a few inches, and stuck his hand out. It was warm outside, surprisingly warm, but also surprisingly windy — probably forty or fifty miles an hour he guessed from the way trees and shrubs were swaying. He feared it might well last all day.

The previous night he had decided he would go for a walk today, perhaps even walk to the Belmont, by way of Harbour Road. That clearly was not an option at the moment and he decided to explore the hotel after breakfast. It might be interesting and it would help pass the time. Maybe he could buy some Bermuda shorts; he had felt so overdressed several times the previous day.

This morning he left his blazer in his room and made his way to the lifts in his shirt sleeves. He felt in better spirits. The fact that he had a grown up daughter had now truly registered, and she was a daughter anyone would be proud of. He was beginning to realise Bermuda was changing his life once again.

There was a young boy, perhaps twelve or thirteen already waiting for the lift. It arrived almost instantly. The boy pushed the button for the ground floor. A recorded female voice told them it was the third floor and the lift was going down. Newman kept a straight face and thanked her. The boy looked at Newman a bit oddly, pushed the button for the next floor, and got out.

A digital panel by the side of the doors gave the outside temperature as 73 degrees and the wind speed and direction. His estimate hadn't been far wrong, it was from the northwest at 42 mph. 'The marvels of modern science' he thought to himself.

When the doors opened again he found it wasn't the floor he wanted. He got out anyway. He could see some shops, he'd see if he could get a newspaper to take to breakfast and perhaps a paperback novel for later.

He entered the newsagent's and souvenir shop. There were several piles of daily papers on a low shelf to his left. He picked up a copy of a London newspaper, *The Times* for Thursday 25 March, the previous day — which had come in on that day's British Airways flight from London — and took a copy of the day's Mid-Atlantic Chronicle. He paid and made his way to Windows on the Sound.

He was half way through breakfast before he turned to the Mid-Atlantic Chronicle. Glancing over the front page his eyes stopped on an item in the bottom right hand corner. It read:

Good news, bad news.

By Tom Palin, Special Correspondent.

Bermuda woman meets father for first time, after fifty years!

Margaret Carpenter, 49, of Flatts, yesterday met her father for the first time. Don Newman was on a New York - Trinidad flight which diverted here the previous afternoon. It was the first time he had set foot in Bermuda since he left in May 1943. Don, an RAF Catalina pilot during the war, didn't know he had a daughter until Margaret introduced herself to him at the Southampton Princess. What a surprise that must have been!

When I caught up with her at the airport last night and asked how she knew he was her father, Margaret said "I did some detective work. My mother had told me a lot about him. It all fitted together like a jigsaw puzzle."

Asked how she felt about it she said she was overjoyed. The bad news is that Margaret's mother Lucy is seriously ill in King Edward VIIth hospital.

Don is staying here a few days, hoping to see Lucy before he leaves. But he has promised to return to Bermuda again before too long.

'So much for keeping it a secret,' Newman muttered to himself. Someone had let the cat out of the bag. He doubted it was his daughter, she would have mentioned it to him — even asked him if it was OK with him first. But it was clear that Margaret had cooperated with the reporter, once the news was out. So she was clearly happy for the news to be reported. That was perhaps the main thing.

"Mr Newman?"

He was leaving Windows on the Sound. In front of him a tall, clean shaven, well built young man, in Bermuda shorts and smart pale blue jacket was addressing him.

"Yes, Don Newman."

The stranger thrust his right hand forward. "Good morning Sir, I'm Tom Palin. I wonder if you could spare me a few minutes?"

Newman took his hand and their eyes met. Newman felt he could trust him. "I should think so, what do you want to talk about, Mr ...sorry what was your name again?"

"Palin — Tom Palin."

"Mr Palin."

"Well — perhaps we could sit for a few minutes. There are some seats by the windows up there." He pointed to an area past the lifts.

Newman was a little surprised that Palin knew his name and imagined that he was going to be asked to participate in completing a questionnaire about what he thought of the hotel, or Bermuda, or both. Ah well, he was in no hurry. He might as well be helpful. He had a lot of time to kill. He could see it was still pouring with near horizontal rain. He took a snap decision to go with it.

"OK, you lead the way."

Palin chose two arm chairs in the wide foyer overlooking the outside pool and the South Shore. He turned his chair at an angle so that it was easier for him to see Newman, then offered Newman a cigarette, which Newman politely declined. Palin put his own back in the packet.

"Mr Newman, did you see my piece in the Chronicle? I see you bought the paper."

So that was what this was all about. "Yes, I saw it, I was surprised. We were trying to keep it a secret."

"Why - it's a good little story. Your daughter seemed only too pleased to talk to me yesterday evening."

"Yes, maybe, but it's not as simple as that."

"That's what I wanted to talk to you about Mr Newman. There must be a bigger story. That's the impression I got from Margaret. I'd like to do a full page for the weekend edition."

"Sorry, no way, Mr Palin, no way!"

"Well that's a good start, Sir. It certainly confirms what I've heard. There is more to this then?"

"Yes and no."

"How do you mean, Sir?"

"Yes, there is more — there is some background, but I don't want it published."

"I see. You realise you can't stop us printing what we already know. The war's over now! If I have to, I'll just have to run with what I've got from other people."

"What other people Mr Palin?"

"We never reveal our sources Sir, but suffice it to say, they're local."

"Well what have you heard from your so called sources?"

"That you were court-martialed by the RAF, here in 1943, for collaborating with a German agent."

"That's complete nonsense and if you print that I'll take you to court!"

"I hope it won't come to that Mr Newman. I'm only trying to get at the truth?"

Newman visibly bristled and stood. "I told you, I don't want to talk about it," and began to walk away.

"Mr Newman, please trust me. I won't say anything you or your daughter don't want me to print. You can see my copy before I submit it. I might add that I've never agreed to that condition before."

Newman paused and pondered.

Palin could see Newman was wavering, and pressed on. "From what I've heard so far, the truth might do a lot of good. Margaret says her mother has suffered terribly because she never knew the whole truth and she suffered because most of her friends thought you had dumped her when she was pregnant — and a lot more things like that! If she recovers and sees that the truth is now down in black and white for the whole world to see, it could work wonders. That's presuming that there is another — might I say better — side to the story. As a reporter I've learnt that there are always two sides with this sort of thing."

Newman returned to his seat. He was looking tired and strained again. The events of the last few days were catching up with him. He leant forward, a hand on each knee, his head bowed and staring down at the carpet. Palin's words 'It could work wonders' had reached him. He might be right and he would dearly love to help Lucy. Nothing could undo the past, but that was no reason for doing nothing now.

"Yes I hadn't thought of it like that — you could be right — but I want to talk to my daughter before I agree to say any more."

❖

The article was the centre spread in the weekend edition. Palin had done his homework and obtained Helmut Schachmann's side of the story as well. He had done some research and included a photograph of the damaged Catalina on Darrell's Island after it had been salvaged in 1943. Also a special photo — which Palin had organised on the Friday afternoon — of Don Newman with his daughter standing at Burgess Point with the Great Sound in the background. The photographer had taken several shots. The paper chose the one in which they were standing shoulder to shoulder and looking at each other smiling, almost lovingly, in the Bermuda sunshine. He was wearing the Bermuda shorts he'd purchased soon after he had finished telling his side of the story to Tom Palin.

It was a week before Lucy regained consciousness and a further week before she could read the article. After that she made a steady and almost complete recovery. She said she was dying to meet Don again. Margaret didn't like her phraseology — but didn't comment. However her mother wouldn't let her bring him to the hospital each time he returned to

Bermuda, which was every two months or so. She didn't want him to see her until she looked better.

In the middle of November Lucy left hospital. The hospital said her recovery was miraculous. Margaret 'phoned her father at his home in England. He caught a plane the following day. It was to be a long time before he returned to London!